THE
THIRD SIN

THE
THIRD SIN

A Sonya Iverson Novel

Elsa Klensch

A TOM DOHERTY ASSOCIATES BOOK
NEW YORK

THE THIRD SIN

Copyright © 2014 by Elsa Klensch

A Forge Book
Published by Tom Doherty Associates, LLC
175 Fifth Avenue
New York, NY 10010

www.tor-forge.com

Forge® is a registered trademark of Tom Doherty Associates, LLC.

Library of Congress Cataloging-in-Publication Data

Klensch, Elsa.
    The third sin : a Sonya Iverson novel / Elsa Klensch.—1st ed.
        p. cm.
    "A Tom Doherty Associates book."
    ISBN 978-0-7653-1446-8 (hardcover)
    ISBN 978-1-4668-1554-4 (e-book)
    1. Iverson, Sonya (Fictitious character)—Fiction.
    2. Women television producers and directors—Fiction.
    3. Inheritance and succession—Fiction.   4. Diamonds—
    Fiction.   5. New York (N.Y.)—Fiction.   I. Title.
    PS3611.L46T48 2014
    813'.6—dc23
                                                                    2014015698

Forge books may be purchased for educational, business, or promotional use. For information on bulk purchases, please contact Macmillan Corporate and Premium Sales Department at 1-800-221-7945, extension 5442, or write specialmarkets@macmillan.com.

First Edition: August 2014

Printed in the United States of America

0 9 8 7 6 5 4 3 2 1

THE
THIRD SIN

Chapter 1

I've never killed anyone before. But I've never needed to.

The pills look innocent. Freshly pried from foil sheets. Enough to stop a heart quickly, painlessly, quietly.

Take the pestle and grind the pills to dust. Mix in some powdered sugar?

No. The ice cream won't be tasted. It will be gulped down, as it is every night, without thought, without a pause to actually experience the flavor.

Carefully scoop out half the ice cream. Sprinkle the powder equally through the chocolate layer. The flavor mustn't vary.

Ladle the rest back into the carton. Open the freezer door. The containers look like rows of soldiers, dressed for war.

Put my special package in the front so it's first to be eaten.

Close the door.

No regrets.

Chapter 2

TV producer Sonya Iverson stared at her computer, intent on the script sent for her approval by one of the writers for *The Donna Fuller Show*. She wasn't satisfied with it, and was annoyed that she would have to stay late to help with a rewrite. She had promised to meet her boyfriend, Keith, for a leisurely dinner, and this meant disappointing him—and herself—again.

The show's writing staff complained that Sonya was too demanding. She knew that behind her back they called her a "tough, hard-nosed, tight-ass." And that was true, at least when it came to work. She was a perfectionist, and proud of it. Almost every year, one of her segments won an Emmy.

Sonya began to add feedback to the script. Her concentration was broken by loud knocking on her door, followed by a shrill, familiar voice.

"It's me. It's important."

When Sonya's office door was closed, it was a signal to leave her alone unless there was an emergency. Even

Donna Fuller, the program's star and Sonya's ultimate boss, respected a closed door. But not Sonya's intern, Kirsten Sacco. Sonya frowned as the knocking continued, already sure that Kirsten was responsible.

With a sigh of resignation, Sonya uncrossed her long legs, got up from her desk, released the lock, and opened the door.

As she'd anticipated, Kirsten stood breathless in the doorway. The tall young woman stepped into the room as Sonya moved back behind her desk and sat down.

"I'm so excited. I've got the most awesome news ever. It looks like the family's going to have to live with Wade selling the diamond. I just hope they stop fighting now that he's made up his mind."

"My door was closed," Sonya said pointedly, ignoring Kirsten's news, "and I specifically asked you not to interrupt me when my door is shut. So say whatever it is you have to say and let me get back to work."

"I just did—I told you about the sale of our exquisite diamond, the Braganza." Kirsten was quite pale as a rule, but today Sonya noticed a tinge of pink to her skin, reflecting Kirsten's excitement about her news.

Sonya felt angry at herself for being impatient. What bothered her so much about Kirsten? Was it that the inexperienced intern assumed she had special privileges because of her mother's long friendship with Donna Fuller? Or was it that Kirsten never missed an opportunity to remind everyone that her grandfather, Daniel Lewis, had started the network news division and made it the success it was today? Or was it Kirsten's naked ambition that set her teeth on edge?

Whatever the answer, Sonya wasn't eager to have one of Kirsten's usual endless chats. She leaned back in her chair and examined the twenty-two-year-old. Kirsten had a beguiling, childish way of dropping her chin whenever she was being criticized, as she was now. Sonya knew it was an artificial, practiced look of vulnerability, but felt a grudging admiration for Kirsten's determination to keep it up.

"Yes, okay, Kirsten." She made an effort to keep her voice low and in control. "What did you say? What is it this time?"

"Mother just phoned me and I knew you'd want to know."

"Know what?" Sonya asked.

Kirsten did a little jig and announced in a triumphant voice, "The Braganza diamond will be sold at auction after all. Uncle Wade decided last night. Uncle Wade told the family he doesn't care how angry any of them are, or whatever they threaten. Harold and my mother, Blair— you know, she's Donna's friend—say he hopes to get as much as thirty million dollars for it. Could be more."

She stopped and smiled. "Then he'll be one of the richest men in New York City." She put a serious expression on her face, one Sonya wasn't used to seeing. "Mother doesn't know I'm telling you all this, but I'm sure I can get us an exclusive. Uncle Wade usually does what I ask."

Sonya remembered when Kirsten had first pitched the story of the Braganza diamond a few weeks earlier. Kirsten had told Sonya, "It has an unbelievable history, you know. It's said to be the biggest yellow diamond ever found, and it once belonged to queens of Portugal and Brazil."

Sonya had briefly researched the stone's history, which was fascinating, but the sale of a single, not-very-notorious diamond was hardly worthy of a block of network prime time. Later, Kirsten told her the sale had been canceled, so she'd put it out of her mind.

Now, apparently, the auction was on again—and this time, there was a family conflict attached. That might make good television.

"What do you mean about the family being angry, Kirsten? Who's angry, and what kinds of threats have been made?"

"Well, not really angry," the intern replied, obviously choosing her words carefully. "It's just differences of opinion. You know, like any family."

Sonya decided not to press for details. There would be time for that later if the story developed.

"It's definitely being put up for sale?"

"Yes. Mother said the auction house is picking it up the day after tomorrow. They want to send it on tour immediately. It'll be displayed at the major branches of the auction house around the world—I think Geneva, Hong Kong, and maybe London. They're announcing the sale and the display schedule as soon as Uncle Wade turns over the diamond on Friday morning."

Sonya sighed at the thought of the problems that lay ahead. Putting together the story would be a lot easier without Kirsten's interference, but she might be the key to getting the family members to agree to interviews.

Now that she had Sonya's attention, Kirsten sat in the visitor's chair opposite Sonya's desk and leaned forward. "I'm sure Uncle Wade will do an interview. He loves being the center of attention and I'm sure he'll understand that appearing on *The Donna Fuller Show* will be great publicity for the sale. He really needs the money, so he wants as many people as possible to bid on the diamond."

Sonya was surprised by the sudden, undisguised malice in Kirsten's voice. Usually the blonde spoke of how close she was to her uncle.

"I'll go talk to Donna," Sonya said. "If we do a story, she may want to schedule it to coincide with the diamond's tour and then air a follow-up when the auction takes place. I'll let you know what she says."

"I'm coming with you," Kirsten said swiftly.

"No," Sonya said firmly as Kirsten rose. "Interns aren't allowed in Donna's meetings. You've been here long enough to know that."

"Well, maybe she'll make an exception in this case, since she's my mother's close friend—and it's really my story."

Sonya flushed and pushed her red curls behind her ears as she stood up. She wanted to stride past Kirsten, who was intent on blocking her path to the door, but given the disparity in their heights, wound up edging around the woman.

"Don't take it personally. It's policy." She escaped from her office into the hall.

Kirsten followed, her voice rising. "Why can't I come? The only reason you'll get an exclusive is because I set it up."

"You've made your point, Kirsten. But the answer is no." Sonya walked away quickly. She could hear Kirsten following her but decided to ignore her.

Donna's assistant was not at her desk and Donna's door was open. As Sonya approached, she saw the television host sitting at her desk, putting files into a Louis Vuitton tote. "Sonya, come in," she called, smiling. "I'm in a hurry to leave but I want to go over several things for Friday's show."

Sonya entered and sank into one of the comfortable, round chairs in front of Donna's desk. Kirsten stood behind her.

"Do you want something, Kirsten my dear?" Donna asked sweetly.

"Yes. Mother told me Wade will auction the diamond after all. She sends her love and wants you to call her tonight."

"Well that's nice. Of course, I'll call." Donna smiled. "Now, Sonya and I have things to discuss."

Kirsten started to speak, but Donna nodded toward the door. The signal was clear and Kirsten left, closing the door behind her. Sonya and Donna exchanged smiles. They both knew that if Kirsten could, she would stand right outside, with her ear pressed against the door, eager to hear what was said.

Donna put another file into the tote before setting the bag aside. "I hope she's not giving you too much trouble, Sonya. I know she's aggressive, but she's also intelligent and ambitious. Her mother expects great things of her."

"She's all of those things," Sonya agreed, "but she's extremely needy. She wants constant reassurance. Maybe her parents' divorce and her mother's remarriage sapped her confidence."

"I don't think so. Kirsten was a baby when her mother and Giorgio were divorced, and she was only around three or four when Blair married Harold." Donna shook her head. "Give her time. I remember what I was like at twenty-two. I wanted the world and I didn't care what I did to get it."

It was hard for Sonya to believe the great Donna Fuller had ever been as neurotic as Kirsten. She thought about her intern's eating habits as an example. A Buddhist and a vegetarian, Kirsten's main source of food seemed to be dark green spirulina balls, which she proudly explained were made from algae grown on a lake in California. Kirsten said they were a great source of protein, but Sonya wondered if the blonde was just dangerously thin or actually anorexic.

She wondered if the way Kirsten ate was a rebellion against her mother, Blair Bruckheimer. Blair was a well-known cookbook author; Sonya had seen her two or three times as a guest on The Food Network.

Kirsten was also a shopping junkie who spent her free hours at H&M, Express, and other stores aimed at young women. Kirsten didn't want her mother to know how much she was spending, so she'd hide her shopping bags in Sonya's closet and take her purchases home gradually. Sonya had no idea where she got the money—certainly not from the little she earned as an intern. Perhaps her father provided it. Or dear Uncle Wade.

Sonya swallowed and flipped open her notebook. This was not the time to tell Donna her opinion of Kirsten's behavior. It could only cause trouble, especially if Donna repeated the story to Kirsten's mother. She would need the family's cooperation for the story.

Donna smiled. "So Sonya, I gather from Kirsten's outburst that you are about to recommend that we do the diamond story after all."

"Yes. According to Kirsten, Wade Bruckheimer estimates the diamond will bring thirty million, so there should be some interest in who buys it. Of course, there's a risk that it could wind up being a private sale with an unnamed buyer. Then there wouldn't be much of a story. Still, the stone has a romantic history and we can cover that."

"Do you really think you have enough to do a full segment of the show?"

"There's an additional angle that makes it stronger—the family. Kirsten says there are lots of hard feelings there. I'd work on the Bruckheimers. Why did Wade decide to sell, who gets the money, how do the Brazilians feel about seeing a piece of their history on the auction block? That kind of thing. Conflict. What do you think?"

Donna stared at Sonya for a moment before leaning forward intently, nodding. "Yes," she said, "that would work. But Sonya, go lightly. I know that family; they're complicated. The fact that Wade kept changing his mind about the sale . . ." Her voice trailed off. "There could be some real anger there."

Anger. That was exactly the way Kirsten had put it. Sonya frowned, musing. It wasn't like Donna to warn her off; usually, the boss insisted on having conflict in every story. That's what made the show successful. She wondered what was in Donna's mind, and was about to ask when the other woman rose to her feet, picking up her tote. Sonya stood as well, saying, "Okay,

I understand. But I need to be able to go where the story takes me. I've gathered from Kirsten's hints that Wade Bruckheimer's high living has made him desperate for money. If that's true, the sale of the diamond could be a real blessing. Others in the family might be hoping for part of the money. At this point, I have to take Kirsten's word for it that the stone belongs to Wade, though I've found dozens of photos of his stepmother, Irina, wearing it at big parties. I wonder how she feels about the auction. "

Donna nodded. "I've seen her with it. I must say it is a spectacular stone."

"What's Irina Bruckheimer like?"

"I don't know her well, just from casual encounters at parties. But Irina certainly behaves as if the Braganza were hers, so I always assumed it was. I know she's used to getting her own way and I'll bet that she'd do anything to avoid giving up that diamond."

"I did a little research on the family when Kirsten first raised the possibility of a sale, and as I remember, Wade's mother—Douglas Bruckheimer's first wife— was a sensational beauty. That's how the diamond came into the family in the first place: Esperanza Dias Bruckheimer's father gave her the diamond and she brought it to New York when she married Douglas."

Sonya had come to the end of her notes. "That's all I've got. I didn't go much further because it didn't seem like we would do the story. Now I'm not sure what happened to her. I remember something about a murder. Or was it just a divorce?"

"No, never," Donna laughed, "not in that Brazilian family. They would have killed Douglas before they'd let him disgrace their family with a divorce. Blair told me Esperanza died in a violent car crash two years into the marriage—shortly after Wade was born."

"Does Blair know all the family dirt?" Sonya asked lightly.

"Only some of it. She told me that Douglas once got drunk and told her about his 'beautiful Esperanza.' She came to New York in the sixties as Douglas Bruckheimer's bride and was an instant celebrity, with her pictures all over the tabloids and fashion magazines."

"Yes," Sonya said, "I've seen some of those pictures online. How does Irina, wife-number-two, feel about worship of wife-number-one? Not happy, I'll bet."

"I'm not sure. Most of what I know is just hearsay from Blair, but she's got a good nose for family secrets."

"Like her daughter, huh?" Sonya joked. "But the more I hear, the more I'm convinced this can be a great story for us."

"Sonya, keep in mind that Blair is married to Irina's son, Harold, and might have her own slant on the family, as well as a stake in the sale."

Sonya responded with a burst of enthusiasm as something leaped out at her from her memories of the research she'd done on the Bruckheimers. "I remember! Esperanza came from a rich, politically powerful family. When she died, her father built a church in a small Brazilian town as a memorial. It's called the 'Church of Beauty' or the 'Church of the Young' or something like that. I'll check on it. One article claimed that many young women go there to pray because they believe it's a shrine with special powers."

"Really?" Donna asked with surprise. "That's odd,

but it adds up. Esperanza's son, Wade, waited until he was in his forties to marry, and then he chose a twenty-two-year-old Brazilian model named Bella, who I hear is the image of Esperanza."

Sonya closed her notebook. "Donna, I'll wrap the story around Esperanza, the history of the diamond, and the conflict in the family. How about this for a segment tease: 'Esperanza—the beautiful ghost that needs to be laid to rest.' Something like that?"

Donna hesitated, turning away and staring out the window. Her voice was low and serious. "Sonya, you may be right. When she died, the story went around that the ghosts of Brazilian queens had cursed her for taking the stone out of the country." She turned back to Sonya. "You never know what the sale and our story will stir up."

"What do you mean?" Sonya asked.

Donna shrugged. "It's just a feeling I have."

The two women walked out of Donna's office together. Sonya was uneasy. More often than not, Donna's intuition was right. She tried not to think about it as her boss headed for the elevators.

By the time she'd reached her office, Sonya had shoved her misgivings aside. The story was good, and she was ready to work on it.

Chapter 3

Irina Bruckheimer clicked off the TV and hurled the remote at the screen. The remote bounced harmlessly off the set and fell to the floor, burying itself in the deep pile of the carpet which had been custom woven in Belgium in the perfect shade of gold to complement her bedroom décor.

"How dare you, you bitch?" she raged at the now-vanished gossip reporter she had been staring at moments before. "Why don't you leave me alone? Haven't I suffered enough?"

The reporter had been careful not to use names as she'd delivered her report with barely concealed glee. But Irina knew the woman was talking about her. Irina's friends would be discreet and not mention the broadcast, but she knew they would all know about it. The noon gossip segment was a must-see for her Upper East Side set.

Tears filled Irina's eyes as she remembered settling in to watch the program. The television had been artfully built into an elegant Louis XVI credenza which Irina had had converted into a media center.

"In the 'right circles,'" the woman had said, "a party isn't a party until a certain self-important socialite shows up, flashing a certain stone." Irina had frozen, staring at the screen as the report continued, "I'll have to let you guess who I'm talking about." Her smile seemed brightly artificial.

The reporter arched a perfectly shaped brow, leaned closer to the camera, and continued in a conspiratorial tone, "Please don't tell this grieving widow that her favorite sparkler may soon be sold. Sold by someone very near, but not so dear. Of course, there's plenty of money in the family, so maybe her daddy could buy it for her? My friends, here's a final question for you all to ponder. If this lady no longer has that big old rock, how many invitation lists will no longer include her name?"

Irina felt as if every word was a blow. The woman had struck at her greatest vulnerability.

There was no way she would let the Braganza diamond be sold. The glorious yellow stone had established her position in New York society from the moment her husband had fastened it around her neck. It had rescued her after the horror of those years in Cincinnati. There was nothing she would not do to keep it.

Irina threw herself onto the antique lace bedspread and rested her head on one of her large, soft pillows encased in fine Irish linen. The spread reminded her of Venice and the island of Burano where she had ordered the coverlet to be handmade.

The comfort and beauty of her bed and bedroom always lifted her spirits. The room was filled with her carefully collected, gilded French antiques. She absolutely insisted on authenticity, so everything was an original, and each piece had been selected for its quality, line, and proportion. Not even the smallest items were copies. She needed to have the best, no matter how expensive.

In the drawer of her Louis XVI desk was a certification of provenance asserting that Marie Antoinette had been the owner of the very bed on which she, Irina Bruckheimer, was now resting. An ornate chest placed in front of the brocaded wall had also belonged to the unfortunate queen. Near the window overlooking Central Park was the Empire chaise that had been in the bedroom of Napoleon's sister, Pauline. It was reputed to be the very one on which she had posed while Canova made that scandalous nude sculpture of her.

She had met Douglas Bruckheimer when she was nineteen. He was a handsome, wealthy man, ten years her senior, who could give her the security she craved. She gloried in his attention and was gladly seduced.

Shortly after they were married, she had bought Pauline's chaise after seeing it advertised in an antiques magazine. It was her first antique, and as it had been set into place, she had unexpectedly felt important. Young and romantic, she had persuaded Douglas to make love to her on Pauline's chaise. Weeks later, she realized her son had been conceived that day.

Irina had soon realized that the marriage would have failed if she had not become pregnant. She told herself that it didn't matter. For her, her husband—and their child—were a way out of the agony of her father's house, and an entrée to New York society.

After Harold was born, Douglas's lovemaking was infrequent and perfunctory. He had fulfilled his obligation by creating another heir—as had she. He moved on with his life, happy to have the generous allowance Irina's father gave them but uninterested in his wife or son. Instead, he turned to other women. Without his love to distance her from the horrific memories of what she had seen as a teenager, Irina sought refuge in the excitement of acquisition. If Douglas refused to pay for something she wanted, she manipulated her father to get it.

Irina sat up and looked around her bedroom. These beautiful objects defined her place in the world, but nothing was as important to her as the Braganza. Now her stepson planned to sell her precious diamond to the highest bidder. She clenched her hands and screamed, "No, I will never let it go."

Getting off the bed, she went to the window, trailing her fingers over the furniture along the way. Fourteen stories below, the sun shimmered on the deep blue of the Central Park reservoir; the leaves on the trees had begun to change color. It was fall, the time she looked forward to every year. She'd recently received the new designer clothes she'd ordered for the season's big parties. The Braganza would complete her look. It was part of her identity. She'd worn it longer than Esperanza—the diamond belonged to her more than it did to Douglas's long-dead first wife.

She knew what she had to do.

She picked up her cell phone from the desk, clicked it open, and started to dial her father's number, then closed it and reached for the landline. Max refused to speak on cells. The FBI could be listening.

The call went through without trouble and soon Irina heard his crusty voice demanding impatiently, "Who is it? Who is it?" He never revealed who he was until he knew who was calling.

"It's Irina, your daughter. Look at your caller ID, for god's sake."

"Yes, Irina, what do you want?"

She knew she had to get right to the point. At seventy-five, Max Lundell refused to waste time on small talk. If she tried to chat with him, he would just hang up.

She kept her voice calm and spoke clearly because she knew he was a little hard of hearing. She began as she had so often before, playing the game, as she had for years. "Dad, do you remember the promise you made in the attorney's office after Mother's murder?"

"Shit. That again, huh?"

"Yes, Dad, that. Again."

"No. I don't remember. It was a long time ago. And you know goddamned well my memory isn't what it used to be." Irina could tell by his tone of voice that he knew very well what she was talking about.

She made her usual reply.

"How could you forget?" she asked.

To her surprise, he cut the exchange short, saying, "I'm tired today. Let's get right to it, Irina. What do you want this time?"

"You said that you could never repay me for what I did. You thanked me for betraying my mother."

"What the fuck do you want?" He was angry and not angry at the same time. This was an old dance for them both.

"Listen to me, Max. I need to own the Braganza

diamond. I've worn it for years. You know that it's important to me."

"What?" he said. "You call me up to talk about some piece of jewelry?"

She heard him sigh. He was probably sitting in the brown leather library chair in his apartment. He'd still be in his dressing gown and slippers, gazing out at the muddy Ohio River as it curved through Cincinnati. The years had not treated him kindly. All his wealth could not protect him from emphysema, caused by years of smoking. His breathing was increasingly labored and every time Irina spoke to him, his voice sounded weaker.

She pictured his veined hand holding the phone close to his face, staying true to his secretive nature. If she had to, she would press him. He would have to listen to her. After all, she had saved him. Because of her, he had not been charged with her mother's murder. And even after all these years, even if the statute of limitations had run out, if she spoke of that day, he would be ruined.

That day . . .

She had just turned eleven, and that day she had run home, excited because she had been elected captain of the basketball team. She was eager to share the news with her German-born mother, even though she wasn't sure how Anna would respond. Anna didn't approve of the American school system or her daughter's love of sport. But she loved Irina, so she might try to be happy for her, just for a moment.

As she always did when she came home from school, she gave the doorbell three quick rings, then waited for her mother to open the door. When Anna didn't appear, Irina tried the knob and was surprised to find it unlocked. Entering the house, she smelled a sickly sweet odor—blood, she quickly found out—and knew something was wrong. She found her mother lying battered and bloody on the bedroom carpet.

Irina didn't know how long she had stood there, frozen, in shock, before panic swept over her. She knew in an instant that her father had killed her mother, as he had so often threatened.

"He'll kill me," Anna had warned her more than once. "If he does, you must tell how violent he was and how frightened I was of him."

That morning he had been in a bad mood, and he and Anna had argued—over what, Irina could never remember. There were so many arguments, so many fights. As she'd left for school, she'd heard Max shout, "Fuck you, Anna, you German bitch. Another word and I'll shut your fucking mouth for good." Irina had closed the door on the sound of a loud slap and her mother's scream and had run all the way to school.

Now she ran that way again, racing back to school and the safety of the classroom. Children were still milling about on the playground and no one noticed when Irina slipped back into the building.

It was some time later when her father and the school principal found her, crouched under her desk. Max walked toward her with his arms outstretched, but Irina screamed and drew away from him.

She knew what he had done.

Somehow, the police had concluded that Anna had surprised someone who had invaded the house looking for drug money. Or perhaps the district attorney had been impressed with her father's wealth and power in his construction business.

Though the police questioned Irina several times, she knew they were not really interested in what she had to say. Not that it would have mattered—she couldn't tell the truth. Max insisted that she tell the police he was a loving husband and father, and the dreadful memory of her mother's body lying on the bloody carpet guaranteed that Irina would stick to this story. The only truth she told was that she had not seen the attack on her mother. With little evidence and no eyewitness, it had been easy for the DA to drop the case.

Anna lingered in a coma for five years. Max lived in fear that she would awaken and accuse him. Irina often went to the hospital to sit with her, staring at her mother's strong hands, useless at her sides. With Anna's death, the case became a matter of murder, but by then, the trail was cold and Max was able to use his money to make sure no one cared.

All these years later, Irina had not forgotten what had happened. She knew Max hadn't forgotten either. Years before, when Anna's murder was officially marked "unsolved" and filed away, Irina's father had told her, "Anything you want, for the rest of your life, I will get for you." She had cashed in on that promise more than once and was ready to do it again.

"What do I want? I want the Braganza diamond," she said, hearing the bitterness in her voice. "Wade has decided to sell Esperanza's diamond. You must buy it for me."

He said nothing.

Angered by his silence, she waited. He had an uncanny ability to sniff out any weakness, and to show anger would give him the upper hand.

"You want me to buy it for you? That's a funny notion," he said at last.

"Yes." She went on, unfazed by the sarcasm in his tone, "I've worn it for years. Since I first married Douglas. It's mine, and I won't be humiliated by another woman wearing it."

She paused, then began again, speaking slowly and deliberately to let her words sink in. "I've had enough of loss and humiliation. You know what my life was after the attack on Mother. How the press never left me alone. Well, they're at it again. They know you have the money to get it for me and they want to know why you haven't already arranged for me to have it. Not ten minutes ago I saw a TV gossip columnist carrying on about my losing the diamond. It was infuriating."

"What do you mean 'carrying on'?" She picked up the tension in his voice and smiled to herself. She had him on the hook now.

"She mentioned you and your money. The sale will be news, and Mother's death will probably be rehashed again."

He sighed. "Why didn't Douglas give you the diamond?" This was his usual tactic—changing the subject.

"The diamond came from the Brazilian side of the

family and Douglas claimed he signed an agreement with the Dias family to ensure that it would go to Wade."

"So let Wade keep it. I'll tell you what—I have friends who can make a perfect copy for you. They make insurance companies happy and no one knows the difference."

"Don't be crazy. Everyone will know it was sold, especially when some other woman turns up wearing it. Mother came from a family of jewelers and taught me that wearing a genuine stone gives a woman confidence. I'm telling you once and forever, I won't wear a fake."

"What do you expect me to do? Call Wade and tell him he's making a mistake in selling it?"

She strained to control her temper. "Why would Wade listen to you? I promise you, Max, you're the one who will be making a mistake if you don't buy it for me. I know you have the money. You're worth close to a billion. Buy the stone. Mother would have wanted you to do this for me."

"Irina." Max's voice softened with the weariness of age. "I can't afford to buy that diamond and neither can you. It could bring thirty or forty million or more. The damn Arab oil people and the Russians have big money now."

"You have big money too."

"You have an over-the-top impression of my money . . . always have. I've got partners, obligations . . . problems."

She interrupted him. "Stop. I'm sick of you crying poor. What you did to my mother ruined my life. How can you deny me what I want?"

When he spoke, she heard the tinge of fear in his voice.

"I'm not promising anything, but I'll give it some thought." That was the concession she had been waiting for.

"I'm sure you'll find a way. Good-bye." She smiled as she hung up. The Braganza would be hers.

She stayed at the window, looking down at the golden leaves below. In the end, Max would buy the stone for her.

But if he didn't, what would she do?

Chapter 4

Jorge Dias felt a jab of pain in his chest and stiffened. The surgeon had warned him that he would feel pain after the bypass operation, but this was sharper than he expected. His wife, Elenora, was right. He had to look after himself—he knew that he wasn't well, yet, and worse, he knew that he looked it. The strain of his illness showed. He knew by the way friends glanced at him, and then looked quickly away.

A few more days of rest would have helped, but there was no time for that. This trip to New York might be his last chance to buy the diamond back from his nephew, Wade.

He walked slowly across the lounge and settled in a chair away from the crowd at the bar, who were sipping drinks and chattering, perhaps getting up the nerve to actually fly in their small, private planes. Jorge reached for the newspaper on the table beside him and opened it to hide his face.

His plane would take off in a few minutes, and in

nine and a half hours he would land at JFK International Airport in New York. Then he would call Wade and they would meet, and Jorge would struggle, as always, with his feelings for his nephew.

From the terrible day his sister Esperanza was killed, he had felt an inseparable mix of love and pity for her son, and too often, that overwhelmed his good sense. Whatever Wade wanted, Jorge gave him, and the grief-stricken boy had grown into a greedy man. But the Braganza was the one thing Jorge could not give him.

Jorge's father, Fernando Dias, had always intended that the Braganza would remain in Brazil and eventually be displayed as a treasure in the national museum. Though Fernando's will had not specified the stone's fate, the whole family knew what he had wanted. A Brazilian aristocrat, bound by honor, Jorge now had to make good on his father's promises.

Fernando had worshipped his daughter Esperanza. On her eighteenth birthday, he had given her the Braganza. She loved wearing the stone, so Fernando had raised no objection when, after her marriage, she took it to New York.

It had been different when Esperanza's son, Wade, married Bella. Jorge, by then head of the family, objected strenuously to the marriage. Bella was Brazilian, but of a different class than the Diases and a gold digger if he ever saw one. Her brothers were ruffians, and Jorge barely persuaded her to sign the prenuptial agreement he had so carefully prepared. At Bella's instigation Wade had sold the beach house his grandmother had left him, and which had been in the family for more than eighty years.

From the day of their wedding, Wade's demands for money from the Dias trust had increased dramatically. Jorge had given him much of what he'd asked for, but recently he had become concerned about the drain on the family's finances.

Now Wade was refusing to sell the Braganza back to the family so that it could be brought back to Brazil, its rightful home. His response to Jorge's last offer had been a vengeful, brief e-mail: "Uncle, I warned you. You have refused to help me since I married. Now I have to put the diamond on the open market. It will bring more than you can pay."

Ignoring his doctor's advice to rest, Jorge was flying to New York to settle the matter once and for all. He was determined to get his hands on the stone before it was advertised for auction. He would insist that Wade sell the Braganza to him and his investors, and at a fair price. It must be returned to Brazil. It was a matter of his family's pride and honor.

Of course he could sue to recover the Braganza, but given the lack of documentation, the outcome in the United States courts might be disappointing, and the public disgrace of a legal battle was the last thing he wanted. Still, if Wade wouldn't sell him the diamond, he would do whatever was necessary.

Jorge put down the newspaper and pulled off the navy cashmere scarf his wife had put around his neck as he bent to kiss her good-bye. "Leave it on," Elenora had insisted as he tried to remove it. "The air-conditioning in those planes is freezing." She had clung to his arm, tears glistening on her cheeks. "I've always come to New York with you. Why are you refusing me now?"

He'd shaken off her hands and climbed into the back-seat of the limo. Through the open window, Jorge had said, trying to be reassuring, "My heart is fine. I'll be back before you know I've gone." He'd seen tears well up in her eyes and had added, "I'll call you when I get to the airport."

Now as he folded the scarf precisely, calmed by the softness of the cashmere, he refused to feel guilty for not bringing her. But what lay between him and Wade was man's business and her constant chatter would disturb them. Perhaps, once he had secured the jewel, he would let Elenora wear it once, before they gave it to the museum.

He put the scarf and the newspaper into his briefcase, took out his cell phone, and pressed his home number.

Elenora picked up after the first ring. "I'm fine," he said. "I've talked to the pilot and we'll take off right on schedule. The next time you speak to me I'll be in New York." She wouldn't let him finish.

"Wade is no longer your motherless little nephew who needs protection," she argued.

As he took deep breaths to ease the tension mounting in his chest, he wondered if she realized how much her anxiety tired him. "Yes, yes, stop your nagging."

"What if we don't get the Braganza back? Who cares? It's been in New York so long that most people have forgotten about it. You have children and grandchildren who love you and need you to guide them, not to mention your wife. Don't be foolish with your old-fashioned talk about honor. Your health is more important."

Jorge spoke quickly, cutting her off. "The pilot must leave on time. If everything goes as planned, I'll see

Wade tonight and have good news tomorrow. You'll see. Good-bye." He closed the phone before she could speak again.

He stood up, steadying himself with his hand on the back of the chair. Elenora didn't understand what the Braganza meant to him. People have *not* forgotten, he thought—at least not the people who mattered to him.

The society-page photos of Irina Bruckheimer wearing the spectacular yellow gem tormented him. Brazilian papers delighted in publishing them, almost always pointing out that the rough diamond had been found by three local prospectors some two hundred years earlier and was rightfully part of the historic heritage of the nation.

Remembering it had been worn by Brazilian and Portuguese queens only increased his anger. Its beauty should radiate in the national museum, not around the neck of a rich New York woman.

At one time Elenora had believed it would come to her. He remembered the dismay on her face when his father told them it was to be a present for Esperanza.

"You are the first son. You should have inherited the diamond," she had said as soon as they were alone. She was right of course, but like the rest of the family, Jorge was bewitched by his ravishingly beautiful sister.

Esperanza had first worn the Braganza to her eighteenth birthday party. The life-sized oil painting of her with the diamond resting on her breast had raised the envy of every woman and the desire of every man who saw it. Newspaper reproductions of the painting caught the attention of readers and made her an instant celebrity.

Photographers followed her day and night, waiting

hours to snap a shot. What she wore was copied by young rich Brazilians, and envied by others. Her quick wit made for clever headlines in the tabloids. Through it all, Esperanza remained levelheaded and dignified.

Though she had taken the Braganza with her to New York, Esperanza knew the diamond belonged in Brazil. Had she lived, surely she would have returned it someday. But she was long dead.

Jorge looked out at the tarmac. The memory of the day his sister had been killed never failed to choke him and bring tears. It had begun at this very airport, over forty years ago.

While Esperanza was still a teenager, disturbing notes began to arrive at the family home, filled with sexual fantasies or driven by hate for the superrich. Some asked for money in exchange for a promise "not to kill her." Once the gossip columns dubbed Esperanza "our princess," the number of letters increased and their tone became darker.

Wealthy Brazilian families were used to such threats and the police said that most could be ignored as the work of "known cranks." Nevertheless, Fernando decided to provide bodyguards for his daughter. They kept her safe until she was married and had moved to New York. When Esperanza left Brazil, the letters stopped coming.

Little more than a year after the marriage, Wade had been born. Fernando Dias had been eager to bring his grandson to São Paulo and show him off to Brazil's aristocracy. Esperanza's birthday would take place during the trip, so Fernando arranged a magnificent ball to celebrate the occasion. Esperanza would wear the Braganza that night.

Fernando encouraged the press to cover her arrival, staged in the style befitting the "princess" she was. Jorge and the director of public relations for Fernando's company orchestrated the drama of the beautiful young woman's return to her homeland.

Once the plane landed and taxied to a stop, Douglas Bruckheimer, Esperanza's husband, would exit first. He would wait for Esperanza to appear at the door of the plane, and if necessary help her down the steps. Wade and his nanny would follow. Esperanza and Douglas would greet her family, then everyone would pass through the terminal to cars that would be waiting for them. Later, there would be a press conference, where Esperanza would answer questions about her glamorous life in New York, followed by a reception for family and specially invited guests.

Jorge had called New York to explain all this to his sister. She was not pleased, and Jorge was forced to report to his father that though Esperanza wanted to keep her visit entirely private, because these were her father's wishes, she had agreed.

"We must forgive her," Fernando solemnly advised. "Esperanza is young, and doesn't understand how important public relations are to a businessman."

Soon after the plans were made public, threatening letters once again began arriving at the Dias residence. "What could possibly happen with so many people waiting at the airport?" Fernando asked.

The day of the flight, Douglas announced that he had an unexpected and urgent business appointment which would keep him in Manhattan. He would follow his family to Brazil the next day. Esperanza, Wade, and the nanny boarded the plane without trouble. The flight was smooth and on time.

At the airport, Fernando waited at the gate. Behind him, photographers jostled one another to get the best position, proof that Esperanza had not been forgotten. Everything seemed normal, except for the extra guards the airport had provided. Jorge, standing near his father, barely noticed the six men in mechanic's uniforms, gathered on the tarmac next to a security van.

The plane taxied to the gate and the steps were lowered. Esperanza appeared in the doorway and a shout went up from the crowd. She hesitated at the top of the steps for a second, then ran down them and toward her father.

Before she had taken more than a few strides, four of the men in uniforms surrounded her, grabbed her, and hurled her into the security van. It happened almost before anyone had time to react.

The nanny, who was holding Wade, had followed Esperanza down the stairs. When she saw the attack—and the two "mechanics" who had moved in her direction—she turned and scrambled back to the security of the plane. She stumbled, but the pilot and a flight attendant kept her from falling. The fake mechanics spun around and raced to the van, which had already begun to move.

Fernando was the next to react. "My god, they've taken my Esperanza. Come back, come back," he shouted as he raced toward the security van. He tripped and fell onto the tarmac, calling Esperanza's name.

Other people were beginning to realize that a kidnapping was taking place. Security guards were grabbing for their radios, the photographers were swinging their cameras around. Suddenly, an airport baggage truck accelerated away from the terminal, apparently trying to get between the kidnappers' van and the airport exit. The van picked up speed, tried to swerve around the baggage vehicle, and smashed into a concrete security barrier with a horrible sound of screeching tires, broken glass, and crumpled metal.

Fernando Dias reached the wreck in moments, but he was too late. There were no survivors. Esperanza was dead, her skull crushed, her dark beauty reduced to a tangle of bone and blood.

Fernando's grief was unbearable. He blamed himself—and airport security—but most of all, he blamed Douglas, his son-in-law. "Why wasn't Douglas there to protect his wife and son? What business kept him in New York? Why did I let her marry him? He has no sense of responsibility."

Douglas took the next flight south. He tried to meet with his father-in-law, but Fernando refused to see him. Without waiting for Esperanza's funeral, Douglas left as soon as he could, with Wade in his arms, the nanny at his side, and the Braganza in his briefcase.

Fernando was determined to obtain custody of his grandson. He pursued every possible legal angle, and Douglas fought him at every turn. Before the struggle ended, it had become a bitter, ugly battle, and the tabloids thrived on it.

The infant Wade became a celebrity, just as his mother had been. The press in Brazil never got enough of him and his poor-little-rich-boy story. The New York papers were almost as greedy. Nine years later, Douglas married Irina, who at nineteen had no interest in being the mother of a spoiled ten-year-old. Though Douglas had fought tooth and nail to retain custody of his son, he allowed Irina to send the boy to boarding school without complaint. That, too, had been covered thoroughly by the press. From school, Wade had sent his uncle Jorge a steady stream of letters of complaint.

For many years, Jorge had believed it was his duty to watch over his nephew; that belief had been worn away by Wade's near-constant demands. Esperanza's son had been trouble from the hour he came so unhappily into his life.

How many times had he flown to New York after one of Wade's urgent calls for help? And how often had he risked customs to bring sleeping pills to his nephew? He patted his pocket. Wade's insomnia was chronic; he no longer achieved relief with any medications available in the U.S. Only the pills Jorge brought him were powerful enough to work; they were so strong they weren't approved for sale in the States.

Jorge saw that his plane's copilot was waiting at the door for him. He picked up his briefcase and began his last journey to New York. Wade's decision to sell the diamond showed how little his nephew cared about Brazil and the Dias family. This was his last trip. Wade would not trouble him again.

Chapter 5

Sonya lay in bed and watched Keith Harris's trim, naked back through the open bathroom door. He leaned toward the bathroom mirror, holding his square chin high as he scraped the shaving cream off his neck. He was a detective with the NYPD and was as meticulous about shaving as he was about his work. He had a heavy beard, she knew all too well; sometimes she felt like leaping out of bed in the middle of the night to massage soothing skin cream into her face.

She swung her legs onto the floor, put on her cotton robe, and went into the kitchen. She could not bring herself to walk naked through her own apartment, though she enjoyed watching Harris do it. It was her upbringing in rural Minnesota. Did her mother ever walk around naked? Sonya doubted it.

Keith had made coffee. Two filled mugs stood on the counter.

Sonya smiled. Keith tried to please her. But then so did most divorced men at the start of an affair. What followed later was something else, something that usually ended badly. Not that she had an unblemished record; her own marriage had ended with a divorce on her thirtieth birthday.

Keith came up behind her, kissed the back of her neck, then gently turned her to face him. He kissed her again, pulled her robe open, and touched her breasts. Sonya shivered and responded by curving her body against his. She could feel his erection pressing against her.

"Come on," he whispered, "it's back to bed for us."

She hesitated, then relaxed and let him guide her to the bedroom, where they made love again.

With her husband it had been different, never satisfying. Sonya had only felt this way with Keith. He was a skillful lover who knew how to please her, and she wanted to do the same for him.

As he lay close beside her, she kissed him lightly on the cheek and whispered, "Keith, we have to get up. We'll be late for work . . ." They laughed together.

"What better reason?" He grinned as he got up and headed again for the bathroom. "I'll just take another quick shower." Sonya went to the kitchen. She stood there, thinking how different he was from her ex-husband. Maybe it would work the second time around.

"Why are you frowning?" he asked as he came in toweling his hair.

She handed him a mug of now-cooling coffee. "Do you want me to zap it for you?"

He took a gulp. "It's okay. What's the matter?"

She sat at the kitchen table, saying, "Nothing you need to know about."

"Tell me."

"It's nothing."

He sat next to her and kissed her on the ear. "Tell me. I want to know everything about you."

She stiffened. She didn't want him to know everything about her. And she didn't like his need to be in control. The pleasure of their lovemaking began to fade.

She decided to let him have it.

"Since you want to know, I was wondering how long you can keep being Mr. Good Guy. You're so perfect; I think you must be making a superhuman effort to please me. One day I'll come in and find dirty dishes piled in the sink and the garbage overflowing. That'll be the day I see the real Keith Harris."

He laughed. "Are you serious?"

She bristled. "Yes. I'm serious."

He laughed again. "Okay then. Here's the answer. I'll be Mr. Good Guy for as long as you want me around." He waited for her response, but she said nothing. Keith continued quietly, "I'm naturally neat and if I learned one thing from being married to a messy woman, it was that it's easier to clean as you go. It's not such a big deal. Are you really worried about dirty dishes?"

She got up and poured herself another cup of coffee, thinking about her ex-husband and his two small children arriving for their month-long summer vacation. Each time they came, everything changed. Out of guilt about the divorce, he gave in to their every demand. She hated it when the kids jumped on her new sofa, when they deliberately spilled sodas to get attention, when they used her lipsticks to draw faces on the bedroom wallpaper.

"But you love his children, don't you?" her mother had asked when she'd complained.

"No," Sonya had answered. "And I doubt I ever will." She had been right about that.

She put her mug into the microwave oven and pressed the beverage reheat button. Keith was silent, and Sonya saw his disappointment that she had not responded to what he said. "Let's talk about it another time. I've got to concentrate on Donna's interview this morning."

He was as willing to change the subject as she was. "You said it's with Wade Bruckheimer, right?"

"Yes, now that he's decided to go ahead with the auction of the famous Braganza diamond."

"It sounds like another lightweight puff piece. I thought you didn't want to do them anymore."

"I've got another angle on it now. The story is going to center on his family. There seems to be a lot of conflict about the sale, and when family members fight, there's nearly always a good story. Wade believes he has the right to sell the Braganza, but it seems that there might be some question about that."

"How did you get the inside stuff on the Bruckheimers?"

"From Kirsten. She mentioned some differences of opinion among them, and that got my snoopy instincts going."

Keith laughed. "I'll bet."

"Besides," Sonya continued, "I went back to do more research on Wade Bruckheimer. He has quite a background. Did you know that he was once part of a get-rich-quick scheme in Brazil? I don't know how involved he was, but there was a plan to illegally export exotic birds to the United States. It didn't amount to much."

"Was he ever formally charged?"

"No, not from what I could find. One article called him a victim because the crooks exploited him and his connections, but the case just disappeared. There was no follow-up coverage that I could find."

"That's odd. Maybe there wasn't enough evidence, so they dropped it."

"I asked Kirsten, but she didn't know much about it. She said the Brazilian police questioned Wade until his uncle Jorge stepped in and settled it. My guess is that Wade got mixed up in it because he was trying to make a quick dollar. Apparently he lives high on the hog and is always short of money. I'll bet Uncle Jorge has a full-time job, keeping Wade out of trouble."

Sonya took her coffee from the microwave and sipped it. It was hot and strong; just what she needed. Carrying the mug, she went into the bathroom, calling over her shoulder, "I've got to finish dressing."

Without moving from the table, Keith shouted, "How does Kirsten know Wade's family stepped in?"

"You don't have to yell—the apartment's not that big," Sonya said, and laughed. She went on, "The *Times* ran an article on the whole affair and Kirsten says she happened to hear the family talking about it. More likely, Kirsten had her ear against a door."

"I see she's on your nerves again. Anyway, the charges can't have been too serious, or it wouldn't have faded away so easily. The Brazilians—and the U.S.—

are hot on protecting those exotic birds. If you're found with an illegally smuggled animal in Brazil, you can go to prison for life. It's heavy stuff."

"Yeah, that's the law," she agreed. "But the Dias family has a lot of influence in Brazil. When I Googled Jorge, I got thousands of hits. He's big in business and in the social world of São Paulo. I'll bet he knows the police commissioner, the cardinal, and every important judge in the country."

Fully dressed, Sonya returned to the kitchen. She was feeling guilty for not responding to Keith's statement that he would be around for as long as she would have him, so she had put on a burnt-orange suit that played up the color of her hair. Keith had often told her the outfit was one of his favorites. She hoped he would understand that it was a peace offering.

"Fantastic," he exclaimed when he saw her, smiling broadly. She could tell from the look in his eyes that he had gotten her message, and just like that, any lingering tension between them was gone.

Sonya smiled in return, then leaned over and gave him a quick kiss. She sat beside him, setting her unfinished, cooling coffee on the table.

"With the Dias clan behind him, nephew Wade didn't have much risk of being sent to jail," she said, then laughed shortly and continued. "Kirsten says Wade has a beautiful macaw that he takes everywhere he goes. Apparently it's really old, smells up the whole apartment, and chatters like crazy with a nasty vocabulary he taught it. No one but Wade likes the bird, but he's devoted to it, and it to him."

"So Wade is the black sheep of both the Dias and Bruckheimer families?"

"Looks that way. Kirsten says he has never worked, but he must have gotten money from somewhere—look at all the lavish parties he's thrown over the years, and he's always lived well."

"How rich is this Uncle Jorge?"

"Very rich; you could even say stinking rich, with many investments in both land and industry. If he doesn't have enough cash to buy the diamond, I'm sure he has friends who would be willing to chip in. Any upper-crust wife in São Paulo would kill for that stone."

"Well if Jorge or his friends have the money, why doesn't he just buy it from Wade?"

"Who knows what's gone on between them? Could even be that Wade won't sell it to Jorge out of spite. There's got to be some bad blood. Anyway, I still have lots of questions, but I think it can be a great story." She kissed him on the cheek. "I've got to do my makeup and get going."

"Me too. Good luck on the interview. Sounds like your kind of fun. Just stay clear of the parrot. They have nasty bites."

"Macaw," she said, smiling, "it's a macaw. I'll be careful. I promise."

She blew him another kiss as she went into the bathroom to apply makeup. Keith Harris was easy to have around. He was great in bed, he took her work seriously, and he cared for her.

Sonya shook her head, chastising herself. No. He could be the greatest guy ever, but nine years ago she had sworn that she would never again get serious about

a divorced man with kids. She wasn't going to break
that promise now.

It's not about the dirty dishes, she thought, or the children, or anything to do with Keith specifically. She was
determined to control her life.

Chapter 6

Sonya opened her boss's door and froze in surprise at the sight of Donna Fuller hunched in her chair, her arms defensively wrapped around her shuddering body. Her head was bent, her hair concealing her face.

At the sound of the door, Donna looked up, revealing swollen, red-rimmed eyes. Sonya stepped back, aghast. She had never seen her boss so distraught. Donna's glamorous façade was gone. She looked like what she was: an exhausted, fifty-year-old woman with skin too tautly stretched over her cheekbones, the result of one too many face-lifts.

What had happened? Was Donna ill? Had she gotten some kind of bad news? Or—Sonya's heart dropped—was there a problem with the show? No, no, it couldn't be that—Sonya would have heard.

All that flashed through her mind in seconds, but before she could follow her instincts and offer some comfort, Donna burst out, "What the hell do you want, Sonya? Can't you give me a moment's peace?"

"My god, Donna, I'm sorry. I never dreamed you'd be at the office this early. I was just going to put these questions for Wade Bruckheimer on your desk." She awkwardly held out the papers as evidence.

Donna gave Sonya a dark, angry look, then lowered her head again with a strangled sob. Sonya closed the door and took a few steps toward her.

"What's wrong? How can I help?"

Donna swiveled her chair, turning toward the window so she didn't face Sonya. "There's nothing you can do." She shrugged. "There's nothing anyone can do. It's my problem. A problem from the past, when I was young and stupid. I thought it was buried for good, but I was wrong." She sighed and straightened her back, then swung to face the room and motioned Sonya to one of the easy chairs that faced her desk.

Sonya was mystified. She had the greatest respect for Donna and regarded her as a mentor. She was a brilliant, successful woman with the number-one magazine show. She had gone toe to toe with world leaders, arrogant celebrities, and industry giants. When she asked someone to appear on her program, it was practically a command performance. It was hard to believe that any mistake in her past could harm her now. Sonya decided that the best way to reassure Donna and help her regain her confidence was to behave as normally as possible.

Sonya pulled her chair closer to the desk and smiled. "Let me get Sabrina in here to fix your face. You need a makeup artist like never before." There was no sting in the words. Both women were well aware that image was everything in their business.

"You're right. I must pull myself together." Donna took a small mirror from a desk drawer and looked into it, poking at her hair. "God, I look awful. But not as awful as I feel." She picked up a tissue and gently wiped her face, then threw the tissue into her wastepaper basket. "I had a fierce argument with an old friend last night. It was one of the worst nights of my life. Our friendship is over, and I was so upset that I couldn't sleep." She glanced at Sonya. "And you know I can *always* sleep, even in a war zone."

Sonya tried to soothe her. "Donna, these things happen. In a few days you'll both get perspective and go on as you were before."

Donna reached for a tissue and gave her nose a hard blow. "I will never forget the things she said." She shook her head.

Sonya wondered if Donna wanted to talk, to relieve herself of some of her anguish. That kind of exposure was almost unheard of—Donna fiercely guarded her privacy. After seven years of working for her, Sonya knew almost nothing of her personal life. "Would it help to talk about it?"

"No, there's nothing to say." Donna put down the mirror, went to the window, and stood looking down at the traffic. She sighed. "My friend was a spoiled brat when we were children. She just had to ask for something and she got it. No one's ever told her any different, so even now, she thinks that if she wants something, it should be given to her immediately." She heaved a deep sigh. "She's a kind and generous woman in many ways, but she lacks depth. She can't comprehend that the world is not so kind to all of us. Most people have had to fight tooth and nail for what they want."

Sonya's mind clicked back to their discussion the day before. What had Kirsten said? That her mother had asked Donna to call that evening. Blair and Donna had known each other for decades. Was Blair Bruckheimer Donna's past, "catching up" with her, and was their argument connected to the sale of the diamond?

"My friend judges people too harshly," Donna continued. "That's what upset me most."

Sonya half-rose, but Donna shook her head and held up a hand to stop her. "I had to talk to someone and I'm glad it was you. Thank you for your concern. It means a lot to me, more than I think you realize." She smiled, already looking more like her usual self, as she went to her desk. She sat, took a deep breath, and with a deliberate change of mood, said, "Now, let's get on with the Wade Bruckheimer story."

Donna reached out and Sonya handed her the list of questions she'd prepared, then picked up a pen and a few sheets of the notepaper Donna kept handy on her desk. She wrote *Wade Bruckheimer* and the date on the top of the page.

"Remember when we first discussed this story and I said that I knew the Bruckheimer family?" She paused.

Sonya looked at her, trying to read her expression.

"Well, the truth is that Blair Bruckheimer is a close friend of mine and has been for many years."

Sonya nodded. So, she was right. It was Blair Bruckheimer who had upset Donna. "Yes, I know. Blair's father, Daniel Lewis, started the news department at the network. You told us you used to work for him."

"I met Blair through her father. He was a great man. He built the department so well that even though he's gone, we still lead in the ratings. He should get more credit. You could say he took me under his wing."

Donna looked away, as if remembering him. "Don't read it the wrong way. He did the same for others. He guided me through many a tough story. But more than that . . ." Donna began to frame each word carefully as she spoke. "When I had personal problems he took me home to his family. So Blair and I began to spend a lot of time together. I was matron of honor at her wedding to Giorgio Sacco, Kirsten's father. As a friend, and on a very private basis, I've stepped in with advice on how to promote her books on TV programs."

Sonya clicked her pen on and off—it was something she did when she was nervous or impatient. "Oh," she said. "Does this have some bearing on the Braganza story?"

"Perhaps."

"I don't understand."

"Let me make myself clear," she responded firmly. "Because of my friendship with Blair Bruckheimer and my past relationship with her father, I must distance myself from the story. You know what the tabloids and blogs are like. They're so quick to jump on gossip and blow it all out of proportion. Nothing pleases them more than finding some conflict of interest that can ruin a career.

"So I've decided not to do any interviews. In fact, I'm not going to touch this story at all until you're done with it. I'm leaving it in your very capable hands. Let's see how it comes out before we decide on how much time we will give it, or even if it's worth airing."

Sonya sank back in disbelief. Not air the story? Donna had never failed to air one of her stories.

"Don't be upset, Sonya; even you didn't think much of it at the beginning."

"True. But that's changed now. I have the angle that will make it dynamite," Sonya insisted with enthusiasm. "Aren't you being overly sensitive? Who could accuse you of having any personal interests in the sale of this diamond?"

"Sonya, believe me, I don't have *any* interests, personal or otherwise. But I know the problems my friend Blair has had with the Bruckheimer family, especially since Wade married Bella."

Sonya shrugged. "I think you're overreacting, but I'll do whatever you say, Donna. And I'm sure you'll be happy to air the piece when it's done."

"Thank you." Donna gave Sonya one of her usual blinding smiles—the one Sonya had seen her use many times to get what she wanted. Donna was her confident self again. "Don't read this the wrong way," she said. "I'm just playing safe."

Realizing she had been dismissed, Sonya moved to the door. Before she could open it, Donna added, "Sonya, one last thing. Keep the story focused on the unfortunate Esperanza and the diamond."

What? Sonya turned back to look at her boss. "But, Donna, you know that's my angle for the story—the family conflict."

"Even though we've fought, I have to look out for Blair's feelings. I owe it to her father."

Sonya frowned. What was Donna afraid of? Didn't she realize Sonya wouldn't be able to do her job if her hands were tied like this? "My appointment with Wade Bruckheimer is for noon," she said. "You're sure you want me to do the interview?"

"Yes." Donna nodded, then visibly turned her attention to some papers on her desk.

Their strange conversation was over.

Heading for her office, Sonya asked herself what could have happened to have affected Donna so profoundly. She was giving Sonya permission to spend time and resources on a story she was reluctant to air—and at the same time, was telling her not to use her best leads. It made no sense.

Had Blair asked Donna to cancel the story?

But it had been Kirsten, Blair's daughter, who had first alerted Sonya to the sale. . . .

Except, Sonya remembered, Kirsten had said her mother didn't know she was passing on the information about the diamond.

It was all very confusing.

Sonya sat down to review her notes. Before she spoke to Wade, she wanted to have a solid idea of the questions she wanted to ask and the information she hoped he would provide.

Chapter 7

Blair Bruckheimer ran her hand over the gleaming sur-
face of the antique farmhouse table. It was a comforting reminder that she was one of many strong women
who had worked at this table to feed and support their
families. She had been a young food writer when her
parents had given it to her, secretly moving it from their
home to hers. Touching the table again, Blair smiled,
remembering her exhilaration that evening, when she'd
gotten home from work and found it.

How different that day had been from when she and
Harold moved into Irina's apartment. Most of her furniture had been left behind, but her kitchen table would
never be abandoned. While the movers were still setting the table in place, Irina had confronted her.

"I had no idea you were bringing *that*," she'd snapped.

"Irina, I told you I was," Blair had responded calmly.

"Well, it's simply too big for this kitchen," Irina had
insisted.

"It's fine, Irina. There's plenty of room for it." Blair

had looked at her mother-in-law steadily. "I need a large table for my work, and I love this one."

Irina had laughed. "You love it? Really? *De gustibus non est disputandum,*" she trilled venomously. "There's no accounting for taste, is there?" Irina waited for a reaction, but Blair refused to be drawn in. Smiling sweetly, Irina added, "Let me remind you that this is my apartment and I say the table goes."

That was too much for Blair.

"Well," she began with calm determination, "let me remind you, Irina, that the money from my work is what your son Harold and I live on, and, as I have already said, I need this table for that work. If I cannot have this table here, Harold and I cannot live here."

"That's hardly a threat, Blair."

"It's not a threat, it's a fact. If you want your son living in 'your' apartment, then my table stays. It's your choice."

"I'll speak to Harold." Irina turned abruptly and left. Later, when Blair asked Harold, he said she'd never mentioned it.

That face-off had set the tone for Blair and Irina's relationship. Irina never again challenged her openly, though Blair knew the older woman whined to Harold, who seldom passed along his mother's complaints.

When he did, he invariably took Irina's side. Though Blair loved Harold, she resented his blind devotion to his mother.

Blair saw Irina as greedy, stingy, and manipulative. She took every opportunity to remind Harold of how little money she had, but Blair knew better. Irina's father had established a generous trust for her; her husband, Douglas, had left her another trust, the proceeds from the sale of his Main Line Philadelphia family's steel business. He'd left his sons only token sums; Irina had received the vast majority of his assets.

Even with Blair's income, she and Harold had to rely on Irina for housing. She let them live with her rent-free and fostered the expectation that when she died, Harold would inherit the apartment along with whatever was left in her trusts. But Irina was capricious and enjoyed teasing her son, saying that there was no money and that the apartment might pass to some charity or other.

Through it all, Harold had encouraged Blair to stay calm, telling her that Wade had promised to leave him the Braganza and had named Harold his executor. Then Wade had married Bella and begun to spend more money than ever before.

Now Wade planned to sell the Braganza, ending Harold's hopes of a big inheritance. Once the diamond was sold, and the money placed in Bella's greedy hands, there would be nothing left for Blair and Harold.

Finding that the tray of cookies that she'd left to cool were ready, she placed them in a jar. Ginger snaps were Kirsten's favorite, so Blair kept a supply on hand in the hope that her daughter would gobble them as she had when she was a child and finally gain some weight.

"Those cookies smell great," Harold said, entering the kitchen. Blair looked at her handsome husband. After eighteen years of marriage, he was still a knockout, tall and lean, with blue eyes that lit up when he smiled. Those smiles were rare—he considered himself a "boring engineer" and a serious person—and Blair treasured each one.

"Are you still upset about the sale?" he asked as he reached for a cookie.

She stared at him. "Angry? No. Furious is more like it. I should have been prepared. Months ago, you told me Wade was broke and would have to sell the Braganza. I just didn't believe he'd do it."

He sighed. "I didn't believe it either."

"We can't stand by—" she began.

Harold interrupted her. "I don't care, my real worry is Mother. She's been depressed since Dad died two years ago. The sale of the diamond is another blow. She's worn the Braganza for so long, she's convinced it's hers. She'll do anything to keep it."

"Irina doesn't deserve any sympathy. Your father said all along that it belonged to the Dias family and would go to Wade," Blair said bitterly. "How about some sympathy for us?"

"Stop it," Harold responded with unusual firmness. "First of all, don't forget that the diamond came from his mother, not mine. It's his by right. I know Wade promised to leave it to me when he died, but is that what you want? My brother dead?"

"You know what I mean. It's only right that Wade give you something from the sale."

"And you know that he'll spend every dollar on himself and Bella. But he's entitled to it. It's his diamond."

Blair picked up the cookie tray and put it in the dishwasher. She knew Harold would never ask his brother for money. She loved him, but . . . "You're hopeless."

"Who's hopeless?" The deep voice came from the

doorway. Wade stood there, dressed in an ill-fitting, blue-striped caftan and holding a bulky cardboard box. On his shoulder sat Cacao, his macaw.

"Wade," Blair demanded, "get that damned bird out of my kitchen."

"Oh, Blair, don't be so uptight."

"Damned tight, tight, tight," Cacao squawked, turning his large bright eye to watch Blair.

"See? He agrees with me," giggled Wade. "Now, help me with this box."

Harold took the box from him and put it on Blair's beloved table. "What's this?" Harold asked as his brother shifted his bulk toward the table and began to encourage Cacao to walk down his arm. Blair realized he was about to let the bird stand on her table.

"No," she roared, startling everyone in the room. "Put that bird near the sink. I don't want it messing all over the place."

Wade chuckled and complied. "Just give him a piece of dried spaghetti and he'll stay there. Won't you, dear Cacao?" Wade pursed his lips and sent a smacking air kiss toward the bird. "I thought I smelled something good. If those are your famous ginger snaps, I want one, and I want it now."

"Okay," Blair said. Her hand shook as she held the jar toward him.

As she expected, he reached in and took a handful. "You can forget about the spaghetti, I'll give Cacao a piece of cookie." He broke the ginger snap in half and held a piece out toward the bird. Cacao balanced on one foot, took the cookie tightly in the other, and nibbled away. "Cacao loves your ginger snaps. Sugary things aren't supposed to be good for him, but once in a while I like to give him treats, don't I, sweetie?"

"Weetie," the bird mimicked.

Blair looked away, hiding her disgust. Harold had once asked her, "Do you want to see my brother dead?" At this moment, her answer would have come easily: "Yes. And that goddamned bird too."

Wade pointed to the box. "This is a treat for you, Blair. I bought it for you as a peace offering. I know I should have asked you and Harold what you thought about selling the Braganza."

"Yes, you should have," Blair replied honestly.

"But I would have had to do it no matter what you said. The truth is I need to raise as much money as I can."

Blair looked at the box.

"Guess what it is," Wade said, spreading his arms with a flourish. Before she could respond, he continued, "Okay I'll tell you. I stopped by Williams-Sonoma, your favorite store, and picked up the latest espresso, cappuccino, latte, you-name-it machine. I promise it's as efficient as you are. You'll love it."

"Thank you," Blair said evenly.

"That's wonderful," Harold cut in with enthusiasm.

Blair reached for a knife and slit the box open. She looked into it, took out the instructions, and whistled. "My god, I've seen this in the shop. It costs four thousand dollars."

Wade waved his hand nonchalantly and sat at the table. "Don't worry. Isn't it a beautiful machine? Just consider it a gift from my Braganza." He took another handful of cookies. "Want another cookie, Cacao?"

The bird moved restlessly from one foot to the other, bobbed his head, and let out a shriek. "See, he wants it. Cacao loves your cookies, Blair.

"I feel bad about Irina. I didn't know what to send her, so I ordered what the florist called 'a tree of flowers.' I know nothing will take the place of my diamond hanging around her neck, but I'm sure she'll love the flowers." As an afterthought, he added, "The diamond wasn't hers, anyway."

Wade struggled to his feet, supporting himself on the back of his chair and leaning against the table to steady himself.

"I've got to go," he wheezed. "My beautiful Bella is expecting me. She gets cranky if I leave her alone too long. Besides, I've got to get ready for my interview. It's for Donna Fuller's show. She's a friend of yours, isn't she, Blair?"

"Interview? You're doing an interview for Donna Fuller?" Blair asked, her voice high and tight.

"Didn't Kirsten tell you? For some reason, Donna herself can't come, so her producer Sonya Iverson will do it. The publicity should definitely help the sale."

Blair tightened her jaw and clenched her teeth to keep from screaming at him.

Wade put Cacao on his shoulder. "Let's go, baby." He shoveled two more cookies into his mouth as he shuffled out.

"Wade's put on more weight, hasn't he? It's harder for him to walk," Harold said.

Blair could barely speak. "He can keep his fucking insulting gift. And I hope Donna and that producer have a second thought before doing that interview."

Harold raised his voice. "Blair, I asked if you think he's getting heavier?"

"Yes, he is, and I hope it kills him before he sells the diamond." She took a moment to control herself, then continued in a near whisper, "He can't last long at this rate, Harold. We just need to find a way to postpone the sale. His heart must be under enormous strain. If he dies before the diamond's sold, you'll control it as his executor. You could negotiate a private sale with the Dias family. The diamond would go back to Brazil. They would be happy, and we . . . we'd . . ." She laughed. "We'd get our fair share and be rich."

Harold turned, fixing unblinking eyes on hers. "Don't you think I know that?"

The strength of his flat, cold voice startled Blair. This was a side of Harold she had never seen.

"Don't you think I know that?" he repeated.

Chapter 8

When Sonya arrived at Wade's apartment she found the front door ajar. She knocked briskly, and after a few moments without a reply, slowly pushed the door open and looked in. The entrance hall was dark, with a black-and-white-checked floor and a chipped ornate gilt console. An empty vase sat on top of the console, holding a few dead branches with crumbling leaves. They gave the space a feeling of neglect.

At the far end of the hall Sonya saw a staircase—probably the one Kirsten had told her led to the penthouse that Irina shared with Harold and his family. Thinking about Kirsten reminded Sonya of their argument that morning.

The intern had offered to assist at the interview. "I can ease the way with the family, show you around, help with questions, assist Perry with the equipment . . ."

Sonya was firm, explaining that, as a family member, her presence would make Wade feel awkward. He would be more careful in his answers, and much less responsive. But Kirsten had continued to plead until, in frustration, Sonya had shouted at her, "No. And that's final."

She was already anxious enough, worrying about Donna's refusal to take part in the story. What had Blair said to her, and would Blair try to be at the interview? The last thing that Sonya wanted was both mother and daughter trying to interfere.

Sonya took a few steps into the foyer, hoping Perry would soon arrive—he and his camera equipment had been sent to the freight elevator. As she opened the door more widely, the light fell on a macaw, which was perched like a sentry on the banister. Obviously startled, it squawked, "Go way go way go way."

The harsh sound made Sonya flinch. She called up the stairs, "Hello?"

No reply.

The macaw tilted his head to the side and looked at her with knowing eyes. It was a beautiful mix of exotic colors. Its head was green, its face white and framed with small black feathers, its wings were blue, and its crest was golden. The colors, shining in the light from the open door, reminded her of the perfectly placed marks in an impressionist painting.

"Go way." The macaw rose to its full height, surprising Sonya with its size. As she approached, it again cried, "Go way," and began to flap its wings aggressively.

Sonya tried to reassure the creature, saying softly, "Hey there, calm down, I'm your friend." She moved closer, hoping to stroke its neck. The bird jerked forward in a flash of color and Sonya felt a stab of pain as its beak clamped down on her index finger. She gasped.

"Cacao! Naughty!" Sonya looked up. It was Wade Bruckheimer. He spoke sharply, but looked at the bird with the proud expression of a father correcting a favorite child. The bird pulled back and Sonya looked down at her hand.

"I hope you're not hurt, Miss Iverson. His beak is strong."

"No, no," she said, recalling how Keith had warned her. She examined her hand. There was no blood. "Only a light nip on the finger," she said. "I was a little startled, but it's perfectly all right."

Sonya looked at Cacao. There was a gleam in his eyes and his quiet cooing convinced her that he was pleased with himself.

Wade wore a wide blue shirt over chino trousers and leather sandals. The shirt was unbuttoned at the neck, showing a thick roll of flesh.

"Well, I'm glad you're not hurt. It usually takes a while for Cacao to make friends, but listen to that cooing. He loves you already," he said. Sonya was not so sure.

He continued, "I must apologize for my wife. Bella wanted to greet you, but she just had to run to an appointment."

Sonya nodded, and then looked toward the staircase. "Kirsten lives up there?"

"Yes," he said. "With my half-brother, Harold, and his wife, Blair. I guess you'd call Kirsten my step-niece but she's more like a daughter to me. She and my wife are friends." He smiled. "You see, our families love each other. We are all close."

Wade offered his arm to Cacao, and once the bird

had taken his place there, man and macaw ushered Sonya into the living room. Wade deposited Cacao on a large perch near the fireplace, then pointed to the portrait over the mantelpiece. A heavy, gold frame surrounded a full-length, life-sized oil portrait of a beautiful young woman. She looked radiantly happy in a flowing white dress. Around her slender neck was the gleaming yellow Braganza, with smaller white diamonds sparkling around it.

"This is my mother, Esperanza Dias, in the white dress she wore on her eighteenth birthday," Wade said, glowing with pride. "It's a very famous portrait and quite valuable, but I'd never sell it. You know she was killed by kidnappers when I was just a baby? I never knew her."

"Yes, I've researched your family and am familiar with the story. It must have been hard, growing up with that history behind you."

"My family is wonderful and supportive."

Cacao interrupted them with a loud shriek, and a "Go way. Go way."

Sonya turned and saw Perry. "It's my cameraman," she said.

"Cacao warns me when a stranger arrives," Wade said with pride.

"Come in, Perry," Sonya called. "We'll start shooting as soon as you are ready." She turned back to Wade. "How does your wife feel about the painting?"

"You know how women are . . ." He paused, waiting for a reaction, but Sonya only smiled. "The women in the family are all a little jealous. My mother was so beautiful and so saintly."

"She is beautiful, and we'll want to get some shots of her, especially since she is wearing the Braganza."

"Her dress is an exact copy of one worn by the queen of Brazil. I see this painting every day of my life, and never tire of it."

"Where would you like to do the interview?" Perry asked Sonya.

It was Wade who answered, pointing toward the easy chair. "I could sit there with Cacao behind me. He'll be upset if he's not on TV."

Perry said calmly, "Having Cacao in the background will cause problems with editing. But we can get some shots of you and Cacao and cut them into the piece."

"All right," Wade said. "Kirsten told me it might be a problem. But Cacao must be in the story. I promised him." He simpered a bit, saying, "Kirsten told me you are the network's best cameraman and said that you'd make me look so handsome all my friends will be envious."

Perry grunted and started to set up the lights.

"I want to make sure that people know I'm so happy about the sale. The auction house told me they've already had inquiries about my beautiful diamond. When I told the family, they were thrilled."

Sonya said nothing.

Wade lifted the bird's perch to move it out of the room. The macaw flapped his wings and squawked angrily. Wade said, "Calm down, Cacao. You'll be on television later."

"That's some crazy guy," Perry said. "And the bird too." He and Sonya finished arranging the chairs and lights.

Wade came back, brushing off his hands. Sonya wondered how often the perch was cleaned.

It was immediately apparent that something had changed in the few moments that Wade had been out of the room. Gone was the affable host. Wade was shaking as he sat while Perry adjusted the lights.

He put his hand up to shield his eyes and snapped, "The lights are blinding me. They're making me feel sick."

Sonya looked at him. "I promise this won't take long."

"You know I'm only doing this to raise the price of the diamond. I hate being interviewed."

Perspiration was beading on his forehead. Sonya decided to keep her questions short and to the point. Perry gave her the signal that they were rolling.

"Why are you auctioning the diamond?"

"When my father died, I decided to change my life. I now have a beautiful bride. And to make her happy I want to sell my Braganza. It will set us up so we can enjoy the rest of our lives together."

"Your mother, Esperanza, was the first member of the Dias family to wear the diamond, wasn't she?"

"Yes, my grandfather gave it to her on her eighteenth birthday and she wore it when she married my father."

"By all accounts, that was quite a wedding."

"Well, of course, I wasn't there, but I've seen all the pictures. It was the wedding of the decade in Brazil— possibly the wedding of the century. The ceremony was held in the cathedral and Mother had twenty-four bridesmaids, all of them dressed in flowing white. It was spectacular. Pictures of it appeared in magazines and newspapers all over the world." Sonya could see that Wade was relaxing as he told the familiar story of his family history.

"Where did she meet your father?"

"It was love at first sight, you know. Mother came to East Hampton for the July parties, then went to Manhattan for the celebration of Brazil's National Day in August. My father, who was going to Rio for the Mardi Gras that year, came to the party and met her."

"And the Braganza diamond? She brought it with her to New York?"

"Yes of course," he answered with a hint of impatience. "My grandfather, Fernando, had given it to her."

"Your family from Brazil visited often?"

"Yes, they did," he replied. "They bought the two apartments below my father's penthouse. This apartment was for me and my nanny. The apartment next door was for my Brazilian family when they visited— which was very often. All three apartments are connected—we are one big happy family."

Sonya paused. "I heard that some members of your family object to the sale of the diamond."

His eyes narrowed. "Who told you that?"

She ignored the question and pressed him, "Was the agreement that the diamond was to go back to Brazil?"

"That's not so," he said, impatience beginning to give way to anger.

"Do you really have the authority to sell the Braganza? Who does it belong to? Your Brazilian family? Your stepmother?"

"Look, if this is going to be one of those 'gotcha' interviews, I'm stopping now." Sweat was gathering in a ring at his hairline. Sonya leaned forward and handed him a tissue. He took it and roughly wiped his face.

Sonya asked, "Has your uncle Jorge spoken to you about the sale?"

Wade flushed. "No."

Sonya waited for him to go on. The silence increased his uncertainty.

"I mean, yes, but not about the sale. He is visiting me and staying in the apartment next door. He entirely approves of the auction. Why shouldn't he? It belonged to my mother, not to him."

"I'd like to interview him, too, to get the Brazilian point of view of the sale."

"My god, leave him alone."

"How about your brother, Harold? How does he feel about your selling the diamond?"

"Why are you asking all this?" Wade started to knead the side of his neck with one hand. "They're just jealous. They're greedy and jealous and they hate me."

Sensing that he was ready to tell the truth about the family reaction to the sale of the Braganza, Sonya leaned in and said, "Why do you say that?"

Before he could answer, the macaw squawked in the background, "Bad girl, bad girl." Wade's eyes lit up and he shouted in relief, "Kirsten's here!"

He ripped the microphone off his shirt as he struggled to get out of the chair. "Kirsten, come here. I need you."

Sonya was furious. Two hours ago she had told Kirsten not to come, and now she had interrupted the interview at the crucial time. She turned and spotted her intern in the doorway with Cacao on her shoulder.

Beside her was a man in his forties, tall, handsome, and stylishly dressed.

"Hi there, Uncle Wade," Kirsten said, walking into the room. "How'd it go?" she asked as she placed the bird on his shoulder.

"Oh, Giorgio," cried Wade as he ran to the man. "This has been hell."

Sonya interrupted to introduce herself. "Excuse me, I am Sonya Iverson. And you are?"

A smiling Kirsten said, "This is my dad, Giorgio Sacco." Giorgio broke away from Wade's embrace to shake Sonya's hand.

As nicely as she could, Sonya asked Kirsten, "What are you doing here? And why did you interrupt me?"

"Sorry. I didn't realize you were still taping." Sonya could tell from the look in her eyes that Kirsten was lying. For how long had she been listening? What was she afraid that Wade was going to say? Why had she stepped in and stopped him?

"Pack up your equipment and let's go," Sonya said to Perry. "There's nothing more for us here . . . at least for now."

Chapter **9**

THURSDAY, 3:00 P.M.
Franklin fashion show, front row

Sonya looked down at her practical slingback shoes showing under her neatly pressed pants and felt an immediate wave of insecurity. The last thing they could be called was fashionable, let alone glamorous. She'd initially chosen them for their practicality, found they fit perfectly, and had gone back to the store for a second pair. In polished black leather, they had a two-inch stacked heel that increased her height to a commanding five foot eight. The comfortable round toes would, she hoped, decrease the likelihood that she would suffer from painful bunions, which had afflicted her mother for years.

The two fashionistas who stood chatting in shrill voices beside her wore minidresses, bare legs, and sandals with four-inch heels. They looked like Manolos to Sonya's discerning eye and probably cost as much as her mother's budget for a month.

But no matter how ridiculous those women were, they had the power to make her feel insecure about her looks and even her life. At thirty-nine, that feeling was something she didn't relish. She looked across the runway to the line of faux blondes established in the front row and pulled herself together. From their long, bleached hair to the deep red polish on their nails, these women were pathetic copycats who relied on glossy magazines for direction. They hadn't the confidence to express their own tastes or senses of style—assuming they had either. She laughed to herself. They were as insecure about fashion as she was.

"Don't those girls look great in their minis?" bubbled Kirsten in the seat next to her. "I wish my legs were as good. My dream is to own a pair of Manolos, they would make my legs look sexy." She gave a giggle of happiness. "I'm so lucky to see all this."

Yes, you are lucky, Sonya thought and you had better realize it. Donna had no right to insist that I bring you and give you one of these precious front seats. You should be sitting in the back. Your seat belongs to an important buyer or editor.

"Enjoy it while you can," she snapped. "Nothing lasts long in this business."

To hide her irritation, she flipped open her program. Then she caught the uncertain look on the intern's face and realized she had touched a sore point. Kirsten wanted desperately to get a job at the network. And she was pulling every string to make sure she did. Sonya softened her tone. "What I meant was that it will be a short show. Just thirty-five numbers and with fast-paced models legging it down the runway it'll be over in less than fifteen minutes."

She needn't have said anything; Kirsten's attention had already been diverted by the latest arrivals.

"That blonde in the red dress is the actress, Jayne Anne Haliday, isn't it?" she said. "She had an abortion and pretended it was a miscarriage. She didn't know a photographer had gotten a shot of her coming out of a clinic." She laughed. "Bad luck, eh?"

Sonya froze. The fact that the actress had lied about the abortion probably meant that she was torn about making the decision. It was a frightful one for any woman to make. And the photographer who had taken the picture of her coming out of the clinic was despicable.

"I wouldn't call it bad luck. I'd call it an unforgivable invasion of privacy," she said firmly.

"Did you know that Donna had an abortion?"

Keeping her face expressionless to hide her surprise, Sonya looked at the intern. Her face was flushed and her eyes were sparkling with excitement.

"No, I didn't know," she said, "but I think that's Donna's business, not mine."

"Oh, don't be such a prude. Everyone knows about it. She got pregnant a year or so after she joined the network and my mom looked after her when she had the abortion. That's why they became friends."

Sonya had heard rumors about Donna but had no intention of discussing them with Kirsten. She looked again at the program.

Short shows were the trend. It took more time to get in and out of the crowded tents than it did to see a thirty-piece collection of mostly outlandish clothing that few people would actually ever wear. The corporations which owned most designers' names wanted as much publicity as they could get. The extravagant outfits made for great video that was flashed around the world. The publicity they got increased the sales of the designers' accessories and perfume. That's what the CEOs wanted. Did the publicity help women to spend money wisely? No, Sonya told herself, it just confused them.

Kirsten was young enough to be a perfect victim. She swallowed every new sales pitch without question, struggling to stay on the cutting edge. Sonya thought of her compulsive shopping and the bags of newly acquired clothes hidden in the office. Kirsten seemed to be ashamed to take them home where her mother would see them and question her. Sonya wondered how many hours a day she spent putting together her outfits.

Kirsten gave her a sideways glance and said, "How do you like my new hairstyle?" She had recently dyed her chestnut hair a light auburn so it was almost as red as Sonya's. She'd also curled it into the loose bob that Sonya wore.

"I certainly recognize the color," Sonya said.

Kirsten had the grace to look abashed. "You know I envy your hair, Sonya. Mine's so dull and mousy. I hope you don't mind, I just wanted to experiment with a look that is more exciting."

"It's okay, I'm not annoyed," Sonya replied, though secretly she was irritated. Kirsten's new hairstyle suited her and the red color made her pale skin look translucent. But it wasn't only her hair and makeup she copied. Kirsten came into her office and looked around. Sonya had caught her going through production notes on her office desk.

"Is your mother as fascinated with fashion as you are?" she asked.

"No, Mom is an old stick in the mud. All she cares about is cooking." Sonya looked at Kirsten more closely, appraising her total appearance. Over her coral T-shirt she wore a micro minidress with a stripe of black, blue, coral, and turquoise running around her hips. On most women that stripe would add ten pounds; on Kirsten it only emphasized her slender, model-like figure. She'd paired the dress with a pair of obviously new sandals with a two-inch wedge and silver straps. Sonya had watched her struggling along the corridor in them and had almost laughed out loud.

Kirsten followed her glance, arched her foot, and said, "My wedgies were a present from my father. He bought them for me in Milan. He likes to see me dressed up."

Sonya was surprised. Kirsten had rarely mentioned her father before. She had once thought he was out of the picture, assuming Harold had taken over as her father figure.

"That's a nice trait for a father to have."

"Yes. He can be generous when he wants. But he's pretty mixed up. You should hear Wade talk about some of the crazy stunts they've pulled."

Sonya's interest started to grow. "They're friends?"

"Mom says more than friends."

"You mean they were lovers? Surely not. They've both married."

Sonya knew she was naïve; growing up in Minnesota she never got used to complicated relationships that were so common in Manhattan.

"What does that matter?" Kirsten made a grimace. "And remember, Wade wasn't always obese with apnea."

Sonya wasn't surprised to hear that Wade had sleep apnea, given his weight and age. She'd seen enough articles to know that it was a potentially serious medical condition that could cause a person's breathing to be irregular while they were sleeping. Some people even stopped breathing entirely.

"Does he need oxygen when he sleeps?"

"Yes. He sleeps with a mask and a machine. Otherwise he snores all the time and could even die. But he wasn't always like this. When Mom married Harold, Wade was best man and the best-looking guy there. You should see the photos. I bet my dad fell for him then."

This was the first confirmation Sonya had that Wade was bisexual. She said casually, "It must have made for an interesting mix in the family."

Kirsten laughed. "It still does. Of course, we weren't all living together then. Mom, Harold, and I had an apartment on the West Side. It was easy for Dad to stay with Wade when he came to town. He did for years, until Bella moved in."

"Do Wade and Bella have separate rooms?"

"Sure, Bella says she can't sleep with the constant buzz of Wade's apnea machine. Wade says he can't sleep without it. Even with it he only gets three or four hours a night."

"So you and Wade are friends?"

"He's always been like an uncle to me. Dad and Uncle Wade used to take me shopping when I was kid. I had a lot of fun with them. Mom said they spoiled me, but Wade used to reply that was what uncles were for."

Sonya thought of her own childhood, growing up without a father. Her mother had had to count every cent. Shopping had never been a pleasure. It was always about finding the cheapest thing.

The music swelled as two muscular men came out and started ripping off the tape that sealed the plastic sheeting that protected the runway. The fashionistas hurried to their seats, the lights dimmed, and with a burst of music the first model appeared.

Chapter **10**

Cacao was dead.

The macaw's body lay in the bottom of the cage, a rigid mass of feathers.

Bella felt herself swaying as if she were going to fall. She had come into the bedroom and seen that the cover on the cage had slipped. When she'd reached the cage, she'd seen the body, with its bright feathers and black beak, frozen in place. She stared and swallowed hard, fighting the nausea that swept over her. She should not have drunk so much whiskey.

From the first day she'd seen it, everything about Cacao had repulsed her. She had wished it dead a thousand times.

Its high-pitched squawking could be heard in every room. The phrases that Wade taught it were rude and embarrassing. Then there was the sour smell that reached into each corner of the dark apartment, permeating the freshly laundered sheets and towels. Even after a shower she felt unclean, as unclean as she did each time Wade touched her. At the thought of his clammy hands reaching out for her, acid rose and burned her throat.

She stared through her tears at its vivid plumage. She should have loved the bird; after all, Cacao had apparently loved her. He had often tried to climb onto her shoulder or to elicit affection from her. Why did she hate it? In a surge of drunken guilt and self-pity, she told herself the bird had been her only friend in this ugly family.

She couldn't bear to look at it any longer. With a shaking hand she pulled the cover over the cage. Stumbling to the bed, Bella sat on the edge of it, as far away from Wade as possible.

An hour ago she'd been at a party, drinking, dancing, and having fun in the few hours she could steal away from Wade. She rested her head against the cool rail of the brass bed and tried to think. How had Cacao been when she'd left home earlier that evening? Had she missed any signs that her husband's companion was about to die?

She remembered going into the library to say good-bye to Wade. Cacao, on her husband's shoulder, squawked a nasty, "No, no, no," at her. Wade saw that she was irritated and tried to make up for it by saying how pretty she looked. Still, the bird had unsettled Bella and she'd fled the apartment for her party, where she had succeeded in making herself feel better.

Until she'd gotten home and discovered Cacao's corpse. Now she would have to wake Wade and tell him that his beloved bird was gone.

Bella kicked off her satin sandals and undid the buttons that fastened the black dress over her breasts. The garment was too tight to be truly comfortable but revealed enough of her cleavage to make her the sexiest woman at the party.

She stood up again and padded barefoot to the nightstand, which held a few bottles and glasses. She poured herself a couple of fingers of scotch and gulped it down, hoping it would give her courage.

Wade lay turned away from her. His face was hidden by the mask of his apnea machine, which Bella could hear clicking and whirring as usual. Somehow, Wade had learned to sleep despite the noise and the constant current of air. He was finally getting restful sleep after years of suffering. Bella wasn't so lucky.

Delaying the inevitable, Bella went back to her side of the bed, sat down facing away from her husband, and softly muttered, "Wade, I'm only twenty-seven and I have no life with you. You are a liar and a cheap bastard. You better fucking well sell that diamond. Wade, you fat hideous slob, I hate you and I'm glad your loudmouthed, stinking bird is dead."

The quiet tirade made her feel better. She glanced over her shoulder to make sure he hadn't heard and was relieved to see him lying still.

Suddenly she was struck by how still he was.

She leaned over and put her hand on his chest. She could feel no movement. But the machine should have kept him breathing.

Adrenaline surged through her, making her dizzy as she got to her feet. Steadying herself, Bella moved to Wade's side of the bed and shook him roughly.

"Wade, wake up. Cacao is sick and needs you."

He didn't stir.

She bent forward and shouted, "Wade!"

He didn't move.

She squatted beside him. Was he unconscious, or could he really be dead? His arm lay over the side of the bed. It felt cool as she put her fingers on his wrist to search for a pulse.

Nothing.

Were the rolls of fat at his wrist getting in the way, or was there nothing to feel? Bella covered her mouth, struggling against the renewed urge to vomit.

He was dead. She was sure of it.

What should she do first? Call the doctor? The police? Rouse the family? Or go into the spare room and try to go to sleep? There was nothing to be done for him now. Let someone else discover the body—Bella would just pretend that she'd never been in the bedroom.

No. She could see the lead story in the tabloids. "Beautiful Bella from Brazil came home from a party and got a good night's sleep in the next room while her husband lay dead in the marital bed." Absolutely not.

It would play better if she discovered him dead and phoned for help. That would be what the police would expect a loving wife to do.

As she struggled to her feet, she touched the sticky ice cream carton he'd left on the floor after his usual nightly binge. As she usually did, she grabbed the carton, then groped around for the spoon he'd used and the top of the container, but she didn't find them before nausea overcame her. Holding the carton she staggered into the kitchen and vomited into the sink.

Relief flooded over her. She turned on the tap and

watched the vomit wash away. The horror of living with Wade in the dark apartment vanished with it.

Lifting the handset for the kitchen phone, she dialed her brother Rico in São Paulo. It rang eight times before he answered, in a voice brusque with sleep.

"Bella, can't this wait until the morning?"

Her eyes filled with tears at the sound of her beloved brother's voice.

"Rico, Rico," she said, "I came home and found Cacao dead."

"Who on earth is Cacao?"

"The macaw, Wade's macaw. You remember."

"You're calling me in the middle of the night because a bird is dead? You're drunk." He sounded angry now.

"No, no. I've only had a little champagne," she said. She mustn't throw up again. She took a glass from the drying rack, filled it with water, and took a sip. "Don't be silly. This isn't about the bird. It's about Wade. He's dead too."

"What do you mean? Wade is dead?" Rico was wide awake now. "Start from the beginning. Where are you?"

She reached for a chair and steadied herself. "I came home from a charity party about ten minutes ago and found Cacao lying on the bottom of the cage. Then I tried to wake Wade to tell him. I shook him and shouted in his ear. He just lies there. He's not breathing. I don't know what to do. Help me."

"Bella, calm down and get help there. Didn't you say he has diabetes? He could be in a coma. Maybe he's taken one too many of those sleeping pills he likes. He was an unhappy man, so maybe it is suicide. But whatever it is, you need a doctor. Get off this phone and dial emergency. Do it now, then go upstairs and get Harold to take over."

He gave an exasperated sigh. "It's bad enough that you went to a party without your husband."

"Wade didn't want to go. He never wants to go. He's fat and lazy and boring. I hate him."

"Don't talk that way. Who brought you home?"

"A good friend."

"What sort of friend? Tell me the truth."

She ignored his question. "Rico, I'm sure Wade is dead. All I want to do is leave this place and never come back."

"Do what I say, call emergency, *right now*. If the police check your phone records for any reason, you don't want it to look like we had a long chat while Wade was dying.

"Do what I say and do it immediately. Go upstairs and get Harold to call for help. I'll talk to you tomorrow, find a New York lawyer for you, and get on a flight there if you need me. And Bella, watch what you say." He clicked off the phone.

She stood staring into the sink, which was still flecked with her vomit. She filled the ice cream carton with water and used it to clean the sink. With it went the horror of her life with Wade. Rico would look after her just as he had when Jorge Dias had forced her to sign a prenuptial agreement. "Don't worry about it," he'd told her. "It's meaningless. We'll contest it when he dies and you'll get everything."

Despite Rico's instructions, she couldn't bring herself to dial 911. Bella wandered through the living room, stopping in front of the oil portrait of Wade's mother. She could finally have that painting taken down. She would be free of the specter of the perfect Esperanza. Bella smiled at the sight of the Braganza around Esperanza's neck. The money from the auction would soon be hers.

Slowly she climbed the stairs to Harold's apartment, thinking about what Rico had said.

Wade was an unhappy man. He had every reason to commit suicide.

She would inherit the Braganza.

At the top of the steps, Bella began to scream, "Help me . . . it's Wade."

Chapter 11

FRIDAY, 4:00 A.M.
Sonya's apartment

The distinctive, insistent sound of a cell phone ring tone penetrated Sonya's deep sleep. Before opening her eyes, she lay still for a moment to be sure she was really awake—that the ringing was not part of the frightening dreams she had been having the past few nights.

Sonya slept with her cell phone on the bedside table and kept it at full volume, a habit she developed in her first job as a producer of local news in Minneapolis. News like fatal car accidents usually happened in the early hours of the morning, and she had to dress and be ready for the crew in minutes.

On a network magazine show in New York the nighttime calls were rare, but she liked to feel she was always available.

"Who is it?" she whispered, keeping her head on the pillow and turning away to avoid waking Keith.

The dramatic sob that answered her could only come from Kirsten.

Sonya kept her voice calm and businesslike, hoping

it would stem the intern's outburst. "What is it, Kirsten? What's the matter? Why are you calling at this hour?"

"Oh, Sonya, I'm so glad to hear your voice," Kirsten said, adding, with another sob, "Wade's dead."

Sonya sat up, now fully awake. "What? Wade's dead? How?"

"We don't know how. And Harold won't let me see him or tell me anything, but I wanted you to know. I'll try to find out everything."

Sonya sensed movement on the other side of the bed. Keith was awake. "Wade Bruckheimer's dead?"

Sonya nodded.

"Just a minute, Kirsten, while I get up and go into another room." She went into the kitchen and settled at the table. Keith headed for the bathroom. Sonya frowned, hoping he wasn't going to try to be part of her conversation. The cop in him would have trouble resisting news of an unexpected death.

"Now, Kirsten, tell me what's going on."

"Is Keith with you?"

Sonya ignored the question and said, "I want to help you. Just be calm and tell me what you know."

"Okay, okay." Kirsten took an audible breath. "Bella came home and couldn't wake him. Then Harold went down and looked at him and called the police." She added with annoying petulance, "That's why I wanted to know if Keith was there. Maybe he can find out what'll be in the police report."

Sonya wanted to blast Kirsten for not knowing that that would be all but impossible and might endanger Keith's career, but realized that the young woman was genuinely upset and needed understanding, not criticism.

As gently as she could, Sonya said, "You know he can't do that, Kirsten. Is everyone else all right?"

The other woman began sobbing again. "Cacao's dead too."

Kirsten's crying was so violent that Sonya began to wonder if it was genuine. Was Kirsten self-centered enough to be weeping over the possibility that the Braganza story would be canceled?

"The bird is dead too?"

"Yes. Yes." Kirsten almost choked the words out.

"Kirsten, take a minute and calm down. Get a drink of water," Sonya said firmly. "I'll hold on. Then you can start from the beginning."

Keith came out of the bathroom and kissed Sonya on the neck. Without thinking, she shrugged her shoulders to shake him off. He stood motionless behind her for a moment, then moved away. Sonya put her hand over the phone, and whispered, "I'm sorry . . . you can see I have an emergency here. . . ."

"Okay. I'll make some coffee."

Kirsten returned to the conversation, sounding calmer, though she still sniffed back tears every few words. "Here's what I know. Bella found Cacao dead in his cage and when she tried to tell Wade, she couldn't wake him. I got up when I heard her shouting for Harold. She was drunk and was sick all over the bathroom floor."

"Did you see her yourself?"

"Yes, and she was hysterical at first. Mom told me to get out of the way. I waited while Bella got cleaned up and put on one of Mom's dressing gowns. Then Mom made her lie down."

"What was your impression of her, besides the fact that she was drunk? And what did you mean about her being hysterical 'at first'?"

"She was calmer after she got cleaned up, but I could still smell the alcohol on her. Of course she was nervous, but she wasn't crying or anything. I wanted to sit with her, but my mom told me to stay away and let her rest."

"Who checked on Wade?"

"I heard Harold go down as soon as Bella came upstairs shouting, before I even got out of my room. After a while, he walked halfway up the stairs and told Mom and me that he'd called the police."

"How long was he in Wade's apartment?"

"He's still down there; he went back down after talking to Mom and me. The police are there now but I don't know if Wade's body has been taken away."

"When did all this start, Kirsten?"

"A little after two A.M., I think. When Bella's screaming woke me up, I looked at the clock."

Keith put a cup of steaming coffee in front of Sonya, then sat down at the table, holding his own cup. Sonya took a drink, then said, "So you haven't seen the body?"

"No. Harold wouldn't let me. He said things had to be left just as they were until the police were finished. That's all I know."

"Think it over for a minute and see if you remember anything else."

"Okay," Kirsten agreed calmly, fully recovered from her tears at the beginning of their conversation. "Oh, Sonya, what about our diamond story? Mom said it would definitely be sold now that Wade's dead. I'll be ready to get to work right away this morning."

"We'll talk about the story later. Just tell me what Harold said, if you remember."

"He said he couldn't find Wade's pulse and was sure he wasn't breathing. Mom went down to him and they walked away from the stairs, so I couldn't hear them. I tried to get closer but my mother saw me and told me to go back upstairs. When she came back and I asked her what was wrong she told me the same things Harold had."

"Where is your mother now?"

"She's sitting with Bella. That's typical of her. Bella's my friend, but Mother pushed me out and took over."

"And Irina?"

"I'm not sure. She always closes her bedroom door and it's really hard to wake her up. Even all that noise downstairs may not have been enough, because I haven't seen her. I think she takes something to help her sleep. I don't think Harold's going to tell her until the police leave."

"Have you any idea what the police are doing now?"

"No, I don't know." Kirsten gave an exasperated sigh. "I don't know why they won't let me see Wade."

"You were close to him. Maybe Harold and your mother are trying to protect you. It's not easy to see the body of someone you love."

"Why do I need protection? I'm not a kid. You know how strong I am. They resent me and Harold treats me like an outsider. I hate him and I hate my mother for marrying him. Wade was the only one who loved me." Kirsten's voice had hardened.

Sonya took another deep breath. "Listen, Kirsten, let's not get into all this now. Have a little understanding. Wade is Harold's brother. He must be in shock."

"Well, I'll give him a shock. I called my father and told him what was happening. My poor dad. He's shaken up. You know he loved Wade and hated Harold, too. He said he was coming right over; he should be here any minute."

"I'm going to hang up now. I don't need to hear all this now. I'll see you at the office, later." Sonya paused for a moment. "Come in late if you have to, and if you decide you need the day off, take it. And damnit, Kirsten, stop making all these thoughtless judgments."

Kirsten's voice rose in anger and the words poured out of her. "I've lived with Harold for eighteen years. The only person he cares for is his mother. He does everything she asks because he wants her money."

"That's enough," Sonya said sharply. "I've changed my mind. Take the day off. I don't want you at work until you calm down." She clicked off the phone.

"What's going on, Red?" Keith asked. "She really knows how to upset you."

"I guess you got the gist of it . . . Wade Bruckheimer is dead. Harold and Blair have kept Kirsten away from the scene, but I'll bet there's a big story here. Wade was about to sell a thirty-million-dollar diamond and now he's dead in a house full of greedy people . . . most of them wanting the stone."

"You suspect murder?"

"Exactly. From the little Kirsten told me, it could be natural causes or even suicide. But my reporter's instinct tells me it may not be."

"They'll do an autopsy on him, so you'll know the cause of death soon enough."

"And his bird died too. What about that?"

"His bird? Suspicious, for sure. They'll do a necroscopy on the bird."

Sonya reached out and touched his hand. "Keith, I'm sorry . . . I mean, when you kissed me, I was upset and tired—a lethal combination for lovers."

"Thanks, Red . . . I understand. It got to me for a while, but I'm okay. How about a little more coffee?"

"I'm wired already. Better not have any more. I've got to get to work early. For one thing, the local station will want some of my tape of Wade for the morning news." She stopped and looked at Keith, suddenly remembering, "Oh, Keith, I forgot you have early shift this morning. I'm sorry my phone woke you."

"That's okay."

"You've been taking care of me." She stood and moved to him. "Now what can I get for you?"

He got up and kissed her. "Nothing, Red. I have to confess I sneaked in an English muffin and juice while I was making the coffee."

She laughed. "I might have guessed. Now go get ready. I'll take the bathroom after you."

On the way, he stopped and turned back, laughing with her. "Come to think of it, there is one thing you can do for me. Change that ring tone on your cell. It's powerful."

She started to reply, but he smiled and added, "Just kidding. It's great."

Sonya looked at the cell phone on the table. She knew he was lying. The ring tone she chose had a special meaning. As a child, she'd often heard her mother humming a song, and she unconsciously learned it. Sonya had had no idea what the lyric was, or even the name of the song. He mother had said she couldn't remember. But Sabrina, who prided herself as an expert on pop songs of the fifties and sixties, knew it immediately when Sonya had hummed it for her, years earlier.

She'd said, "Sonya, for sure that's Paul Revere and the Raiders, from the sixties. It's 'Hungry.' "

"Are you sure? It doesn't sound like my mother's kind of thing."

"Absolutely sure."

Soon after that conversation, Sonya had found the song online and downloaded it to her phone. It had been her ring tone ever since. As if on cue, the melody played as her phone lit up. Caller ID told her it was Donna. She answered, "Good morning."

"You heard from Kirsten, I'm sure," Donna said without any greeting.

"Yes, I have. Did Kirsten call you?"

"She's sure it's murder. What do you think?"

"Donna, it's too early to come to any conclusion. Let's wait for the police report."

"Kirsten sounded sure, but you know what she's like. We can discuss it as soon as you get in."

She abruptly clicked off, leaving Sonya still holding the silent phone.

Chapter 12

Sonya was surprised to see Kirsten waiting near the reception desk when she arrived. Her head was tilted downward in the pose Sonya had noticed she often used to elicit sympathy. At least, thought Sonya, she's not gossiping with the receptionist, for a change.

"Is Donna in yet?" Sonya asked the security guard.

"No," was the reply.

Deciding to wait to speak to Kirsten, Sonya nodded in greeting and said, "Give me fifteen minutes to get settled, then come see me." She walked briskly past the young woman, heading for her office.

She wondered which Kirsten she was about to see— the grief-stricken woman who had called her in a panic early that morning or the television professional. Kirsten's sorrow had seemed genuine, but Sonya wasn't sure how deeply she had been affected by Wade's death. One thing was obvious, though: Kirsten's competitive drive.

Sonya slung her bag on the desk, sat down, and unlocked her file drawer. Kirsten appeared in the doorway and asked, "Do you want coffee?"

Despite feeling sorry for what she must have been through that night, Sonya felt a spasm of anger. She had asked for fifteen minutes and been given two. It struck Sonya that Kirsten was as greedy as any of the Bruckheimers. Not just for money, but for attention, to satisfy an insatiable need for approval.

"Do you want coffee?" Kirsten repeated. Sonya realized that her voice was trembling.

Despite her determination not to mother the intern, Sonya felt swamped by a wave of sympathy. "I had some at home, but another cup would be great, thanks."

Encouraged by Sonya's reply, Kirsten stepped completely into the office. "How about a doughnut? There are a lot left from the early morning show."

Sonya shook her head. "Just coffee."

"Are you sure? They're awesome. I ate three while I waited for you," she said cheerfully.

"Coffee's fine," Sonya said.

Once Kirsten left, Sonya tried to start preparing a log sheet for Wade's interview, but found herself worrying about the intern. Kirsten's usual favored snack was high-protein spirulina balls; she had to be feeling frantic to have eaten so many doughnuts.

Sonya had noticed Kirsten's pale face and the dark circles under her eyes; probably signs of a sleepless night. She had dressed in keeping with the somber mood of a death in the family. Her shirt dress, which was long and shapeless and so loose it probably belonged to her mother, was dark green. With it she wore black leggings and flat shoes. The only bright spot in her look were her large gold hoop earrings.

Sonya switched on her computer monitor and scrolled through the overnight reports. The wire services knew less about Wade's death than she did, except for one that speculated that an overdose of drugs was a possible cause of death. Wade, who was known to have taken social drugs, had possibly killed the bird and himself.

It was the curious death of the bird that had Sonya convinced Wade's death was murder. It was too much of a coincidence to believe that both had died of natural causes on the same night. She knew that Wade loved his bird; he would never have killed Cacao.

Sonya found the tape Perry had neatly labeled #ONE and put it in the machine. A quick fast-forward showed the camera following Wade as he showed Sonya around the living room. At that point in the interview, Wade had been friendly enough, and certainly not depressed. He had said he was selling the diamond so he could enjoy good times with his wife. Things were going his way. Why would he kill himself?

Sonya hit pause as Kirsten returned with the coffee and sat on the opposite side of the desk. Kirsten peered at the image on the monitor. "Uncle Wade," she said softly. "I can't believe that was only yesterday. I miss him already. He understood me." Her eyes began to tear and Sonya offered her a tissue.

They sat in silence for a moment while Kirsten wiped away her tears. Her reaction seemed real enough. Maybe I've been unfair, thought Sonya.

"My mother said I must apologize for calling you that early. I was so shocked, I didn't think about the time.

I knew you would understand and that you'd want to know because of the story." Sonya wasn't surprised that Kirsten didn't mention that she'd also called Donna.

"Uncle Wade has been part of my life forever," Kirsten continued. "I just wish they'd have let me see him. That would have made it seem more real. This way, I feel like he just disappeared. Even after his body had been taken away, the police wouldn't let me go into the bedroom or see Cacao's cage. I couldn't say good-bye to them."

As she spoke, Kirsten tugged at one ear. She whined, "It's hurting," as she yanked off the earring and pulled on her earlobe in what Sonya recognized as an attempt to ease the pain. Sonya looked closely. She'd never seen Kirsten wear those earrings before. The gold circles were studded with small diamonds and rubies. She wondered who the jewelry belonged to—perhaps her mother or Bella. Surely not even Kirsten would have the nerve to raid Irina's jewelry box.

"Pretty, aren't they," Kirsten said, holding up the earring. "Usually not my thing, but I couldn't resist borrowing them for today. They're like an homage to Uncle Wade. He loved beautiful things."

"Borrowed? Who lent them to you?"

"Uncle Wade always said that they would be mine when he died," she said defensively. "They belonged to his mother. He let Bella wear them, but he promised them to me. She won't mind that I took them."

The intern shifted uneasily in her seat.

"You can't imagine how furious Mom is with me. She almost lost it when I told her I'd called Donna to tell her Wade died."

Sonya's throat tightened and she leaned forward, ready for a confrontation. But Kirsten was oblivious. "Mom said Wade's death was a family matter and I was not to talk about it to anyone, not even to a family friend like Donna. How am I supposed to avoid it when I'm working for her, and she's my godmother?"

Sonya responded through clenched teeth. "Easy! If you have anything to say, you are to tell me. I'm doing the story. Do you understand?"

Kirsten picked up the earring and twisted it in her fingers. For a moment Sonya thought she would bend the fine gold circle out of shape, but she gave her earlobe another pull before putting the earring back on.

"I just don't understand my mother," she continued. "One day she is crazy happy about my doing the internship with Donna and the next she says not to talk to her. When I said I hoped Donna would still do the story, she said not to make trouble. Mom and Donna are supposed to be great friends, but there's something going on between them. I don't know what it is. Do you?" Kirsten looked at Sonya through her eyelashes, inviting confidences Sonya had no intention of giving her.

"If I were you, Kirsten, I'd follow your mother's advice. Don't get mixed up in it."

"My mother has no respect for me. I intend to make a career in this business, and I can't even get my mother to give me moral support. Now that Wade is gone, I only have my father on my side and Mother doesn't like him."

She dabbed her eyes again, but this time Sonya was sure that there were no tears.

"She blames me for everything," Kirsten went on.

"Sometimes I think she hates me. She certainly doesn't love me as mothers ought to love their daughters."

Sonya remembered something Sabrina had once said: "Who really understands anybody's secrets? Or what another person really wants."

Sonya felt sympathy for Kirsten—and for Blair— both unfulfilled and needing approval. That's what Kirsten really wants from Donna . . . and from me, she thought.

"Let's get some work done before the morning meeting," she said, and was pleased to see Kirsten straighten up and reach for her notebook, ready to start. Sonya decided to say what was on her mind. "Before we begin, I want to get something straight. This is my story, not yours. If you have anything for it, you come to me, not Donna, not Perry, not Sabrina. Understand?"

Sonya assumed that Kirsten was rarely spoken to so plainly, that in her family, everyone played secret games. She could see by the intern's expression that she was unhappy with what had been said. Sonya crossed her arms and waited until Kirsten spoke.

"I understand, Sonya."

Sonya had no illusions that this would permanently change things between them, but it cleared the air for the moment. Given that Donna was committed to keeping Kirsten as an intern, Sonya would have to continue to find ways to make their relationship work. But she realized that she had no reason to feel threatened by or jealous of this needy, determined younger woman.

"I'll call and see if Donna is in. She wanted to see me right away."

Her secretary said that Donna had changed her mind

and that she would see Sonya at the morning meeting. She had not offered any explanation.

"We have a couple of minutes before the meeting, so tell me why you think Wade was murdered. You seem to have convinced Donna."

"I got the idea from Giorgio. When I called my father, he said that he had been afraid that someone might try to kill Wade and that he had warned my uncle to straighten out some family matters. He was very upset; he told me he was sorry he wasn't more insistent with Wade. Giorgio would have done anything to protect Wade."

"I'd like to interview your father. Can you arrange it for me?"

Kirsten frowned. "I'll try," was her terse answer.

"Let's go to the meeting. We'll pick up on this later."

Sonya and Kirsten joined the rest of the staff in the conference room. Sonya enjoyed the customary exchanges of morning greetings and minor jockeying for seats. As usual, Donna arrived on time, smiling as she took her place at the head of the table. She seemed in good form, apparently completely recovered from whatever had happened with Blair.

Since the executive producer was away, Sonya led the meeting. Despite being distracted, she was able to muster her usual discipline and focus on each story as the staff discussed it, but she was anxious to hear what Donna had to say about the Braganza piece. Would Donna give the go-ahead even without autopsy results?

Of course the diamond story was last on the agenda. Donna opened the conversation by saying, "I might run a short piece on Wade Bruckheimer on our Tuesday show. We have your interview, Sonya, and I assume it has some good sound bites. Do you know if the diamond will still be sold?"

Before Sonya could speak, Kirsten piped up from her seat at the end of the table. "I think it will—" At Donna's gesture of dismissal, the intern fell silent, looking startled.

Sonya said, "We don't know anything yet about the diamond. I'll try to confirm the sale today."

Donna nodded and continued, "All right, let's keep going on it, but we'll wait for the autopsy results before we make a final decision. Sonya, have you any idea when we'll get that?"

"It's getting media attention, so it could be pushed to the top of the list. I'll look into it."

"And the bird?" Donna flipped through Sonya's report. "It died at the same time as Wade. It will be autopsied too?"

"I believe so," Sonya said, nodding.

"I saw it once when I was visiting Blair. It was beautiful."

"Wade was crazy about Cacao. It's more than suspicious that they died at the same time, don't you think?"

Sonya was a little surprised when Donna replied, "Yes, I do." Her boss went on, "But let's stay away from that for now. Let me know when you get the autopsy results. That is, if you get them to me before Kirsten does." Donna laughed, as did much of the rest of the staff. It wasn't like Donna to make those kinds of bullying "jokes." Sonya decided Donna must be feeling the strain of having a murder strike so close, in the family of an old friend. She decided to ignore the remark and just do her job.

Chapter 13

FRIDAY, 8:15 A.M.
Blair's kitchen

Harold Bruckheimer looked up from reading *The New York Times* and held out his coffee cup for a refill as Blair crossed the kitchen. "It tastes stronger than your usual brew. Did you use your new do-it-all coffee machine? The one Wade gave you?"

Blair stifled her groan of annoyance. Just yesterday Harold had helped her repack the machine to return it to the store. He'd agreed with her that any machine that needed such a thick operating manual was a waste of time and money. It was typical of him to forget all about it. He had a brilliant mind for engineering but that was about all. Even so, sometimes she wondered if it were an act, if he used his apparent confusion as a way to avoid any unpleasant interactions.

She knew better than to try to argue. If she criticized him, he would clam up and not speak to her for hours. It was his habit whenever she tried to discuss a problem.

The phone on the table rang. As usual, she moved to

pick it up, but to her surprise, Harold threw down his paper to grab the handset. "For me," he said, putting his hand over the speaker. "It's the attorney returning my call."

Blair reached for the last piece of french toast on the hot plate. She bit into it, comforted by its warm sweetness. The dish was one of Harold's favorites and she'd made it to give him energy after a sleepless night.

Disappointingly, Harold was not in the mood to eat, while Blair wound up eating all but two pieces. That was another difference between them. She ate like a fiend when she was stressed, while his appetite disappeared completely. That was why he was slim and she had to watch her weight.

He ignored her now, turning his attention to the phone. "Thank you for calling back so quickly." Blair swallowed, listening to her husband's side of the conversation.

"Yes, it was an enormous shock. Wade was happy with Bella, happier than I had ever seen him. Of course she's devastated. She was distraught when she came to wake us."

He listened for a moment and then went on. "The police came immediately. The detective in charge said he expects the autopsies will be done today and we'll know the cause of death. I'll call you as soon as I hear." He shook his head. "No, we don't know when he died exactly; just the time when Bella found him."

Blair prompted him from across the table, "Tell him it was about two o'clock."

Harold glared at her for a moment while saying, "The autopsy report will reveal all those details. But I need to see you as soon as possible about Wade's will."

Blair frantically signaled to him that she had something to say.

"Just a moment." Harold put his hand over the mouthpiece. "What is it, Blair?"

"Tell him that we want to get probate started immediately. I'm worried that things will start disappearing around here. Both Bella and Jorge have itchy fingers."

"Three o'clock this afternoon would be fine." He paused for a long moment. "The diamond?" he asked. "It's in the safe where it's always kept."

Panic gripped Blair. In the shock of Wade's death, she had forgotten the diamond. Now she remembered that both Irina and possibly Bella had the combination to the safe.

"Harold, tell him we'll check on it immediately," she interrupted.

Harold nodded and repeated what she'd said into the phone. Then, apparently in response to something the attorney said, he added, "I haven't seen it lately because Bella doesn't want to wear it and Mother hasn't been going to many parties. But it must be there. Wade told us the auction house would send an armored van to pick it up today. Should I call them and stop that?"

Blair interrupted again, this time letting her anxiety ring out. "We are not making final decisions yet. After we've checked the will, we'll decide about the sale."

Harold covered the mouthpiece and shouted at her, "For god's sake, Blair, shut up! I can't hear what he's saying." He removed his hand and spoke into the phone. "Okay, thanks again. I'll see you at three. Right."

He crashed the receiver back onto the cradle. "Good god, Blair, your behavior embarrassed me. The only saving grace is that the old guy has known me for years. He understands that I'm perfectly capable of taking care of this. I don't need your interference."

Blair lowered her head to hide her face. "I'm sorry, darling. I spoke out of turn. It's because I'm tired and upset. I know you can handle everything. You always have." She gave him a quick look to see if he had forgiven her, and then continued, "You have to admit that the lawyer raised a good point. I can't remember the last time I saw the Braganza. Let's check on it."

Harold said brusquely, "It's in the safe, in the den. Where else would it be?"

Anxiety tightened Blair's chest. "Do you remember when you last saw it?"

After a pause, her husband said, "I can't remember, but I know it's there." He looked straight into her eyes. "Only Wade, Irina, and I know the combination."

You're wrong, Blair thought, I know it, too. You've forgotten that you gave it to me years ago, when Douglas first got sick and you went to that conference in Seattle. And if I have it, I bet Bella has it too.

She shuddered. Bella had slept in the den last night. And she'd sobered up; she could easily have opened the safe.

"Harold," Blair said, "finish your coffee and let's check the safe." He stared at her for a moment, then took a long, obviously reluctant drink of coffee. He slowly and deliberately folded his newspaper and set it on the table, then stood up, carried his mug to the sink, and turned on the water to rinse it out.

Blair waited patiently. She'd put up with Harold's passive aggressiveness for years and knew any attempt to speed him up would only make him stubbornly slower. She told herself to be compassionate. It was clear that Harold had not fully accepted Wade's death—not a surprise, since less than four hours had passed since his brother's body had been carried out of the apartment.

Finally, Harold said, "Let's go," and Blair walked with him to the den.

Bella had slept on the pull-out sofa in the den, and when she'd gotten up, she'd made no effort to straighten the room. The sheets were a crumpled mass on the bed and the pillow was streaked with black mascara. Blair pulled the sheets and pillows onto the floor and folded the bed back into the sofa.

Harold went to the ornately framed Bavarian landscape painting which hid the safe. As he maneuvered it off the hook, the picture slipped through his fingers and fell heavily to the carpet.

"Be careful. That's one of your mother's favorite paintings." Blair stooped and picked up the picture, then carefully set it down, leaning it against the sofa with the back of the canvas facing into the room.

Harold had paused to study the face of the safe. He asked Blair for a tissue and wiped the dial. The tissue came away clean and Blair saw that there was no dust on the front of the safe. Trying to control the fear in her voice, she said, "Someone opened it recently."

She could hear the stress in her husband's voice as he replied, "Wade probably opened it—he had to show the diamond to the executives at the auction house. Or maybe Irina wanted a piece of jewelry for some reason."

Irina, Blair thought, grasping at anything that might relieve her dread. Irina kept some of her fine jewelry in the safe.

Harold breathed heavily as he slowly punched in the combination. His hand shook; Blair was tempted to tell him to let her take over. Finally he swung open the door. The safe was full of jewelry cases of various sizes. A folding file of documents sat atop the heap. Harold carefully began removing things from the safe and handed them to Blair, who set them down on the coffee table. First the folding file, then the small boxes that contained Irina's jewelry, and finally, the large, ornate, red velvet box stamped with the Brazilian royal crest in gold. The Braganza.

"Ha, you see, it's here, just as I said." Harold couldn't contain his glee as he turned to face his wife.

Blair reached for the box. "Let me see it," she said, unfastening the clasp and lifting the lid.

The box was empty; its red velvet peaks and valleys seemed to be screaming at the loss of their usual contents.

"Mother must have it," Harold said after a long silence. "Although I can't understand why she would keep it in her room."

Blair couldn't control her anger. "It's not hard for me to explain. Irina is desperate to keep the diamond. She's stolen it."

"Don't be crazy," Harold said. "What could she do with it if she took it? She couldn't sell it—it's too recognizable. Besides," he said, glowering at Blair, "all Irina ever wanted was to wear it. The stone gave her an identity. Something she never got from her husband or her father."

"An identity? That's a load of crap. She's a rich woman who has been given everything she wanted."

"For Christ's sake, why are you so hard on her? She had a rotten childhood. A German mother who never adjusted to this country and a father who was too busy chasing other women to pay her any attention."

"So what," Blair stated flatly. "That's everyone's story. Whose parents didn't have problems?"

Harold exploded. "You've never understood how important her jewelry is to her! I know it's irrational, and it's hard for you to understand. But try.

"Irina's mother came from a family of jewelers who worked for the tsars. Growing up in war-torn Germany, glittering Moscow, fabulous jewelry, and the work her family did for the tsars was all Irina heard about and all she fantasized about. Think about what those stories must have meant to her—try to put yourself in her place for a moment."

Blair heard real fury in Harold's voice and answered quietly, trying to appease him. "I understand. It must have been awful to have such an unhappy mother. Irina went through hell."

Harold visibly relaxed and Blair went to him and kissed him on the cheek. He responded by putting his arm around her waist. "Thank you," he said softly, and Blair knew the fight was over.

Together, Harold and Blair repacked the safe, leaving

the box for the Braganza on the table. Harold closed the safe door and spun the dial. He picked up the jewelry case. "I'll go and see her and get the diamond back."

"I'll come with you," Blair said.

He turned to face her and said firmly, "No, she's my mother. I'll handle her."

Okay, Blair thought, I'll stay out of it—for now.

Chapter 14

FRIDAY, 8:45 A.M.
Wade Bruckheimer's apartment

Jorge was cold with fear as he went through the door that connected his apartment to Wade's. No, not Wade's any longer, he thought, trying to calm himself. His emotions had been out of control since his confrontation with Wade the night before. When the younger man had refused to sell him the Braganza, Jorge had been almost overcome with rage.

Then there had been the shocking sight of the black body bag being wheeled to the elevator and out into the darkness of the early morning.

Now Jorge had to be strong enough to take back the antiques that had been in the Dias family for generations. His father had been foolish to let Esperanza have them, but how could he have known she would die so soon and leave so much unsettled?

And the Braganza, that rare, exquisite diamond. He would have that too. Jorge took a few tentative steps into the living room, then stopped to listen. The silence encouraged him. He felt no guilt for what he was about to do, but he didn't want to face Bella. That would come later.

He had been in this apartment countless times and always felt free to come and go as he wished. After all, the Dias family had paid for the apartment, and as a resentful Elenora had reminded Jorge, their family had supported Wade all his life.

"So," she had said with typical assurance, "the apartment and everything in it belongs to us."

Now, standing in an apartment that seemed different, unknown, and unwelcoming, Jorge knew that his nephew's death had altered everything. Bella was Wade's wife, and despite a prenuptial agreement, she would claim all of his estate. And, Jorge knew, her family had connections in Brazil. They would stand behind her, happy to snatch a victory over the Dias "aristocrats."

Irina would be an even fiercer adversary. Wade's death was the opening she needed to raise the question of who owned the heirloom collection of silver and gold—and the diamond.

As Douglas's second wife, Irina insisted the diamond belonged to her, not Wade, and she and Douglas had fought endlessly about the stone, even while Douglas was dying. In his last days, Irina pressed him hard on the question of ownership of Esperanza's jewelry, but Douglas seemed to take pleasure in denying her the satisfaction of an answer.

"My will," was his weak but terse reply. When he was gone and the will was read, to Irina's fury, a codicil explained that the diamond and antiques were not part of her husband's estate. That they had belonged to Wade since his mother's death.

Jorge drew from his jacket pocket a carefully preserved birth announcement from Esperanza. On the
back, she had written a private note, telling Jorge how
happy she was to have brought Wade into the family
and that her son would be brought up to respect the
family traditions. She'd added that the family heirlooms
she'd brought to her marriage would someday belong to
her son, to ensure his connection with the Diases. Esperanza and Douglas had both signed the note and Douglas had added, in his own hand, the words, "I agree."

Even back then, Jorge had not completely trusted the
Bruckheimers, so he had sealed the note away in Mylar
and preserved it against the day when it might be
needed. He looked around the room and his gaze settled on the portrait of Esperanza. At the sight of his
sister's lovely face, Jorge felt his strength return.

"For you, my beautiful sister. I do it for you. Our
family will reclaim our treasures and I will take your
portrait home to Brazil," he murmured.

He'd decided to begin by inventorying the most valuable pieces, which were kept in a nineteenth-century
Portuguese sideboard in the dining room. Many times
when Jorge and his wife had visited Wade, Elenora had
asked Wade to unlock the cabinet for her. Jorge had
often watched as she had taken obvious, greedy pleasure
in touching the antiques, caressing each piece and mut-
tering "beautiful" and "lovely" half under her breath,
clearly mesmerized by their workmanship.

The night before, when Wade had refused to give up
the diamond, Jorge had called Elenora. She had been
angry but not surprised. "Give him some time to think

it over," she had counseled him. "Perhaps you rushed him. Try again tomorrow."

It had seemed like a good idea at the time.

But now Wade was dead and everything was in doubt. Jorge had called Elenora again this morning, to tell her the sad news. He had heard both grief and fear in her voice when she said, "Jorge, you didn't do anything foolish, did you?"

He spoke as firmly as possible. "I did nothing foolish. What makes you ask?"

"How many times have you said you wished him dead? Have you ever said that in front of anyone?" she asked.

"No, Elenora, of course not. I said that only to you, and you know I never seriously meant it."

"Jorge, the police will be investigating. They will discover that you bring him those strong sleeping pills. He could have taken an overdose."

"Elenora, stop talking nonsense."

She hesitated a moment before continuing. "Jorge, I'm worried. They could accuse you. I'm getting on the next plane."

"No. No, Elenora. I'm sure there is no need for you to come. I will be leaving as soon as I've done what needs to be done."

"I insist, Jorge, so say nothing more. I need to be there to take care of you and to see that we get our heirlooms back. Until I get there, you must make the inventory—and keep your eye on Bella. She knows you opposed her marriage and she will get great satisfaction if she can take those pieces from us."

Elenora believed that Jorge's inventory, and especially any photos he could take, would discourage Bella from removing anything. It was necessary to make an inventory since there was no official list of the contents of Esperanza's dowry, and without a list, it would be easy for Bella to hide choice pieces and claim she didn't know where they were. During the phone call, Jorge had promised Elenora he would have the inventory finished before she arrived. Now, standing in the dining room, he found himself hoping that nothing had already been removed.

Jorge slipped the blade of his pocketknife between the doors of the carved Portuguese sideboard and started to pry at the lock. He didn't want to force it too hard. Not only would marks be noticed, but the sideboard was an antique, deserving of respect. Remembering that it was one of the pieces Esperanza had brought from Brazil, Jorge pulled out his cell phone and took a picture of the sideboard before returning to his task.

One more twist of the pocketknife and the door swung open. He could see the dull sheen of the unpolished silver service on the lower shelf. Reaching in, he took out a silver tray with shaking hands. His grandmother had used this to serve afternoon tea for the family.

Jorge recalled how Esperanza's wedding gifts had been laid out on covered card tables so her guests could admire them. Many of the relatives had given family treasures, saying that they wanted the bride to remember her homeland.

In his memories, Jorge heard Elenora whispering resentfully to him, as she had on that day, "Esperanza has charm as well as beauty, and I know it is impossible for you not to love her. But she is greedy and uses her charm and beauty to get what she wants."

How pleased Elenora would be to have these beautiful things restored to Brazil, to polish them back to life and be able to hand them on to their children.

Absorbed in photographing each precious piece, Jorge failed to hear the light footsteps behind him. He had no idea he was being watched until he was startled by Bella's harsh voice demanding, "What the hell are you doing?"

How long had she been at the door? No matter. Now was as good a time as any to settle with her.

"Hello, Bella, my condolences on the death of my nephew." He always spoke to her with the cold tone he used when disciplining servants and he never referred to Wade as "her husband." He knew that it irritated her to have him call Wade "my nephew," and he used it to remind her that she had not been accepted by the Dias family. He wanted there to be no mistake—he wanted her to be aware of her lower-class standing. They were not equals. In Brazil, he would not even have acknowledged her. In Brazil, she would never have been permitted to marry Wade.

"What are you doing with my things?" Bella stepped farther into the room, looking closely at the silver that Jorge had spread out on the table in order to get clear pictures. "In fact, what are you doing here at all? When did you get here?" She paused. "Were you here last night?"

"When I arrived is not your business. I will stay here

to arrange family matters with my nephew's estate. I am beginning with an inventory of the Dias family heirlooms."

"Listen to me, old man," Bella said angrily. "This is not São Paulo, so you had better drop the fucking superior attitude. I want you out of this apartment. You have no permission to even touch my things, never mind take pictures. Now leave or I will call the police and tell them that you are trying to steal from me."

Jorge rose and stepped toward her. "You will do nothing. Read the agreement you signed before you married my nephew. You own nothing but your personal belongings." Jorge spoke with conviction, intending to settle the issue. "I will decide later if you can remain in this apartment. You know it was purchased by the Dias family and is in our name. Now leave me alone and go mourn my nephew, as you should."

Bella laughed harshly. She glared at Jorge, and he began to think that she would not be easily intimidated. "Watch what you say to me. With my husband dead, everything's changed."

Jorge's heart began to beat faster and he felt the familiar pain in his chest. He fought back the weakness—he would not appear vulnerable in front of her. "Whatever you think you are entitled to get, you already have," he said, pleased that his voice held steady and strong.

He took a deep breath, fighting the pain, and struck back. "Isn't it strange that he died so suddenly? I saw him just hours before, and he was well and happy." Jorge felt a clutch in his chest and was forced to sit in one of the dining chairs.

Bella watched him. "Not feeling well?" She started toward him and he was surprised to find that he detected some sympathy in her expression.

"I am fine, thank you." He would never accept help from this woman.

"It's strange," she said, standing still again, "that just before my husband was to send the diamond to the auction house, you show up and he dies. You brought him sleeping pills and you wanted the auction stopped. I wonder what the police will say about that."

"What are you saying?"

Bella looked at the ornate pieces on the table. "Don't bother to put these away. Go back to your apartment and don't come in here again." She pointed to Esperanza's portrait. "You can have that. I give it to you willingly. I never want to see it again."

Jorge said nothing. The pain told him he must leave and rest, before he fainted. He had the photos of the antiques. He would deal with Bella later.

Wade was dead, and Jorge swore to himself, on his family's honor, Bella would get nothing.

Chapter 15

Irina knew her voice was shrill and growing louder but she couldn't stop. "What do you mean, 'missing'? How can it be missing? A stone like the Braganza doesn't just get mislaid. Someone has stolen it and we'll never get it back." She held her head in her hands and rocked against the sofa. "Oh no, god, no, no, no."

Harold put his arms around her and spoke quietly. "Mother, please be calm, everything will work out. But first, you must tell me where you put it."

"Harold, please believe me, I don't have the Braganza, and I don't know where it is. If I did, I would tell you." She pulled away from him as she felt him stiffen with anger.

"Mother, don't play games with me. I have an appointment with the attorney to discuss Wade's will at three this afternoon. He's already asked about the diamond. If I tell him it's missing, he'll call the police and the insurance company. That means more police and more questions about Wade's death. It'll keep the story alive and reporters will be all over us. You don't want that, do you?"

The last thing Irina wanted was reporters waiting on the sidewalk to question her. She broke away from him. "I told you, Harold. I don't have it."

She gathered her confidence; a flick of her hand dismissed him. Irina rose and went to the window overlooking Central Park, signaling that the conversation was over, but Harold followed her across the room and stood towering above her.

"I don't believe you, Mother. I know you would do anything—anything—to keep that stone."

She looked out at the gently falling leaves, wishing she could be in the park, sitting on a bench and enjoying the soft air. She remembered a day many years earlier, when Harold's nanny had been ill. The little boy had cried to go out, so Irina had dressed quickly and simply, with no makeup, and taken him to the park. Harold had been happy playing beside her and she had enjoyed that time with him more than she'd thought possible. But soon she'd begun to worry that one of her friends or worse, a photographer, would see her, and she had taken Harold back inside.

"Mother, are you listening? I am deadly serious." She looked at him and smiled.

"Harold, please, if I had the diamond, I would tell you. Now calm down and let's discuss who might have taken it." She smiled brightly at him.

Harold brushed her off. "Stop it. Don't try your charm on me. I've had enough. Just give me the stone. As the executor of Wade's will, I demand it. I'm warning you, you'll be in serious trouble if you don't hand it over."

"I am your mother!" Irina said, offended. "Don't you dare speak to me like that! I won't let you treat me so rudely." She rushed into the bathroom, slammed the door and turned the lock, then leaned against the wall.

She knew his habits. He was smart, but predictable. In a few moments he would regret his rudeness, then sit down and wait for her. She sighed.

He had been a difficult child most of the time and was more difficult as a man. He knew how important her antiques were to her and she suspected that he secretly coveted them. When she asked him what he thought, he would say he had no opinion, but when he visited her, Irina often saw his gaze wandering around the bedroom that had become her sanctuary. She could tell from the way he touched her Marie Antoinette bed that it fascinated him.

Apparently, her orderly, exquisite room, so different from Blair's messy kitchen, appealed to his engineering mind. Yet he never gave her a single compliment.

But he did love her, she knew. The night after Douglas died, Harold had surprised her by offering to spend the night in her room. He said he would not mind sleeping on the chaise or even the floor. She had been touched, and had thanked him, but said she was content to be by herself.

Several days later he and Blair had suggested that they move into Irina's apartment "to ease her loneliness." At least that was Harold's excuse; Blair said nothing. Irina knew the real reason behind their plan. They were short of money.

Her first instinct had been to tell the truth—that she

wanted peace and quiet after the struggle of Douglas's protracted illness and death. That she preferred her personal life to remain hidden from his difficult wife and stepdaughter. It was bad enough having Wade living downstairs in the connected apartment.

The more she considered the offer, however, the more it appealed to her. Having Harold near would mean she could talk to him every day and reignite the warm relationship they had once had. Not wanting to appear too eager, she had waited a week before agreeing, and within days, they had moved in.

Her relationship with Harold had improved . . . but Irina knew his money troubles had persisted. Had he taken the Braganza and decided to try to blame her for its disappearance? Perhaps she had failed to realize how deceptive and greedy he was.

Ready now to deal with her son, Irina took a bottle of water from the small refrigerator in her bathroom and poured herself a glass. She returned the bottle to the fridge, then picked up the glass and opened the door. As she anticipated, he was sitting and waiting for her.

"You are being ridiculous," she said, speaking as calmly and clearly as possible. "Tell me what would be the point of my taking it? I couldn't wear it, couldn't sell it. It is ridiculous to think I have it. Besides, I asked your grandfather Max to buy it for me and he promised that he would."

"That's hard to believe," Harold replied with sarcasm. Irina ignored him.

"Who could have my beautiful Braganza? We must

find it. Maybe Wade hid it. Let's look everywhere in his room. Everywhere.

"Maybe Bella has it. Maybe Blair." She took Harold by the arm, urging him to his feet.

"Mother," he protested, "don't be crazy. You know that's not so. Blair doesn't know the combination for the safe." He rose and moved away from her.

The phone rang. Irina froze for a long moment, afraid of more bad news, then went to answer it. A woman spoke, a voice Irina had heard many times before, always with the same news. She replied, "Thank you. I know he has been unwell. Tell him I will call to check on him later in the day."

She hung up and turned to Harold. "Max is sick. He's got a fever . . . it could be flu." She knew her fear was clear in her voice when Harold came and gently guided her to the chaise. She looked at him, eyes wide and mouth quivering. He knelt beside her, took her hand, and held it against his cheek.

"He's your father, go to him and make up for all these years. You may regret it if you don't." He gave a strained laugh. "And stop calling him Max."

Irina took a sip of her water, pleased that her hands were not shaking. She tried to get control of herself, to remember that she had been through this so many times before. But Wade's death had unsettled her, disturbing her usual calm. "Harold, you'll never understand what an actor Max is. He takes to his bed every time I ask for something. He wants me to suffer. I could tell you a million stories of the cruelties he inflicted on your grandmother. I hate him for killing my mother, and he hates me for knowing that he did it. I will never forgive him."

To Irina's irritation, Harold took his grandfather's side. "Mother, you have no evidence that he killed my grandmother. And he's been very generous to you. Without the money he settled on you, you would not be living in this luxury." He swept his hand around the room. "My grandfather deserves some thanks for that, at least. Believe me, I know what it's like to be without real money."

She refused to respond to his shot about the settlement. "Don't fool yourself, my dear. I got it because I kept my mouth shut. But his money is not so important now. With Wade dead, there's no reason to sell the diamond."

"Oh, yes, the diamond." He laughed loudly. "Yes, poor Wade is dead, so now where, oh where, could that little stone be? Shall we go on a 'treasure hunt' to find it?"

Irina shouted, "Harold, there is no cause for your nasty attitude!" Needing a moment to get control again, she took another sip of the water.

"My guess is that Bella has it, that she got the combination to the safe from Wade. I'm afraid she will send it to Brazil to have it cut into smaller stones so that she can sell it. If any of her family is coming to the funeral, that would be the way to get it to São Paulo." She felt that she had convinced Harold.

"Well, Mother, that's one possibility, of course . . . if not a very good one. Blame it on Bella. Or Jorge. Or whoever."

Irina could not stop her hands from shaking.

"Let's go, Mother. Let's look around Wade's apartment to see if there are any hidden diamonds. Isn't that your idea? But watch out. The police may want to come back, and we wouldn't want our prints all over his things, would we? So let's go see if you've got any latex gloves in your closet . . . or better yet, you go look while I'm off to the attorney."

She had never seen him this way. He reminded her of her father—hard and cruel.

"Go?" she roared. "Harold, I don't need your sarcasm. I won't have you treat me this way."

"Shut up," he shouted as he strode out of the room, slamming the door behind him.

Irina knew what had given her son this new, tough attitude. He was the executor of Wade's estate and could do what he wanted with the Braganza.

She would have to be careful now. Everyone would want to get their hands on the diamond now that Wade was dead. But she would win. The Braganza would be hers in the end, just as she'd always intended.

Chapter 16

Sonya smiled in gratitude as Sabrina, her friend and favorite makeup artist, placed a salad on her computer keyboard and perched on the edge of her desk.

"I know you skipped lunch, so eat this. Now. You're looking tired and you're getting too thin. If you keep starving yourself, that handsome detective you're so crazy about will move on."

Sonya peeled the plastic cover off the cardboard container and bit into a slice of cucumber. "Maybe it would be a good thing if he did. His kids are coming for a long visit and I'm not crazy about the role of stepmother."

"Then forget him and make your favorite cameraman happy."

"Don't start on me about Perry. He's a great cameraman and a friend, but that's it. I am not, repeat, *not* attracted to him. And stop taking his side—you're *my* friend."

"You ought to reconsider your feelings about him.

He's mighty talented, you've said that yourself. He's also dependable and has great values. Okay, he'll never be a millionaire, but he's a guy you can respect. And you can work together; you can set up a company of your own with him and do pieces for private companies. With your work ethic and his eye, you'd make a fortune."

"I don't have to marry him to do that."

"Oh yes, you do. Perry won't be able to work that closely with you without falling even more in love with you than he already is. Reject him and he'll find someone else. He's a young, healthy male, remember. How will you feel when he falls for some pretty young thing, gets her pregnant, and marries her?"

Sonya thought about that for a moment. She would feel put out, no doubt about it. But would it change her relationship with Perry? She certainly would miss his devotion, the way he was always there when she wanted him, the way they were so comfortable together. But that wasn't love, wasn't enough to build a whole future on. And she was in love with Keith. Wasn't she?

"You're almost forty and you're working in a young person's industry," Sabrina went on. "You might be happy here for five more years and then what?"

Sonya laughed. "Marrying Perry isn't the only option I've got."

"I know what you think your options are. You're thinking of getting serious about Detective Keith Harris, your lover with the ambitious ex-wife and the kids who are coming for a two-week visit with their daddy."

Sonya took a deep breath. She knew Sabrina meant well, but enough was enough. "Honestly, Sabrina, don't you think that my relationship with Keith is my business?"

Sabrina's voice rose. "Oh, really? Remember, I'm the one whose shoulder you cried on after your disastrous marriage. You made me promise to stop you if you ever got mixed up with a divorced man with kids. And that's what I'm doing now—stopping you. You know in your heart that this is a mistake."

Sonya sank back into her chair. Sabrina was right. She remembered how bitterly she'd fought with her ex-husband over his ex-wife and his two kids and their constant demands for extra money. Their marriage had been a disaster almost from the beginning, and when it had finally fallen apart, she had been brokenhearted. And she had vowed to never date married men again, to never get involved with a man who already had children.

Yet here she was, living with Keith and trying to prepare herself for a visit from his kids. What was she thinking?

Sonya sighed. She'd never had much luck with men. Or perhaps she just didn't know how to relate to them. Her father had left when she was three years old and she'd never seen him again. Her mother had never re-married, and hadn't even dated much after that. But after the divorce, Sonya's father had quickly married again and started a second family.

He'd ignored his first wife and daughter as completely as if they'd never existed—no birthday cards, no Christmas gifts, no communication at all. And when Sonya tried to contact him, when she was in college, his second wife told her that they'd gotten divorced years earlier. She told Sonya that her father had moved to

New Zealand. And Sonya had decided not to chase him any further. He'd gone halfway around the world and she had to think that was a message of some kind.

Since then, she'd dated, and married, and divorced, and dated again. None of her relationships had lasted longer than a few years, and most had lasted only a few weeks or months. She was living with Keith, but she'd known and worked closely with Perry longer than her last two or three boyfriends put together.

"Oh god, Sabrina," she said. "You're right. I didn't think."

Sabrina softened. "It's okay, I'm not criticizing you. I just want you to remember what you went through and how you hated yourself for it." And Sonya knew that Sabrina knew what she was talking about. They'd met when Sonya first joined the network, a year after her marriage failed. The increase in Sonya's salary had paid for her divorce.

She and Sabrina had bonded when the makeup artist caught the producer sobbing in the restroom. Sonya's ex had gone back to his first wife and kids and she was in shock.

"He used to tell me what a demanding bitch she was and that he could never live with her again." She'd sobbed on Sabrina's shoulder. "He told one of my friends that he never really loved me and that marrying me was a dreadful mistake that almost ruined his life. I was so humiliated. I could have killed him."

Sabrina's advice had been to forget him, but to learn a lesson and never again get entangled with a divorced man with kids. And Sonya had made that vow . . . yet here she was, in the same situation, with Keith's kids about to arrive on her doorstep.

Her appetite gone, Sonya pushed the salad away and was about to speak when someone knocked on her door and then rattled the handle. Sonya raised an eyebrow, glad that Sabrina had locked the door behind her when she'd come in.

"Damn, it can only be Kirsten," Sonya said angrily. "I guess we have to let her in."

Sabrina reached over, unlocked and opened the door. Kirsten stood there, her arms clasped to stop her shivering, tears running down her red and swollen face.

"Oh, Sonya," she cried. "I can't believe it. It's too horrible to believe."

"What's too horrible to believe?" Sonya snapped.

Sabrina frowned at Sonya and then put her arm around the intern and drew her into the office. "Sit down, Kirsten, try to stop crying and tell us what's upset you."

"It's Wade. The police say someone murdered him and Cacao. They both died of an overdose of sleeping pills." Kirsten started to sob again. "Why would anyone murder Wade?"

Sonya ignored the weeping. She knew she was being hard on the young woman, but she was fed up with Kirsten's unpredictable and overemotional behavior and her interference in the story. "How do you know all this? The police haven't released the results of the autopsy yet."

"Mom," Kirsten said, as if it explained everything, which it nearly did, Sonya thought, knowing Blair.

After a few more sobs, the intern continued, "The police told Harold and he told Mom. The release will be out in an hour or so. The detective wanted to warn Harold to expect calls from reporters."

"In time to make the five o'clock broadcasts," Sabrina added. "That's the way they usually do it."

"This changes everything." Sonya couldn't keep the eagerness out of her voice. Wade Bruckheimer—and his unpleasant parrot—had been murdered. What a story.

She smiled. "Well, at least we have a head start. I'd better call Donna. Kirsten, go find out where Bella is. I want to interview her tonight. Tell her we're eager to get her side of the story." She looked at Sabrina and smiled again. "Tell Bella if she wants a hair and makeup artist, I'll be happy to bring her the best in the business."

"Happy to oblige," Sabrina replied with a grin. "But first, I'll repair Kirsten's face. Go wash and put some cold water on those eyes. Come back when you're finished and I'll do your makeup."

Sonya waved Kirsten out the door, then punched out Donna's number. The office line was busy and so was Donna's cell. Trying to decide if a text or e-mail would reach Donna faster, Sonya turned to Sabrina and explained, "Kirsten and Bella are extremely friendly and that's why I want her to make the first call. Bella told Kirsten that Wade was unable to perform in bed. She was heartbroken—she wanted to get pregnant as fast as she could."

Sabrina nodded. "Sounds as if Bella has a good head on her shoulders. With all that money in the family, having a child would guarantee that she'd get some, whatever happens."

"I don't know about 'all that money,' " Sonya replied. "The Bruckheimers live high and spend big. My guess is the only member of the family who has real money is Irina, and even that comes from her billionaire father, who is known as the most secretive man in Cincinnati."

She tried Donna again. This time her assistant answered the office line and said that Donna was on the nineteenth floor in an executives' meeting but was due back any minute.

"I'll come and wait for her," Sonya said. She linked her arm with Sabrina's as they walked out of her office. "Thanks for everything. You are a pal. I'll call you as soon as I have the time of the interview."

Sabrina kissed her on the cheek. "All I want is your happiness. You know I don't approve of Keith, but if you are really serious about him, go for it."

"I won't see him tonight. He's working and I have a hot story to keep me busy."

Sabrina shook her head. "Talk about history repeating itself. Remember your ex-husband? You told me you worked so hard while you were married that you were too tired to have sex with him."

Sonya hardly heard her as Kirsten approached, waving an assignment sheet. "Bella at seven? Great. I'll tell Donna." She left Kirsten to Sabrina's tender loving care and headed for Donna's office.

Chapter 17

FRIDAY, 7:00 P.M.
Wade Bruckheimer's apartment

As she climbed out of the van, Sonya looked up at the Bruckheimers' impressive Fifth Avenue apartment building with its dark blue awning. In the autumn twilight, the gray stone structure had the solid look of unostentatious wealth.

Bella had been eager to set up the interview. Sonya wondered why this was such a high priority, given that her husband had been dead less than twenty-four hours.

Kirsten appeared to have recovered from the impact of learning that Wade had been murdered. Sabrina had done a good job of giving her a fresh look. Kirsten flashed Sonya a smile as she climbed out of the backseat of the van and began to help Perry with the equipment.

"Thanks for pitching in. You're a great helper. I wish you were around all the time," Perry said. Sonya could tell from the pitch of his voice that he meant her to hear and she almost laughed, knowing he was trying to make her jealous. Sonya was sorry that their genuine friendship had become strained as her relationship with Keith had developed.

Kirsten grinned at Perry, obviously enjoying the attention. She turned to greet the building's doorman, who confirmed that the police were gone. She asked him to keep an eye on the van, then swept past him, leading Sonya to the passenger elevator while Perry pushed his equipment cart toward the service entrance. Sabrina was at his side, carrying her makeup cases.

Bella was waiting when Sonya and Kirsten stepped off the elevator. She cried, "Oh, Kirsten, at last you're here," and rushed into the other woman's arms. Kirsten embraced her tightly for a moment.

Then Bella pulled away and turned her attention to Sonya. "I feel so alone. I talked to my brother Rico when it first happened, and he promised he'd take care of things, but I haven't heard from him again."

Sonya wondered if Bella was as naïve as she appeared. If Rico hadn't called, it was probably because he was in an airplane. If what Bella was saying was true in the first place, she thought. Someone must have encouraged Bella to act the grieving, helpless widow. The logical suspect was Rico; perhaps he was advising her secretly and Bella's complaints were all an act.

Seeing the look of disbelief on Sonya's face, Kirsten put her hand up to stop Bella. "This is my boss, Sonya Iverson. She'll interview you as soon as the cameraman sets up."

Bella brightened and offered Sonya her hand. "Pleased to meet you. Is it all right if Kirsten waits with me and helps me get myself together?"

"Yes, of course. But Sabrina, our makeup artist, should help you too. She'll be here in a minute and I'll send her right in to you."

As she and Kirsten moved away, Bella thanked Sonya and added, "I'll send Kirsten back as soon as I'm a little calmer. I know you can't get on without her; she's always telling me what a help she is to you." Sonya didn't know what to say, but was saved from the necessity of replying when Bella shut the door between them.

Perry and Sabrina arrived just as the door closed. "Wait a minute, then go in and work your magic on Bella. The better she looks, the better the piece will be," Sonya said to Sabrina.

"How *does* she look?"

"Well I may be unkind, but I think she's putting on a great act. She may have shed a few tears but I'm sure they are of the crocodile variety. You won't have to cope with red and swollen eyes."

"Thank goodness," Sabrina said. She knocked on the door and was told to come in. Perry had already positioned the chairs they'd use for the interview; Sonya sat in hers and reviewed her questions while Perry set up and adjusted the lights and positioned his camera.

When the door reopened, Bella had been transformed. She now wore a black, form-fitting turtleneck sweater and a knee-length skirt. Sabrina had given her a soft, natural look that played up her dark, Latin beauty. After Perry had rigged up her mic, Sonya asked her to sit in the chair where she would do the interview and stepped back to check the monitor. Bella was as photogenic as she was beautiful.

Sonya knew that Bella was one of those women

whose beauty carried them nearly effortlessly through life. Friends, money, and anything else Bella wanted would come easily—all she had to do was smile. It was easy to believe that Wade had needed lots of money to give Bella the kind of life she felt she deserved.

As if she knew what Sonya was thinking, Bella looked serious and said, "I'm not the party girl everyone thinks I am. Wade was the playboy. I just went along with him. Modeling would be more fulfilling and more fun. And maybe I could become an actor."

Perry signaled that the tape was rolling, so Sonya began. "First, let me say how sorry I am about your loss, and also let me thank you for doing this interview."

"It's been the worst day of my life," Bella began. "All I can think of is how I came home last night and found my dear, dear Wade dead. He meant everything to me."

Sonya asked gently, "How long were you married?"

Bella's voice was husky. "Almost three years. The happiest time of my life. We met in Rio and had a simple wedding. All I wanted was to come to New York and be with Wade."

"You like living in New York?"

Bella didn't respond for a moment, perhaps choosing her phrasing. "Yes, I had a wonderful social life here with Wade, but that's not all. There's energy in New York that I didn't find in São Paulo. It's not all about the parties—it's from the active people who do things with their lives."

Sonya nodded. "That's the way I feel about New Yorkers, too. Tell me, Bella, when did you last see the Braganza?"

Bella frowned and shifted uneasily in her seat.

"Honestly, I can't remember. I know Wade showed it to me a month or so ago, one night when his friend Giorgio was here. Giorgio wanted to see it as they were discussing how to sell it. I think that's the last time I saw the diamond."

"Where is the jewel now?"

"I assume it's in the safe where it is usually kept. I've been so upset over Wade that I haven't thought to check on it." Bella's voice broke. "My husband was charming and generous and I adored him from the first moment I saw him. He was my world."

"Have you any idea who would murder him?"

"No." She shook her head vehemently. "Of course not. When I went to say good-bye before I went to the party, he was in the living room with Cacao as usual. He was fine. He said I looked pretty and told me to enjoy myself."

Sonya allowed her a moment to relax, then asked, "Do you believe it was murder?"

"Yes, yes. Why would Wade commit suicide? We were so happy! We were about to sell the diamond and were planning to take a trip as soon as the sale was done."

"Tell me what happened last night when you got home. How did you find him?"

Bella hesitated. "I can't say much about that. I told the police the whole thing and my lawyer advised me not to say anything to the press for fear of compromising the investigation." The way Bella said the words, Sonya knew she was reciting exactly what her attorney had said to her. "My brother Rico said the same. I'm sorry, but I know you understand."

"Tell me as much as you can."

Again Bella hesitated, and then peered into the darkened room as if she was looking for help from someone, perhaps Kirsten, but the intern had not returned to the room for the interview. Sonya said nothing; experience had taught her that silence usually got her some kind of answer.

Bella licked her lips and said, "It started with the bird. Usually when I get home, I get some kind of greeting from Cacao—a beautiful macaw. I'm the only one in the family Cacao greets like that, you know. But there was nothing, so I checked on him and saw that he was dead. I ran to Wade's bedside, to tell him about Cacao, but Wade was dead, too. Then I woke everyone, and Harold came down and the police came."

"Anything else you remember?" pressed Sonya.

"No, nothing, Sonya. But if it were suicide, why would he kill his bird?"

Sonya didn't respond—this was an interview, not a conversation. "Going back to your getting home—what time was it, and where were you coming from?"

"I don't remember the time. I didn't look at the clock, but it was after midnight. Probably about two."

"Coming from?" Sonya asked again.

Bella's answer was very soft, as if she hoped not to be heard, "A party. A charity party."

"Really?" continued Sonya. "Did you go to the party alone?"

"It was the annual ball to raise money to help children with speaking difficulties. Wade's supported it for years. As a child, he was a stutterer and he wanted to help children with the same problem. But last night he couldn't go, because his uncle was flying in from Brazil and he wanted to be here to meet him. He insisted that I go with our friends."

"You went with a friend."

"Yes, a friend. . . . No, I meant friends."

"Who?"

"I can't say."

"Why?"

"I can't say. Ask my lawyer."

"Did you have anything to drink?"

"There was champagne, but I didn't have much. I wasn't feeling well. . . ." Bella looked directly at Sonya with tears glittering in her eyes. Sonya wondered if they were real. "You have no idea how badly Wade's family are treating me. This morning I found Jorge Dias photographing the silver. He said I had no right to it, that it had belonged to Esperanza, Wade's mother, and that now that Wade was dead, it had to go back to the Dias family.

"And my brother Rico, who has always taken care of me, promised to come, but he's not here." Sonya could see real emotion in Bella's eyes now and was not surprised when the woman said vehemently, "Wade is dead and I can't help that, and the diamond is mine, and I'll be damned if they ever get a cent from it."

Even as Bella spoke, the expression on her face told Sonya that she realized she had gone too far, spoken too openly. She tried to rise from the chair but only succeeded in tangling herself in her mic wires. "No more, please," Bella said with a tinge of hysteria in her voice.

Sonya signaled Perry to stop the tape and helped Bella with the microphone. Kirsten had just stepped back into the room, probably attracted by Bella's raised voice, and Bella ran to the younger woman, who comforted her with a long hug.

"You were awesome, Bella," Kirsten said, but Bella only laughed despairingly and ran out of the room even as Sonya drew near to thank her for the interview.

Stalled in the middle of the room, Sonya suddenly realized that Giorgio Sacco was standing next to Kirsten.

"Quite a performance from Bella," he offered. "You know, you ought to interview Kirsten. She's the smartest one in this family, and you'd be surprised how much she knows."

"Thanks for the advice, Mr. Sacco," Sonya replied. "I'll think about that."

Chapter **18**

Jorge Dias stood among the crowd coming into the carousel area to collect their luggage. His regular car service driver was beside him with a large sign saying DIAS. But Elenora was nearsighted and he wanted to make sure she arrived safely and was calm.

When Elenora told him she had used family influence to get on the next plane to New York, Jorge felt a rush of concern. He did not want his wife involved in the aftermath of Wade's death. But, as always with Elenora, once she had made up her mind, she was as immovable as a concrete wall. He consoled himself with the thought that she was closer to the Bruckheimers than he was, and it might be useful to have her with him to keep an eye on the family.

Luckily she had gone through customs in Miami when she'd changed planes, but she would be tired from the long day of travel—and very hungry. Elenora mistrusted airline food and refused to eat it even though she flew first-class. Though she would be anxious to hear the news, Jorge planned to insist that she have something to eat and then go to bed. When she was rested, there would be time enough to bring her up to date.

Standing in the airport reminded him of his own arrival, the night before. He'd called Wade from the terminal and his nephew had answered with a cheerful "Hello," laughing when the macaw repeated it. But as soon as he recognized Jorge's voice, Wade's mood changed noticeably.

"Oh, yes. Welcome," he said in a hard tone.

"Nephew," Jorge said, ignoring his coldness. "As always, I'm happy to hear your voice. I've come especially to see you and I hope we can meet tonight as we arranged. I'm at the airport and will be coming directly to the apartment."

A loud, impatient sigh was Wade's response.

"I've brought your sleeping pills," Jorge added, knowing Wade would be pleased.

Wade brightened. "Thank you. You know how difficult it is for me to sleep with my apnea. I'll be waiting for you."

When Jorge reached the Diases' Fifth Avenue apartment, he was pleased to find it in perfect condition. The nanny who had carried Wade the day of Esperanza's death was still in the family's employ and made weekly visits to keep it ready for unexpected arrivals.

Jorge tossed his bag on the bed, then opened it to remove the box containing the sleeping pills. Traveling by private plane, he had never experienced any problems with customs, though he had a letter from his doctor saying he carried large quantities in case he was delayed on the trip.

As he opened the door to Wade's apartment, he heard Cacao's annoying squawk, "Go way, go way, go way."

Without bothering to greet his uncle, Wade admonished the bird, "Now be quiet, Cacao. It's Uncle Jorge. You know he doesn't like you." As if it agreed, the macaw stopped calling and hid its head beneath the top of one wing. "Poor Cacao. You don't like Uncle Jorge either . . . do you, sweetie?" Wade asked, rubbing his finger along the bird's head. "I'll put you on your perch."

It was a bad beginning. Jorge felt a twinge of chest pain. "Do you mind, Wade, if I sit?"

With a sweeping gesture, Wade indicated the chair opposite his own.

"Thank you, nephew," Jorge said brightly, trying to relieve the tension. "Is your wife here?"

"No. Bella is out at a charity event tonight. I preferred not to go."

"Won't that seem odd, nephew, to have her out partying with others? Is that usual among New York society these days?" Even as he spoke, Jorge regretted not curbing his tongue—Wade couldn't possibly miss the dislike in his voice.

"I don't care, and I pay no attention to gossip." Wade sat down so that the two men faced each other. "Now, Uncle Jorge, let's cut through the shit so we can both get some rest. I'm glad you came, so I have the opportunity to tell you face-to-face that I'm going to sell the Braganza. It goes to the auction house tomorrow.

"So thank you for coming, and I'm delighted to see you and listen to all that blah and blah. But you should know, I've made up my mind."

Jorge was stunned. "I'm your uncle. Please don't be rude to me, Wade."

"I'm sorry, Uncle, I really am, but I want to be clear with you. Everyone has been after me about the diamond and now you, too. I just can't take it."

Jorge saw Wade's momentary weakness as an opening. "Yes, nephew, I understand that you are under pressure and need money. Our family wants to help you, as we have so often in the past."

"Why do you bring up the past? I have never asked for more than I deserved. The money I received was the rightful share of my mother, Esperanza. I was entitled to it."

"Of course. I just want you to know that we are always behind you. Owning the Braganza is a matter of pride for our family. Everything can be arranged behind the scenes."

"You can bid on it at the auction if you're so hot to have it."

"No, Wade. It will be so much better if this transaction remains a private matter. You and I can agree on a fair price, you will have your money, and the diamond will go to the national museum in Brazil as a gift from the Dias family."

Wade sat up. "What do you mean, a 'fair price'?"

"Fair, is what I mean. Whatever's fair. We are businesspeople. But, of course, we're dealing with friends here, so we will expect to pay what's fair among family."

Wade's eyes narrowed. "Uncle, we should stop talking."

In retrospect, this should have told Jorge to back down, but last night, he had been determined to continue, to make his nephew truly understand. "Wade, you know this is a matter of family honor, but we have always been flexible. I forgave you for selling our grandmother's house at the beach, remember? When that house was left to you, it was meant to be kept in the family. But you sold it without telling me, and I tried to understand why."

"Understand?" Wade cut in, his voice rising. "You've never let me hear the end of it. And now you are bringing it up again. I had to sell that house to keep up with my expenses. If it were up to you, I'd be out on the street."

"How can you say that? When did I ever deny you anything? You are repeating lies from the mouth of that greedy woman you married." Jorge knew he had gone too far, but could not stop himself. "Your mother, Esperanza Dias, would be disgraced to have such a daughter-in-law. A wife who goes 'partying' with other men."

Wade struggled to his feet and loomed over his uncle. "That's enough," he shouted. "You dare call Bella greedy when you've come here to bargain over your oh-so-precious diamond?

"You never change. Yes, you've sometimes given me money. Money that would have been my mother's." Wade gave a predatory smile. "Money I was morally entitled to and would have gotten if she had lived. All my life, you've doled it out in little bits, using it to hold me under your thumb. But that's finished. I'll get enough from the sale of the Braganza so that I'll never have to listen to your lectures about Dias family 'honor' again.

"You and the Dias family will be out of my life."

As Wade ranted on, Jorge pressed his body against

the back of the chair, afraid that his nephew might hit him. He tried to speak, but a weak guttural whimper was all that came from his throat.

"You think honor is so important," Wade continued, "but you are foolish. You think others respect you, but that's not so. When people hear your old, aristocratic, pretentious nonsense, they laugh behind your back and call you ridiculous. What century do you live in, Uncle?"

Deeply wounded, Jorge found the strength to force himself out of the chair.

"You are a Dias," he shouted, "and honor is in your blood."

Wade laughed. "You think so? I say, fuck what you call honor. I am no Dias—I'm a *Bruckheimer*." His voice rose again. "I swear to you that your precious Dias family will never again lay hands on the Braganza. I'll make that a condition of the sale if I need to."

He had stormed out of the room, leaving Jorge exhausted in his chair.

Now, waiting for Elenora, Jorge decided that he would not tell her the details of that meeting with Wade.

His driver interrupted his thoughts, saying, "Mr. Dias, isn't that the señora?"

Jorge looked where the man was pointing and saw his wife standing by her little suitcase and looking around. He waved and called, "Elenora, we are over here," but his voice was drowned out by the din in the baggage claim area. He waved again as she walked toward the barrier where the drivers were waiting.

This time she saw him and her face creased in anxiety.

"Oh, Jorge, why are you here? Surely you can trust me to find our driver by myself and get to Manhattan." She shook her head as he bent to kiss her. The driver took her luggage and led Jorge and Elenora to the car.

The backseat of the limo was separated from the driver by a glass panel, and once they were settled in their seats and on the way to Manhattan, Jorge, as was his habit, checked to make sure the mic was off so the driver couldn't hear them.

Elenora kissed her husband on his cheek. "I want to hear everything. So start right now." He put his hand on her knee and squeezed it.

She took his hand and smiled. "I worry so much about you. It's like a miracle to see you well."

"I'm fine," he said. "It's hard to believe Wade is gone. But I tell myself that in the long run, it will be for the best."

"Perhaps so. I always said he was too much trouble for you."

"Trouble he was, and will continue to be."

"What do you mean, Jorge?"

"The autopsy revealed he died of an overdose of the sleeping pills he used—the kind I gave him. At first, the speculation was that he committed suicide, but now the police are saying he was murdered. I don't know why they think that or what evidence they have."

"Murdered." Jorge felt his wife's grip tighten on his arm. "You must stay out of this. Let the police do their work. Think of your health."

"Yes, but he was Esperanza's son. I had to look after him." He sighed.

"And the diamond?"

He shook his head. "As I told you on the phone, he was adamant about auctioning it. He wanted the most he could get for it. He's spent every penny he had on Bella, starting from the time he first saw her parading on the beach in a bikini. Do you remember when he told us she was the love of his life and he wanted to start a family with her?"

Elenora snorted. "I should live to see that happen. All Bella wanted was his money. The only reason she'd have his child is to get more money. Have you talked to her?"

"Unfortunately, yes. She caught me photographing our family silver and told me to get out."

"We'll see about that," said Elenora, emphatically. "What about Blair and Harold?"

"We are invited to eat with them. We have to be careful with them—Harold is Wade's executor and controls the fate of the diamond. You can be helpful there, Elenora. They both like you and might confide in you. We need to find out what they know about Wade's death and where things stand with the diamond."

"Don't worry, Jorge. A little confidential gossip with Blair should do the trick."

Chapter 19

FRIDAY, 8:30 P.M.
Blair Bruckheimer's kitchen

Blair dropped the slices of bacon into the half-full pot of cold water, put on the cover, and turned up the heat to let it boil. A few minutes of simmering would remove the strong salt taste and some of the smoky flavor, making it just right for the coq au vin she planned for tomorrow's dinner.

The dish was a favorite of Jorge's and Blair often cooked it for him and Elenora when they came to New York. She liked to see them and to catch up on family gossip; Harold usually wanted to learn why they had really come to visit.

Even so, they met as friends, as people who shared similar interests, and were genuinely glad to see one another. They rarely talked about Wade and when they did, neither Jorge nor Harold would say anything derogatory about him. Still, Blair had the impression that Jorge wished Wade were as easy to deal with as Harold.

Over the years she had grown fond of Elenora, whom Blair found to be a sensible woman. Blair was surprised the first time she heard Elenora criticize the much-loved Esperanza—the only Dias ever to say a bad word about the dead woman. Elenora said Esperanza was not the angel her parents made her out to be. In Elenora's eyes, Blair learned, Esperanza was a calculating woman who had used their love to protect her while she scooped up family heirlooms that should have gone to Jorge as the eldest son.

Blair had become used to the constant presence of Esperanza in their lives—the portrait of her that dominated Wade's living room, the magnificent treasures she had brought to her marriage, the Braganza. The stories told about Esperanza were already legendary and seemed to grow in power each year. Blair had recently read that women who worshipped at the chapel her father had built in Esperanza's memory had begun to claim that she had worked miracles, healing their pain and solving their problems with lovers and husbands. Elenora had been a pleasant counter to the worship of Esperanza.

Would Wade's death put an end to the endless discussion of his mother, Blair wondered. One thing she was sure of: if Bella continued to live in Wade's apartment, she would remove the portrait of Esperanza from above the mantelpiece.

The intercom buzzed and the doorman announced that Mr. Sacco was there to see her. Blair shook her head. She and Giorgio had little to say to each other. Both she and Harold disliked him for the way he spoiled Kirsten.

"Let me speak to him," she said, then waited to hear his voice with its slight but pleasing Italian accent.

"Hi," she said. "Kirsten isn't here. She's at work. Call her on her cell."

He laughed easily. "I know our daughter's schedule as well as you do, Blair. It's you I want to see."

"Why?" She was wary. Cooking relaxed her and she disliked being disturbed while she was making a special dish.

"I've got something to give you, something I know you'll be glad to get."

This time it was Blair who laughed. "Don't be childish, Giorgio. There is nothing you have that I want and I certainly don't need any presents from you. Give it to Kirsten. She's the only thing we have in common."

"No, it's too valuable for that. I insist on coming up to give it to you personally."

She sighed. "Okay. But I'm busy. You can't stay long."

Minutes later, when Giorgio walked into the kitchen, she had a sense of déjà vu. He looked the same as he had when she'd fallen in love with him twenty years earlier. He still had that appealing northern Italian look, though his black curly hair was receding and there were a few more wrinkles around his deep-set blue eyes. And he still radiated the charm that she had found irresistible.

She had thought him rich when they married, then discovered he was just extravagant and often close to bankruptcy. Worse, he was bisexual and more attracted to men than to women.

"So what is it that you have for me?" she asked as she turned her cheek to avoid his unwelcome kiss.

He pulled out a chair and sat down. "Are you still mad at me?"

"Giorgio, I'm busy. I'm preparing a special dinner for tomorrow night and I want it to be perfect. At the very least you could have called and asked if it was okay to come."

"I thought of calling but I knew you'd put me off. I wanted to see you alone and Kirsten told me this would be your night for cooking, so I tried my luck."

"Why do you want to see me alone? I have no secrets from Harold. Are you trying to make problems again?"

"My god, Blair, can't you trust me a little? I'm here for your benefit. I care about you as well as Kirsten." She shot him a disbelieving look. He raised his hands in a helpless gesture. "Blair, you really are tough. You told me once that you never forgive or forget an injury. I didn't believe you then, but I do now."

He pulled a crumpled red linen handkerchief from his pocket. Blair recognized it in an instant.

"That's one of Wade's. What are you doing with it?" she snapped.

He held it out to her, but she made no move to take it and after a moment he set it on the table, where it became clear to Blair that the handkerchief was wrapped around something.

"Open it, Blair, and see the present I brought you. Not just you, but the whole Bruckheimer family."

Blair carefully set her hand atop the handkerchief, feeling the object underneath. It was oval and about the size of a quail's egg, with smooth faces. Suddenly afraid, Blair flipped the handkerchief open, revealing the gleaming yellow facets of the Braganza.

With a cry that was half astonishment and half disbelief, Blair fumbled for a chair and sat down. "My god,

Giorgio, it's the diamond. How did you get it? Don't tell me you stole it?" She gave a huge gasp of relief. "You can't believe how frantic we've been, looking for it. Harold was convinced Irina took it, but she denied it. I was beginning to think we would have to tell the police it was missing. Can you imagine the scandal? Especially if Harold's mother was the main suspect."

Giorgio reached over and patted her hand. "Wade gave me the stone for that very reason. He knew Irina had the combination to the safe and was desperate to keep the diamond. He asked me to hold it until it was time for the auction house to collect it.

"I was nervous about having it in my home, but Wade assured me it was safe there; after all, no one would imagine the diamond was in my care. When Wade died, I didn't know what to do at first, but then I decided it was best to put the stone in your most capable hands."

He picked up the diamond and held it against the light. "It's extraordinary, the way it's faceted, isn't it?"

Blair reached over and took the Braganza from her ex-husband. "When did Wade give it to you?"

"Five or six days ago. I know you'll find it hard to believe, but Wade was deeply troubled about selling the stone. His marriage wasn't working out and he believed that was because he couldn't give Bella all the things he'd promised her. So he was desperate for money."

The diamond was heavier than Blair expected. She realized, sitting there, holding the stone up to the light and watching its facets spray sparkles throughout her kitchen, that she had never touched it before. She'd seen it many times, of course, in its red velvet box or hanging around Irina's neck. Now she realized what

pleasure sprang from its mysterious beauty. She tilted
and turned the stone, studying its shifting colors, sometimes the paleness of a summer lemon, sometimes the
brightness of a fresh winter orange.

Giorgio took the diamond from her and replaced it
on the red handkerchief.

"Let's talk about Kirsten and her problems," he said.
"First, I want to say I'm sorry I didn't listen to you the
last time we discussed her. Tell me, is she seriously in
trouble?"

Blair didn't answer. There was no way she could de-
scribe everything that was going on in Kirsten's life in a
few minutes. And she knew there was no quick solution.

Giorgio must have seen something in her expression,
because he sighed. "Hear me out. I give her money because I want her to think of me as a kind and generous
father and to love me. She likes shopping and I enjoy it
too. I like her carefree approach to life. She's the reason I come to New York.

"I know I've made a lot of mistakes in my life. I
don't want losing my daughter to be one of them. She's
the only family I have."

Blair knew that was true; his parents were dead and
he had no siblings or other close relatives. But she felt
that Giorgio had no claim on Kirsten. For one thing, she
thought with bitterness, he had never paid child support.
And Blair had done the hard work of raising their
daughter.

But now, she knew she had to be more generous. She
had to have Giorgio's help with Kirsten. She fought to
keep resentment out of her voice when she finally spoke.

"It's her health that worries me. Giving her money

and encouraging her uncontrolled shopping may make you feel good, but it does nothing to help her. If you really care for her, then help me get her into treatment."

"Yes. I will do that."

He sounded sincere, but Blair was not convinced. "I hope you mean what you say."

"Of course I do." Giorgio looked directly at Blair. "You have nothing to fear from me. I'll never be able to take her away from you. Kirsten complains about having a restricted life with you and Harold, but I know she will never leave you. Wade and I both suggested she move to Milan with me, but she always rejected the idea. She loves you and she knows she needs the stability you give her."

He looked sad; his voice softened, showing his grief. "With Wade gone, Kirsten needs you more than ever."

"She needs you, too," Blair said.

He stood up and carefully pushed his chair against the table. "I promise I will help her in any way I can."

Blair heard sincerity in his voice and nodded. "I'll call you later. We'll figure out what to do about Kirsten." She escorted him to the elevator and let him kiss her good-bye, then returned to the kitchen.

The Braganza was waiting for her on the table, sparkling.

For a moment Blair stood still, mesmerized by its light. Then, overcome with a sudden longing, she picked it up and put the cool facets against her cheek. If everything went as she planned, the stone was about to change their lives.

Chapter 20

FRIDAY, 9:00 P.M.
Sonya's office

When Sonya called Keith to cancel dinner, his response was clipped and pointed. "Again? Okay. Bye, then. See you when I get home."

She was annoyed. His attitude was unfair, since he was working a late shift himself and had planned to just squeeze in dinner with her. But she knew that her schedule was an increasing problem between them. Keith often complained that she spent too many evenings working.

It was a fair charge. Sonya had reservations about their relationship and had to admit to herself that she sometimes used long workdays as an excuse to keep from facing him. Still, with the murder of Wade Bruckheimer foremost on her mind, she had no patience for Keith's tantrums. It was just as well they were not meeting.

There was a pile of unmarked tapes on her desk, which probably meant she'd be spending many more hours at work, since all the tapes had to be checked and logged. Perry usually labeled the tapes before he gave them to her, but lately he had begun to play little games with her. Sonya assumed he was jealous of Keith and no longer bothering to hide it. If only he knew how rocky things were between them. . . .

Sonya knew she could ask one of the assistant producers to check the tapes, but she wanted to do it herself. She'd been mentally reviewing her interviews with Wade and Bella and was convinced that she had missed something. Maybe those tapes would help identify the murderer. Whatever time it took, she wanted to review the video herself.

Kirsten volunteered to help, but Sonya did not completely trust the intern. After all, Wade and Bella were her family. She might fail to log something she knew the family was trying to hide. Sonya would figure out what to do with Kirsten once the younger woman arrived.

Fortunately, Perry had numbered the tapes so she could create some order out of the chaos. She'd done the interview with Wade first, so it had to be on tape number one or two. She would start with those.

As she reached for the first tape, Sonya checked her watch. It was 9:15 and still no sign of Kirsten, who always seemed to be absent when wanted, yet underfoot when told to stay away.

The interview she was trying to find was a perfect example. Kirsten had been told not to be there, but she'd come anyway. Why? Sonya asked herself, as she had many times during the past two days. Why had Kirsten been there, and why had she suddenly interrupted the conversation?

Sonya found Wade on the second tape, with his blue

shirt open at the collar; he looked even heavier than Sonya remembered. The first shots showed Sonya and Wade looking at the portrait of Esperanza. Then Perry had panned the camera around the room before pushing into the adjoining den.

At the time, Sonya had been concentrating on the painting and hadn't paid much attention to what Perry was doing. Now, she paused the tape, looking closely at Wade. She realized that he was taking quick glances at Perry. Studying his expression as she played the tape again, Sonya began to suspect that there was something Wade didn't want Perry to film. What that was, she couldn't say. Just then Cacao started squawking and Perry smoothly swung the camera over to take a shot of the macaw flapping its wings.

The next shot began after the bird had been moved to another room. Sonya saw herself and Wade, seated, before Perry zoomed in on a nervous, shaking Wade Bruckheimer. Off camera, Sonya heard her voice. "Why are you auctioning the diamond?"

As if on cue, a breathless Kirsten appeared in Sonya's doorway.

"Oh, I'm so sorry to be late, Sonya. My mom met with Giorgio earlier tonight and she wanted to talk to me about what they said. I couldn't get away from her."

"I don't need to know why you were delayed, Kirsten," Sonya said. "I'm glad you made it in at last. I can use your help. Let's get to work."

Kirsten persisted in explaining as she took off her lightweight coat, revealing a shimmering emerald-green dress. "But I want you to know that I really tried to be on time. It's important to me that you understand

that I'm trying to do a good job. I've got a party tonight, and had to dress."

"Yes, I see. You look pretty in green."

Kirsten continued, "Thanks, I just got it, and I think
the color goes well with my hair, don't you?"

"Yes. As you've observed," Sonya responded with
more than a twinge of sarcasm, "I like that combination myself."

"I was about to walk out the door when my mom
called. She wanted to tell me what Giorgio had said. I
said I was going to be late but Harold thought I should
stay a few minutes to listen, and I thought we were going to have a fight. Fortunately, Irina popped in to com-
plain about Bella, and I reminded them that you were
counting on my help, so finally they let me go." Kirsten
smiled. "That's why I'm late."

"Okay," Sonya said with as much patience as she
could muster. "Let's just get going. I was looking at the
interview with Wade."

"Have you found anything yet?"

"What do you mean by 'anything,' Kirsten?"

"Well, I know you're looking for clues to Wade's
death—or murder, I mean."

Kirsten was right, but Sonya did not intend to share
her thoughts with Wade's niece. "Just start on the other
pile of tapes, and log the B roll. I'll look at the interview and let you know if I want you to log anything."

Kirsten was uncharacteristically silent as she began
to stack the tapes.

Sonya turned back to the monitor. Wade relaxed and
became genuinely warm as he answered the questions
about his mother and how she had met his father. The

first signs of renewed tension appeared when Sonya asked how the Braganza came to New York and how the Brazilians felt about the diamond leaving their country.

Then she'd brought up the connecting apartments and Wade had insisted they were all "one big happy family." A lie if ever there was one, Sonya thought.

Kirsten interrupted, and Sonya paused her tape. "Should I log Bella's interview?"

"No. As I said, just do the B roll. I want to see everything Perry shot. We can do Bella's interview later."

Sonya hit play and heard herself ask whether Wade had the authority to sell the Braganza. She listened to his claim that he could do what he liked with the diamond and then to their conversation about his uncle Jorge. Sonya could hear the strain in Wade's voice, a tightness she hadn't really noticed during the interview. Questions about Harold and Blair upset him the most. He called them greedy and jealous and insisted that they both knew about and approved of the sale of the diamond.

That was when Kirsten and Giorgio had come into the room. Though the interview had been interrupted, Perry had kept the tape rolling. He'd gotten a good shot of Wade going to Giorgio for comfort. On the screen, their closeness was obvious.

Surely, thought Sonya, there was no reason for Giorgio to kill Wade. And, as far as she knew, he had not been in the house on the night of the murder. Not that that would necessarily have stopped him, but it seemed unlikely.

She rolled the tape back and looked again at Kirsten and Giorgio as they entered the room. She paused the playback to study Giorgio. He was certainly attractive, and what a contrast to Wade. Had their personalities been as different? What had kept them so close to each other? Sonya wondered if Bella had said anything about the men's relationship.

"Kirsten, let's see if we can locate the tape with the interview with Bella," she said.

"Awesome," Kirsten replied. "I've been dying to see that."

The phone rang and Sonya answered. On the other end was one of the guards in the network garage. He'd found one of her tapes. Sonya thanked him and said she'd be right down, then explained the situation to Kirsten. "I wonder how the hell that happened. Perry's not the type to lose track of a tape. You'd better go get it."

"Sure," Kirsten said, jumping to her feet. "If a tape goes missing, it's my fault, not Perry's."

As the intern reached for the closet door, Sonya wondered for a moment about her willingness to take responsibility, then said, "Wait, take my coat." She stood up, took her coat off the back of her chair, and tossed it to the other woman.

"Yours is too thin for the weather and the garage can be freezing." She might not like the intern, but that was no reason to let her freeze.

Kirsten grinned and shrugged into Sonya's coat, saying, "See, I'm already rewarded for good deeds. Your coat's awesome. Thanks for letting me wear it."

"I'll wait for you before I start on Bella's interview," Sonya said, feeling magnanimous. It wouldn't take long for Kirsten to run her errand and Sonya could log some

B roll while she was gone. Kirsten grabbed her hand-bag and rushed out.

Sonya found Bella's tape, then laid it aside and went to work on the B roll. She was startled when she looked at her watch and realized that thirty minutes had passed since Kirsten had left. She knew that only one elevator was turned on at that time of night, so getting down to the garage would take longer than usual. Even so, half an hour seemed like a long time to be gone. Maybe, Sonya thought, Kirsten had stopped to chat with some-one from the staff of the network's late-night interview show. The intern had made friends there.

With growing impatience, she started to log Bella's interview. Nearly an hour later, she finished, but there was still no sign of Kirsten. Probably the woman had gotten the tape, realized how late it was, and headed out to the party she had mentioned. But she should have let Sonya know. Frustrated, she decided to go home and wait for Keith.

She reached for her coat automatically before re-membering that she'd lent it to Kirsten. For a moment Sonya thought about taking the intern's coat, but de-cided against it. Realizing that Kirsten still had her coat gave Sonya pause. Surely she wouldn't have worn Sonya's coat to her party?

She looked around the office. Kirsten's bag was gone, too. Sonya's anger flared—so Kirsten had used the missing tape as an excuse to leave!

Then she remembered how contrite the intern had been when she'd arrived, how she'd insisted on telling Sonya every detail of her excuse. Either Kirsten was a fabulous liar, or she'd really felt bad about being late.

And she *had* been determined to watch Bella's interview. . . .

Sonya began to worry. She called the garage. The guard who answered the phone had only just started his shift and had not seen Kirsten; the man he'd relieved hadn't mentioned the intern.

In an instant, Sonya's worry dissolved, replaced by anger. As much as she hated the thought, it seemed that Kirsten had in fact used picking up the tape as an excuse to get to her party on time. It was too much. Sonya dialed Kirsten's cell. It rang once, then switched to voice mail. She left a message. "This is unforgivable, Kirsten. I need that tape. You should have brought it to me before you left."

Sonya put her scarf around her neck and grabbed the extra sweater she kept in the office. Luckily, she was able to quickly hail a cab, so she didn't get too cold on the street. At home, still fuming, she poured herself a glass of cabernet even before taking off her sweater.

She called Keith on his cell, hoping he could get off early and come home, but her call went straight to voice mail. That usually meant she wouldn't hear from him for hours yet. Feeling tired and upset, even though it was barely eleven, she left a message that she was going to sleep.

By the time she'd finished her wine and gotten ready for bed, her anger had begun to fade. Realizing that she missed Keith, Sonya called again, and again got voice mail. This time, her message was, "Good night, sweetheart."

She quickly fell into a sound sleep. The phone rang; she grabbed it and saw Keith's image on the screen.

Not fully awake, she wasn't sure if he was calling because he was mad because of her first message or pleased by her second.

"I'm in bed, Keith," she mumbled.

"I've got some bad news." His voice was sober.

Sonya immediately thought of her mother—was she okay? Then, as she finally woke up, she realized that Keith couldn't possibly be calling about her mom.

"What is it?" she demanded, fully awake now.

"It's Kirsten," Keith said briskly. "Someone shot her. She was found in the network garage."

"Shot her? Oh, no. Is she okay?"

"I think so. The ambulance just left. The paramedics said she'll pull through."

"What happened? Do you know who tried to kill her?" Sonya heard a tinge of hysteria in her voice. She sat up and spoke more slowly. "Why would anyone shoot her?"

"We don't know. She was shot in the shoulder. She's lost a lot of blood, but the EMTs said they didn't think any organs were damaged. I'm sure they'll check everything out at the hospital. We're not sure when it happened. The guard didn't hear a shot; he found Kirsten during one of his routine patrols of the garage."

Sonya cried out, "Keith, it's my fault. I got a call asking me to come down and pick up a tape. I sent Kirsten and when she didn't come back after a while, I left. I thought she had gone to a party or was playing one of her games. I should have gone down to check."

"She was wearing your coat, and her bag looked like one of yours," Keith said. Sonya heard the questions he wasn't asking.

"I gave her my coat since the garage is so cold and she had on the barest minidress. I didn't realize her bag was like mine, but lots of women have similar bags."

Belatedly, Sonya realized that Kirsten would have naturally taken her bag with her so she would have had her identification with her if the guard wanted to see it.

"Red, when I saw her lying there, with that red hair and your coat, I was convinced it was you."

"Oh, no, Keith."

He spoke softly. "I think the killer was after you."

Chapter **21**

"Keith, please come home now. Get them to let you off duty now . . . right away," Sonya pleaded, feeling her heart pound in her chest. "I can't be alone." She knew he would hear the fear in her voice.

"I already asked, and they're arranging for one of the other guys to fill my spot tonight. I just need about five to sign off on my report, and then I'm heading home. I'll be there in a few minutes. Try to stay calm and wait for me, honey."

"Hurry, Keith." Sonya felt like shrieking into the phone. "I know this is my fault. I let Kirsten go to the garage. When she didn't come back, I thought she was just being irresponsible and I went home without checking on her.

"Now Kirsten is suffering because of me. Instead of me."

"Honey, honey," Keith said soothingly. "Don't blame yourself. You told me it's part of her job to get the tapes together. It was natural for her to do it. There's no way you could have known."

Realizing that if she had gone to get the tape, she would now be wounded, perhaps dead, Sonya started to hyperventilate. She clenched her hand so that her nails bit into the soft flesh of her palm. The pain made her breathe easier. Guilt over Kirsten and fear for her own safety threatened to overwhelm her.

"Tell me she'll live," she demanded shrilly.

"Honey, she was unconscious when we got to the garage," Keith said. She could tell he was trying hard to be patient with her. "The paramedics said the bullet damaged some blood vessels, so she lost a lot of blood, but they thought she would be okay."

Sonya realized Keith had said all this before but she was having trouble taking it in. "Have you got a report from the hospital?"

"She's in surgery."

"I feel as if I've murdered her."

She pictured him shaking his head as he replied, "You haven't murdered anyone. This is not your fault, and I love you. I'll be there before you know it. In the meantime, be sure your door is locked and don't open it for anyone other than me."

As soon as he hung up, Sonya became frantic. Her apartment seemed unfamiliar and filled with frightening dark corners. Overwhelmed with a need to be surrounded by light, she rushed from room to room and lamp to lamp, turning everything on until the apartment was blazing.

She set a chair close to the front door and sat there, trying to control her fear, waiting for Keith. She tried not to think of the dark garage and what had happened there.

It seemed like an eternity before she heard a soft knock on the door and Keith's voice saying, "Honey . . . Red . . . it's me, Keith. You can open the door." She leaped from her chair. Her cold hands fumbled with the locks but at last she managed to let Keith in.

He closed and locked the door behind him, then took her in his arms and kissed her. Still holding her close, he half-led and half-carried her to the sofa. He kept one arm around her as they sat, pressed close together. She looked up at him and said, "I just couldn't be alone."

Keith replied by leaning down and gently kissing her. Sonya rested her head on his shoulder. The feel of his solid body gave her comfort. For the first time since he had called with the news about Kirsten, she felt safe.

"I'll pour you a glass of wine," he said. "It'll relax you."

She watched him cross the room, open a bottle of her favorite red, and pour it. Despite all her reservations about their relationship, she realized she was deeply committed to him.

"What you've got to do is to tell me exactly what happened," he said as he sat down again and handed her the glass. "Take your time, and if you feel upset, you can stop until you feel better. But I need to know what happened tonight." He took his notebook and pen out of a pocket.

"What happened?" She sipped the wine and shook her head, trying to focus her thoughts. Keith had a job to do. She didn't know if she could help, but she would try. For Kirsten's sake.

"You said you got a call saying there was a tape in the garage and to come and get it," Keith prompted.

"Yes," Sonya said, nodding. "I was going through a pile of tapes that Perry left on my desk. They weren't as well-organized as usual, so I wasn't surprised to hear that one was left in the van. It does happen from time to time."

"Did you recognize the voice on the phone?"

"No, I assumed it was one of the guards. I rarely speak to them, so there is no way I would recognize it." She stopped for a moment, trying to remember the exact conversation. "But now that I think about it, his voice was not very clear."

"What did he say?"

She took another sip of wine and spoke slowly as she "heard" the man's voice again in her mind. "He said he was going off duty, that the company messengers had all left, and he didn't want the responsibility of leaving it in the guards' station all night."

"Did you ask who had given him the tape?"

"No. I assumed Perry had found it when he was re-stocking the van and had left it for me. I was annoyed that he hadn't brought it to the office as he usually does. I didn't want to stop what I was doing to go get it."

Sonya's voice shook and Keith put a comforting hand on her arm. She took a deep breath and continued, "I was concentrating on the interview with Bella Bruckheimer. I wanted to get a better idea where the story was going."

"So you asked Kirsten to get the tape?"

"Yes, Keith, I did. And now I'll never forgive myself," Sonya replied hoarsely.

"Go easy on yourself, Red. You had no way of knowing this wasn't a normal occurrence. There was nothing about the call to make you suspicious." Sonya shook her head, not ready to let herself off the hook.

"Well, whoever he was, he's a professional. No one saw him come or go, so we have no description, unless Kirsten can give us one when she recovers. The guard heard nothing, so we are assuming the gun had a silencer, since normally shots would have echoed loudly in that mostly deserted concrete garage."

"Why would anyone want to shoot me? The main thing I'm working on is the diamond story." Sonya stopped, realizing what she had said. "The diamond story," she repeated. "Is that a murder story, Keith?"

He nodded. "Yes, it's definitely a murder story. We got the first results of the autopsy on Wade Bruckheimer. He died from an overdose of sleeping pills in his ice cream."

"In his ice cream?" she asked.

"That's what we think. Under his bed, we found a spoon and the top to one of those special cartons of custom-made ice cream he ate every night. And there was melted ice cream in the bird's water pan. The ice cream in the bird's dish and the residue in the spoon were tainted with sleeping pills. We're checking the container lid and the spoon for prints and the crime-scene team is reviewing everything else they gathered, looking for more evidence."

"So, that's how it was done—ice cream laced with sleeping pills," Sonya said.

"Yes. That's it."

"But why would anyone want to kill me?" she asked.

"Something you did, or something you know—or just the story itself—is a threat to the murderer."

"I can't imagine what or who that could be. I've only done two interviews—the one with Wade and one with Bella."

"Who else have you talked to about the murder?"

Sonya thought for a moment. "No one except Kirsten and Donna." She paused. "Obviously it's not Donna, and it doesn't make sense for it to be Kirsten—she wouldn't have gone down to the garage if she'd planned for me to be shot."

"Any idea who might have wanted Wade Bruckheimer dead? Because it's likely that the same person went after you."

"No idea. But I had a nagging idea, when I was looking at the tapes, that there was something in the apartment that might be a clue, something I wasn't seeing clearly. I have to go through all the tapes again." Mentioning the tapes reminded her of Kirsten. She stood, saying, "Keith, I want to go to the hospital now."

"Red, it's four in the morning. The hospital's not going to let you in; you're not family." He got up as he spoke, then kissed her. "You need to rest. I'm here and I'm going to keep an eye on you, and after we've both gotten some sleep, we can go over there."

"Yes, I guess you're right," Sonya said reluctantly. "Should I call Donna?"

"One of the other detectives probably took care of that." Keith stroked her hair for a moment; Sonya rested her head on his shoulder and put her arms around his waist. He whispered, "Now before we go to bed, can

I get you something? Tea? Another glass of wine? Scotch?"

"More wine would be nice."

He refilled her glass, then poured some for himself. Now that the shock was receding, the wine warmed her as she drank. For the first time since she had picked up the phone and heard Keith's voice, Sonya began to feel that she could cope. They walked into the bedroom together.

"This will cause a tremendous stir at the network," she said. "All the executives will want to have their say; Kirsten's granddad was the founding father of the news department."

"You're right," he replied. "But the killer was after you, not Kirsten. He phoned you and he was expecting to see you. He made the same mistake I did, because of Kirsten's hair and the fact that she was wearing your coat. He knew what you looked like, and he saw what he was looking for.

"Hell, when I first saw her lying there, *I* thought she was you. I went through hell in that minute—I thought I had lost you."

She put her wineglass on the bedside table and hugged him.

He shook his head. "Whoever did this must think he got you. He'll be very disappointed when he hears the news. You have to be careful from now on, until we catch him. You must never be alone."

Chapter **22**

It was absurd to cry over the diamond now that it had been returned. But, as Irina told herself many times, the Braganza was more than the most beautiful yellow diamond in the world. It was her life, bringing her comfort in the worst times. Now that Wade was dead, the Braganza was in Harold's hands. Irina smiled to herself. Harold was her loving son. Surely he would let her wear the stone whenever she wanted. Harold would never betray her.

She cradled the diamond in her hands, remembering how excited she had been at nineteen, when the charming, eligible bachelor Douglas Bruckheimer had first let her see it. They had been in the study, in his penthouse, and she had lifted it into the beams of late evening sunlight that had streamed through the window. The jewel's brilliance had illuminated the whole room. Such beauty was a miracle.

Irina had held it against her cheek, enjoying its cool hardness against her soft skin.

"Oh, Douglas, it's divine," she had cried. "My mother came from a family of jewelers and she has told me stories about gemstones like this, but I never dreamed that one day I would hold one in my hand."

He laughed at her, saying, "Maybe one day you'll wear it." He bent and kissed her lightly on the lips. "Stones like this are meant to be worn by beautiful women." He proposed a few months later and for once in her life, Irina was deliriously happy.

As Mrs. Douglas Bruckheimer she quickly received social recognition and made the A-list of important parties. She always wore the Braganza, even after Douglas resumed his series of affairs with other women. Divorce would benefit neither of them. He would lose the allowance her father had given him as part of the marriage settlement, which covered their living expenses and more. She would lose her place in New York society and access to the Braganza, which she had regarded as her property from the first moment Douglas had handed it to her.

When Harold was born, she thought of taking the baby and running, but never had the courage to do it. Where would she have gone? She was not close enough to any of her New York friends to seek sanctuary with them, and she had no family to offer advice and support.

She'd stayed, and made her peace, such as it was, with Douglas's behavior. She'd made sure that her son appreciated her. For years, Irina Bruckheimer had been a name to reckon with—her appearance at a party, charity fund-raiser, or other event made the occasion something truly special. And she'd worn the Braganza with pride, knowing that she had earned it.

Blair's sharp voice startled Irina out of her reverie. "Irina, what are you doing? Put the diamond back in the safe."

Irina jerked up and saw her daughter-in-law standing in the doorway. She looked exhausted and Irina knew she had spent the night at Kirsten's bedside. Blair's beige duffle coat was buttoned haphazardly and her untidy blond hair was escaping from the brightly patterned scarf that sagged half off her head. No matter how worried she was about Kirsten, Irina thought, Blair should have taken a moment to make sure she looked good before leaving the hospital, in case any paparazzi were around to see her.

"Harold didn't tell me that he'd found the diamond," Irina said. "I was frantic with worry, and came to see, if by a miracle, it had reappeared in the safe. And by a miracle, it had."

Blair strode into the room and reached for the diamond. For a moment, Irina wanted to strike her. Why Harold had married her was still a mystery to Irina. Blair was rude and bossy, ten years older than her husband, and divorced. And her daughter was no prize either—a difficult young woman who was out of control as far as Irina could tell.

As calmly as possible, Irina handed the diamond to Blair. "Can't you trust me with it for a minute? The Braganza has been mine for many years," she said. She heard her voice rising and took a breath, desperate not to lose control in front of Blair.

"I'm sorry, Blair," Irina continued. "I don't know what came over me. It's been a difficult time for all of us." She handed Blair the Braganza. "Here. Put the diamond in the safe and tell me how Kirsten is."

Blair took the stone and quickly restored it to the safe, saying, "She's out of intensive care. She lost a lot of blood but she's young and healthy and will recover. But the doctor said she has to be watched—as usual, it's her eating that is the problem. They won't let her go unless she eats properly—she won't heal well if she's not eating well. And knowing how stubborn Kirsten is, that could take a week or more." Unsaid was the thought that once Kirsten was out of the hospital, she would likely revert to her usual diet.

Irina shivered. She looked out the window at the trees in Central Park. The leaves were beginning to turn and soon it would be winter, the harsh season that she most disliked. Her mother had died in late fall. Now Wade was dead, murdered in his bed, and Kirsten was in the hospital, recovering from a gunshot wound. It was an unlucky time of year. Who knew what would happen next? She blinked hard. She mustn't cry. She'd cried enough for one lifetime.

"I'm glad Kirsten is recovering," she said. "I hope the police will soon find out who did this terrible thing to her. When can I visit? I'd like to take her some magazines."

"That's kind of you. I think Kirsten will be ready for a visit by tomorrow, and looking through fashion magazines will lift her spirits. But I think we should space out visits. We don't want to overtire her."

Irina thought of the last time she had seen Kirsten, standing at the top of the stairs, trying to see what the police were doing in Wade's apartment. The T-shirt and shorts she slept in had revealed her gaunt body. Blair should have looked after her properly, instead of spending her time dreaming up recipes.

Irina put her hand tentatively on Blair's arm. "Now let's hear the good news. How did Harold find the diamond?"

"He didn't find it," Blair said simply, then looked away. Watching, Irina wondered if she was about to hear Blair lie, but what she said next had the ring of truth. "Wade gave the diamond to Giorgio for safekeeping and Giorgio returned it to me."

"Safekeeping? From the family? What do you mean?"

"I gather Wade was suspicious of Bella's family. Jorge has mentioned several times that they have a shady reputation."

Irina thought back to Douglas's reaction to the announcement of Wade's marriage to Bella. It was two years before his death, soon after his cancer had first been detected, and he had been in no mood to put up with Wade and his problems. Douglas had suspicions about Bella's family and hired a detective to check them out. The detective came up with rumors, but nothing firm. He did confirm that Bella had attended a convent and gone to drama school. And so, despite Douglas's misgivings, the marriage took place.

"Wade should have taken Douglas's advice and had an affair with Bella," she said. "We all knew she was only interested in his money. And while an affair can be complicated, it has none of the legal problems of a marriage."

Blair shook her head as if to dismiss all thoughts of Wade and Bella. "I'm too tired to talk. I want a shower and some sleep." She went to the door, then paused and asked, "Were there any phone calls?"

"Yes," Irina replied, "Donna Fuller. She said it was urgent and asked you to call her immediately."

Chapter 23

Leaving Irina alone in the den, Blair hoped the older woman would leave the diamond in the safe, then dismissed Irina from her mind. She had to decide what to do about the unexpected message from Donna. Though they were friends, she couldn't forget that Donna was a journalist. She didn't want to return the call when she was this exhausted, but Blair knew it was important not to let too much time pass or Donna would think she was reluctant to talk.

First, she had to be certain she could speak without being overheard. She knew where Irina was and there was no sign of Bella. But . . .

"Harold?" she called, "are you here?" There was no answer. "Harold," she called again as she went through the apartment.

On the kitchen table she found a note saying he was restless and had gone for a walk. While she found it surprising that he was not waiting at home for news from the hospital, she was relieved to have the apartment to herself.

The attack on Kirsten must have prompted Donna's call, but it offered Blair the opportunity to make up—which would not be easy after what had gone between them. She hoped their long history of friendship would bring them together.

Anxiety dried her throat; as she went to the refrigerator to get the pitcher of cold water she always kept there, she was interrupted by a familiar voice calling her name.

"I'm in the kitchen," she said loudly, allowing her anger to show in her voice, and a moment later Giorgio rushed into the room. She held up a hand to keep him from embracing her. "Giorgio, what the hell are you doing here and how did you get in?"

"I want to know how Kirsten is doing. I came in through Wade's apartment—I still have my key."

The stress of the last hours suddenly became too much and Blair lashed out. "Giorgio, I told you last night you can't walk in on me unannounced. You must phone before you come. I can't deal with you right now." She turned away.

Giorgio put his hand on her arm. "I heard about the shooting on the news and I've been crazed. The hospital refused to give me information because you listed Harold as Kirsten's father. I left a message on your cell but you didn't call me back and I didn't know where you were. So I came here in the hope of finding someone, anyone who could tell me how my daughter is."

His distress broke through the haze of exhaustion

and worry that enveloped Blair. "I'm sorry. Of course you are concerned. It's just that I'm tired and worried and have a million things on my mind. I need to make an important call right now. Having you show up on top of everything else is more than I can take."

"Just tell me how Kirsten is and when I can see her. Then I'll leave you."

"The surgeon assured me the operation on her shoulder was successful. She should be out of intensive care in a few hours. She'll be moved to a private room then. The duty nurse told me that now was a good time to go home and rest."

"Thank god she's okay."

"Yes, it looks that way. When I go back, later this morning, I'll add your name to the family list. Then you can check with the hospital about visiting."

"Has there been any word on who might have done this?"

"No."

"Is Harold here?"

"No. He's gone for a walk. Now, please let me get back to my call."

"Can I do anything to help you?"

"No, but thanks." She looked at him and said nothing more, hoping he would get the hint and leave.

"Let me know if you want friendly company at the hospital. I'm available," Giorgio said gently.

"Thank you," Blair said as she walked him to the door. "That's kind."

He gave her a quick hug and left.

Blair returned to the kitchen and sank into her favorite chair, resting her head on her hands. She hated hospitals with their cluttered, impersonal hallways, the constant hum of machinery, the voices of nurses doing their rounds day and night, and the inescapable smell of bleach.

Seeing Kirsten just out of surgery, barely conscious, reminded her of those unbearable days when she had watched her father die. Consumed with terminal cancer, heavily sedated, tubes and beeping monitors attached everywhere—it had been horrifying. Her father had been a difficult man in many ways, but he didn't deserve that suffering.

Earlier that night, Blair had barely been able to look at her daughter's fragile, painfully thin body, her face almost gray against the white sheets. She had had to lean against the wall to keep from falling.

Torn between the urge to escape and her need to be with Kirsten, Blair had forced herself to follow the gurney down the corridor until it disappeared through the doors to intensive care. Then she had turned away and gone to the nurses' station, where she had requested extra security for her daughter. The hospital had been eager to comply—Kirsten's case was high-profile because of her connection to the network and because she was part of the Bruckheimer family. Wade's murder still dominated the news.

She could not delay calling Donna any longer. Blair's hand shook as she punched in the number.

The phone rang twice, then Donna asked, "Is that you, Blair?"

Blair found herself unable to speak, unable to find the right words to heal the rift between them.

"Please, Blair, talk to me," pleaded Donna. "I'm

desperately worried about Kirsten. I've always thought of her as more than my goddaughter. I love her as if she were my own child and I can't believe she was put in harm's way working for me. This terrible thing has happened to her and I can't tell you how much . . ." Donna broke off. Blair could hear tears in her voice and felt her own throat growing tighter.

"Donna, Donna . . ." Blair began, "I understand, and I appreciate . . ." She paused to try to control herself. "Oh, Donna, we'll get through this, like always."

Donna's reply came with a burst of sobs. "I won't let you go through this alone. I'm coming right over, Blair."

The last thing she wanted was Donna in the apartment right now. "No, no, Donna," she said quickly. "You can't. I just got here from the hospital. I want to shower and change and then I'm heading right back to Kirsten. I promise I'll call you later today."

Donna had recovered her composure; she spoke now with her usual take-charge attitude. "No, Blair. I don't want you to be alone right now. We can discuss what has to be done for Kirsten and then go to the hospital together. Why don't you come to me? My driver and I will pick you up in twenty minutes. You can shower and change at my apartment and if you want, you can have something to eat while we talk."

Blair sighed in resignation. "Okay, Donna, since you seem so settled on it."

As she packed a change of clothes, Blair wondered— not for the first time—why she always gave in to Donna. It went back to when they first met. Donna graduated summa cum laude from journalism school and had been hired as an assistant producer at the network. As a promising newcomer, she was assigned to work with Blair's father, then the head of the news division.

Already planning on having her own cooking show someday, Blair had convinced her father to take her on as an intern as well, so she could start to get television experience. Not wanting to be accused of nepotism, her father went out of his way to be demanding of her. During those difficult days, Blair and Donna became close friends and Blair often turned to the other woman for help and sympathy, just as she was doing today.

When Blair stepped off the elevator into the lobby, the doorman nodded and opened the door, then gestured to the limousine waiting at the curb. The driver got out and swung open the car's back door, revealing Donna waiting inside. Donna held out her hand to Blair.

"Oh, Blair," she said, "I've missed you so much."

Blair sat beside her and tilted a cheek toward her friend, waiting for the obligatory kiss that would signal forgiveness, but Donna held her by the shoulders. "We can solve any problems between us. You mean so much to me. When I thought I had lost you, I didn't know what to do."

Blair shook herself free. "After what happened to Kirsten, nothing else matters in the slightest. As long as she pulls through, I don't care about anything, past or present."

That seemed to placate Donna and the two women spent the short ride to Donna's apartment in silence.

Moments later, Donna was leading Blair into the guest room. "I know Kirsten will be okay. Now, after you've had a shower, some food, and a little rest, we'll go over everything together. And when she's fully recovered,

I'll get the best plastic surgeon to repair any scar," Donna stated briskly.

"Thank you," Blair said quietly. She set her bag on the bed and walked into the bathroom. "I'll take a quick shower and then head right back to the hospital."

Donna wouldn't hear of it. "You must get a little rest first."

"I'm worried sick about Kirsten, and I want to be there when she wakes up," Blair said. Looking at the firm expression on Donna's face, she knew she had to give in or face another battle. "Okay, a few minutes of rest before I go."

There was no use arguing with Donna. There never was.

The only time Blair had beaten Donna was yesterday, when she threatened to go public with the scandalous photos of a nude Donna Fuller unless Donna killed the diamond story.

Donna had begged her not to, citing freedom of the press and journalistic ethics. But for once, Blair had stood firm. And Donna had backed down.

Chapter 24

The hot, pinpoint shower was so relaxing that Blair had felt tempted to stay under it forever. But she'd resisted and now welcomed the delicious coolness of the linen sheets on the bed in Donna's guest room. Though she'd known Donna for decades, she'd never stayed overnight in her friend's apartment.

She closed her eyes and thought about her argument with Donna. She had forced Donna to abandon the story on the Braganza. For the first time, she had gotten Donna to bend to her will. Now she had to reverse her plea and persuade Donna to run the story after all. It galled her, though she knew it had to be done.

At first she had been frantic to stop any publicity that would spread the word about the sale. She knew that Wade would spend all the money to maintain his extravagant lifestyle with Bella. Blair and Harold would get nothing.

Now Wade was dead, and as his executor, Harold would control the sale. He would get the money. She hoped that this meant that for the first time in their married life, they could buy a home of their own. Maybe she could open the restaurant she had been planning for years.

She regretted using the photographs to threaten Donna. Now Donna knew she had them.

Blair had found the photos in her mother's safety deposit box after her mother's death. She had known about her father's affair with Donna from the beginning and knew it had destroyed her parents' marriage. But the photos had been a shock. There was no mistaking that Donna was the pretty blond woman enjoying sex with Blair's father.

Lying in Donna's guest room, Blair remembered the first time Donna had come to the family home. Brilliant and strikingly beautiful, with an instinct for the news business that put her on the fast track for promotion, Donna had quickly become a star reporter. She had even filled in once or twice at the national anchor desk. It wasn't unusual for Blair's father to invite young reporters to dinner, but this time, he asked Blair to let her mother know that Donna was coming.

"Wouldn't it be better if you asked her?"

"No," he replied sternly, "I want you to do it."

By then, she and Donna were close friends, so Blair happily alerted her mother, who was not pleased to have an unexpected guest. Trying to smooth things over, Blair offered to prepare her coq au vin for the occasion.

"It's not the cooking, it's the guest," her mother replied, "but I'm delighted to have you cook for us."

The food had been delicious, but her mother had

been reserved throughout the evening and Blair felt an odd undercurrent to the stilted conversation around the dinner table. She decided that Donna just felt uncomfortable in her boss's home and looked forward to the end of the meal, when she hoped she and Donna would be able to go to her room for some girl talk.

But after dinner, her father said, "Donna and I mustn't be disturbed. We'll be in the study behind a locked door. We need privacy."

Disappointed, Blair chalked her father's announcement up to his obsessive attention to work, even though her mother's scowl should have told her that something else was going on. After two hours, they emerged. Donna left immediately, after the briefest of thanks for dinner and a quick "I'll see you tomorrow."

That first evening set the pattern—an awkward meal with the family followed by Donna disappearing into the study for several hours. Occasionally, after she emerged, Donna would stay late to chat with Blair; sometimes they would meet the following morning for coffee, but they never discussed the dinners or what else happened on those evenings.

The affair between Blair's father and Donna was a constant source of gossip around the network. Blair resented the relationship, but more disturbing were the changes in her parents. They rarely spoke to each other anymore, except for essential discussions of household matters. Even if they attended business events together, they came home to separate bedrooms.

Blair expected her parents to divorce at any moment, but they remained together. She was never sure why.

Remarkably, her friendship with Donna continued. Looking back, Blair realized that it was Donna who encouraged the friendship. She called Blair regularly to arrange meetings saying she had free tickets to movies or the theater.

Then Blair got a producer's job with a public television cooking program, left the network, and was able to move out of her family's apartment. Around that time she met Giorgio and began an affair with him.

Donna warned her against Giorgio.

"He is not really committed to you. He spends money like crazy. And I hear that he swings both ways—women and men."

"Where do you hear all this?" Blair demanded.

"Around town. Friends. Please don't get angry, Blair. I love you and I'm just trying to keep you out of a bad scene."

"I understand, but I don't believe all this stuff. We're great together. He's got a sensational body, and we have great sex. He's attentive and sweet, and we're going to get married."

"Married?" Donna asked, incredulous.

"Yes, and I want you to be my maid of honor."

Once Donna saw there was no dissuading Blair, she helped plan the wedding, and later proudly stood to be named godmother at Kirsten's christening.

When faced with divorce from Giorgio, it was Donna to whom Blair turned, and it was Donna who warned her about the difficult Bruckheimer clan. Donna had comforted Blair when her mother had a fatal heart attack, just as she had been at Blair's side earlier, through her father's last illness.

The thought of her father eased Blair's conscience as she contemplated her scheme to influence Donna. Some of the photos had been taken in his library—she recognized the bookshelves in the background. Others were of Donna in a variety of erotic poses in hotel and motel rooms. There were also three pictures of Donna and her father taken by surprise in the middle of a sex act. Blair assumed her mother had hired a private detective to provide her with unequivocal evidence of the affair.

Also in her mother's safety deposit box, Blair had found a document that transferred her father's property to her mother on condition that they never divorce and that she would never make the photos public. Each photo was numbered and listed on the agreement, which had been signed by both of her parents.

The document and photos told the whole story of the relationship between Donna and her father, and the way her mother had dealt with him.

Blair had put the photos in her mother's chest and never mentioned them to Donna—until this week. She had called Donna on Wednesday night, feeling her heart race as she dialed. For the first time in their relationship, the upper hand was hers.

After an exchange of greetings, Donna had said, "You know, we may do a story on the sale of the diamond. If I tape any interviews at your apartment, maybe afterwards we can have a glass of wine and a good chat."

"That's why I'm calling," Blair had replied. "I hope you will agree not to do that story."

Blair heard hostility in Donna's reply. "Why? Why

on earth would you ask that? You know very well that I have to be free to make all decisions about what stories I cover. I can't be influenced by anyone's personal request. Your father was a famous journalist. You should know news standards."

Blair exploded. "I know my father's standards—and I know yours. I have the pictures to prove it."

Donna sputtered, "What . . . what . . . do you . . . how could you mention that?"

That had answered Blair's last question: Did Donna know about the pictures and the agreement? She clearly did. Blair had smiled to herself as she continued, "I mean this: either you cancel this story, or you will see some of those pictures in a tabloid. They'll probably put a black bar over the important parts, but no one could fail to recognize the great Donna Fuller."

"Why are you doing this to me?" Donna had cried out. By then, Blair had begun to shake from the power of her emotions. She had hung up before Donna could convince her to change her mind.

How things had changed in the three days since that call, Blair thought. After causing such anguish for them both, here she was—resting in Donna's bedroom, being pampered.

And now she was about to reverse herself and ask Donna to do the story. She'll think I've gone crazy, was Blair's last thought as she drifted off.

She was awakened by Donna gently shaking her. "Blair, you said you wanted to go back to the hospital as soon as visiting hours began. Get dressed, have something to eat, and my driver will take us over."

Still half asleep, Blair stood up and slipped into her

jeans and a clean blouse. Donna was seated at a small table nearby.

"Here," Donna said, gesturing at the chair opposite her, "sit down and have some coffee to help you wake up. And I brought sandwiches—you should try to eat. Are you feeling better?"

Blair was able to reply with genuine feeling. "Oh, yes, much. Thanks for the TLC." She sat down and sipped her coffee. Without looking at Donna, Blair continued, "I need another favor from you, Donna. I know this will be a strange request under the circumstances . . ." She paused and looked up, meeting her friend's gaze. Donna's face was expressionless but Blair had the sense that she was bracing herself. "I want you to do the story on the Braganza after all."

Whatever she had expected Blair to say, it obviously wasn't that. Blair saw Donna's eyes widen very slightly and the woman took a deep breath before answering. "And if I don't? What else do you have to threaten me with? How do you plan to punish me for what I did when I was young and ambitious?"

Blair reached across the table and took her friend's hand. "Donna, I am so sorry. Forgive me."

"I do forgive you," Donna replied. "But I must tell you that I could never compromise my principles and give in to blackmail. I had already decided to go ahead with the story." Blair saw determination in her eyes and realized that she hadn't won after all. Donna always got her way.

Donna continued, "It's time we went to the hospital. If Kirsten isn't awake, I won't stay. We can stay in touch by cell."

Blair grabbed her coat and bag. Just before they got into the car, Donna paused where no one could overhear them and said, "Blair, I would like to have those pictures. I promise I'll destroy them. They're too dangerous to leave around."

"Of course. I'll give them to you later," Blair answered. But she knew she was lying. As long as she lived, Donna Fuller would never get her hands on those photographs. Blair owed that to her mother.

Chapter 25

As she hastily gathered her notes, Sonya glanced at her watch. Almost eleven thirty, and she was running late. Usually she was passionate about being on time, but she and Keith had been up most of the night before and though Sonya had eventually fallen asleep, she had slept only fitfully. Keith had slept soundly, but had kept his arm around her the whole night. Each time she had awakened, the warmth of his naked body pressed against her had reassured Sonya and she had quickly drifted back to sleep.

Still, she would have liked to have stayed in bed even longer that morning. She had a difficult day ahead and would need all her energy.

When they'd been awakened by her alarm, Keith had held her close for a long moment. "I'm afraid for you to be alone," he'd whispered in her ear. "I'm going with you to the interview."

She had replied, "Thank you, Keith, but I'll be fine. And I won't be alone—Perry will be with me." Sonya had meant it as a joke, something to lighten the mood, but Keith didn't laugh.

"This isn't funny," he said as he sat on the edge of the bed. "Somebody tried to kill you last night. They got the wrong person, but that doesn't mean they've given up. Besides, your interview is in that rat's warren of apartments where there's already been a murder this week."

"Keith, you can't go with me. Your presence will kill the interview. I promise to stay in touch by cell and we can meet after I visit Kirsten. Why don't you shower while I call the hospital?" He had grumbled but complied.

Sonya had shivered nervously while she waited for the call to be transferred to the nurses' desk on Kirsten's floor. A sympathetic voice eased her fear. "She's doing great, Ms. Iverson," the duty nurse assured her. "She has a couple of tests this morning, but she'll be ready for visitors by early afternoon." Sonya thanked her and hung up.

"Good news, Keith. Kirsten is doing well," she shouted through the bathroom door.

"Great," he shouted back.

The thought that she was the one who should be in the hospital clung to Sonya as she prepared for her day. When Keith joined her at the kitchen table, he watched her closely. Sonya could tell he was about to speak. Wanting to forestall him, she sighed heavily and put her hand on his.

"I hope you can understand that I need you to give me space today." He frowned, but she kept talking. "Honey, it's not just that I have work to do and that some of the people I need to talk to will clam up if there's a cop around. I feel guilty about Kirsten and I would like to see her alone so that I can talk to her about what happened. I promise not to go down any dark alleys." She smiled. "Please . . ."

He shook his head. "I don't like it, but I get it. Okay. Just keep your promise to stay in touch."

Sonya took a last long drink of coffee and went to dress. She had scheduled an interview with Blair at noon, but given everything that was happening, she wasn't surprised that she hadn't gotten a message confirming that. She had tried Blair's cell as well as the apartment, but all she had gotten was voice mail. She was planning to just go to the Bruckheimer apartments and see what happened.

But nothing would happen if she didn't get over there and fast.

Perry had texted her several times; he'd been waiting for her since ten o'clock. She met him at the van, grateful he had parked in the parking lot rather than the indoor garage. She was not ready to face that.

"How are you?" Perry asked. "I've heard the whole story, and was worrying about you."

"I'm fine, maybe a little tired and shaky, and most of all, upset about Kirsten." Sonya's cell phone rang; the display read PRIVATE CALLER.

She picked up and was not surprised to find Donna on the other end. "Sonya, I'm really concerned about you. I want to get a bodyguard for you." Sonya grimaced. She had to nip that in the bud right away.

"No, Donna, thank you, but no. I'm fine. I don't need a bodyguard. I just couldn't work with someone watching me all the time. Perry is here, and when I'm not with him, I'll be sure to stay where there are other people." She paused for a moment. "All I can think about is Kirsten."

"She's doing well," Donna said in a reassuring voice. "Are you and Perry ready to talk to Blair? We are definitely going to run the diamond story and I've gotten her to agree to an interview. She's expecting you and Perry at her apartment at noon. I took her to the hospital this morning but she promised to be home in time."

"Donna, I still wish you would do the interviews. I miss your famous touch."

Donna ignored the compliment and hung up without another word. Sonya knew her well and realized that whatever had upset her was not fully resolved.

Sonya turned to Perry, who was patiently sitting beside her. "It's a go." He smiled at her and put the van into gear.

When Sonya rang the bell at the Bruckheimer apartment, Blair opened the door immediately. Sonya was struck by the resemblance between mother and daughter; though Kirsten was much thinner than Blair, they looked remarkably alike.

Sonya held out her hand. "Though we've never met, Mrs. Bruckheimer, Kirsten has told me so much about you that I feel that I know you. And of course I've enjoyed watching your cooking programs."

"Thank you, and please, call me Blair," was the reply. "Kirsten adores you, Sonya."

"I can't tell you how terrible I feel about the shooting."

"I saw her, very briefly, this morning, before she was

taken away for some tests. She seems to be resting comfortably. She's still a bit groggy, but I'm sure she'll be happy to see you if you have a chance to stop by."

Sonya thanked her, then asked to see possible sites for the interview.

"Let me show you the kitchen. It's very much my workshop. We've filmed in there before, for some of my shows."

The kitchen was perfect—large enough, with the table making a good focal point. "It's great, just what we need. I'll get Perry to set up the moment he arrives." As usual, Perry was taking the staff elevator.

"Before we start," Blair said pleasantly, "I want to let you know that I am doing this interview so that collectors know the importance of the Braganza. You control your story of course, but I know your reputation for digging into mysteries." She paused, then continued with an air of confidentiality. "I know that Kirsten would appreciate it if I could count on you to keep our interview focused on the diamond. And that my old friend Donna would feel the same."

Sonya was in no mood to be bullied. "Blair, I understand what your goals are, but I'll follow this story where it takes me. You can refuse to do the interview, but I would have the right to make that refusal part of the story." She paused to give Blair time to think. She could practically see the wheels turning in the other woman's mind and was not surprised when Blair decided to go ahead.

Perry stepped into the room and Sonya wondered if he had overheard them talking and waited in the hall until Blair had made up her mind. "I need a couple of minutes to set up the lighting," he said as he began to unpack his gear.

As Perry worked, Sonya and Blair took seats at the table. Blair said, "Thank you for the help you've given Kirsten. I know she can be a trial at times. But she is a good and hard worker."

Sonya nodded in agreement. "She's very smart and I think she has a talent for television. . . . Like her mother."

Blair smiled at the compliment and then became serious, in contrast to the false congeniality she had shown before. "I'm worried that Kirsten is on the verge of anorexia and I'm afraid that getting shot will be too much for her, physically. She's told me many times that she won't go to a therapist. She admires you. Perhaps you could convince her to get help?"

Sonya was struck by Blair's concern. From what Kirsten had said, Sonya had assumed that Blair was uninvolved and unaware. Clearly that wasn't true, and Sonya warmed to Blair. "Yes, of course. I've talked with her, but I'll do it again. I'm not sure it will help— you know she has her own ideas about what is good for her." Blair nodded ruefully.

Perry signaled that he was ready and that the tape was rolling. Experienced with television production, Blair sat a tiny bit straighter as Sonya began the formal interview.

"Since Wade Bruckheimer died, there seems to be a question about who owns the Braganza. Can you shed some light on that?"

Blair bristled and spoke firmly. "There is no question. My husband is the executor of Wade's will and controls the diamond and its sale. The question of who gets the money from the sale is confidential."

"Irina Bruckheimer, your mother-in-law, has worn the diamond for decades. You say she doesn't have a claim on the Braganza, but she's said in various press reports that the diamond belongs to her." Sonya smiled. "Irina has also said that she doesn't want it sold."

Blair narrowed her eyes. "You will have to ask her about that. I can only speak for my husband and myself."

Sonya pressed on. "And Bella Bruckheimer, Wade's wife?"

"Yes, what about her?"

Sonya could tell that Blair was trying to stay calm but that her questions were not what Blair had expected. "She told me she expects to keep the diamond."

"I've already explained the circumstances," Blair said. She took a breath; Sonya saw a change in her eyes and was not surprised when Blair's next sentences felt a little scripted. "The diamond is fabulous, and I can understand why many people claim some interest in it. Have you seen it? Its color is magnificent."

"I've only seen photos," Sonya said quickly before returning to her planned questions. "Let's talk about the rest of the family for a moment. I understand the Diases also have some interest in returning the stone to Brazil."

But Blair had steadied herself. Her reply was perfectly calm. "As I said, many people would like to possess the Braganza."

Sonya realized she had gotten all she could on the

family. "Changing the subject, your brother-in-law, Wade Bruckheimer, was murdered." Blair tried to interrupt, but Sonya continued, "And you were here, in this apartment, the night of the murder. Can you tell me what happened?"

"I was here, but asleep. All I know is that Bella came screaming up the stairs; we woke up and she was practically hysterical, saying that Wade was dead." Blair relaxed, obviously pleased by the shift in the conversation.

Sonya leaned forward. "Tell me about the special ice cream Wade ate each night."

"It was custom-made just for him, a special kind of vanilla with a rich chocolate sauce running through it, and some of those Brazilian acai berries, handpicked in the rain forests. You could say he was addicted to it. His parrot was crazy about it too.

"Of course, that bird would eat anything. It was a foulmouthed, unfriendly creature that would scream at any stranger who went near it. I felt sorry for it. Poor bird belonged at home in a jungle, not in a New York apartment."

"Do you have any idea who might have wanted Wade dead?"

Blair stiffened. "Of course not. And I really have nothing more to add." She looked away.

Sonya had gotten everything she needed. She nodded to Perry to stop. "Thank you, Blair. It went well."

"I hope so," Blair responded with hesitation.

"If you do sell the diamond, what will that mean for your family?" Sonya asked, genuinely curious.

Blair's demeanor changed completely and she spoke heatedly. "That's a no-brainer for me. My food has never gotten the attention it deserves, and I'm sick and tired of being in the shadow of male chefs. I want to open a restaurant. This sale will give me the money to do it."

Sonya was surprised by her passion. Given the right circumstances, would Blair kill to have the restaurant and the recognition she thought she deserved?

They left as soon as Perry had packed the gear. When Sonya got off the elevator, she found Bella waiting for it.

"Hi," the young woman said, teetering forward in high heels and clutching Sonya's arm to steady herself. "I had a wonderful lunch with friends." She lowered her voice to a whisper. "I hate this place. I don't want to go up to that apartment and those evil people. I'm going to leave here and never see them again. Poor Kirsten is stuck here. You heard they tried to kill her."

Sonya didn't have to smell the alcohol on Bella's breath to know that the woman was drunk. She wasn't sure Bella knew who she was, but she said, "Yes. Whoever shot Kirsten mistook her for me."

"You? I thought they wanted to kill Kirsten." Bella punched the up button and got into the elevator.

"Why would someone want to kill Kirsten?" Sonya asked.

But the door closed, leaving Sonya without an answer.

Chapter **26**

Perry gave a hoot of surprise when Sonya asked him to make a detour and drop her off at Cornell Medical Center. Kirsten had texted her as she was getting into the van, asking Sonya to come visit.

"You mean Kirsten has recovered that fast? It's not twenty-four hours since she was shot." Perry turned the van onto Second Avenue.

Sonya snapped her phone shut. "I'm as surprised as you are. Her message is a bit cryptic, though. She said that she needs to see me as soon as possible. She wants to ask me something, she said, and whatever it is, she doesn't want her mother to know about it. She says I have to come see her before Blair gets back.

"She's so ambitious! I can't believe she's in any condition to talk about work. I wish she would realize how lucky she is to be alive and just forget about the Braganza for a while."

Without taking his hands off the wheel, Perry

shrugged, a gesture of mock disbelief accented by his raised eyebrows. "Well, how is she? Did she say?"

"According to Keith and Blair, she lost quite a bit of blood," Sonya said. "Kirsten's text said that when she passed out from being shot, she hit her head on the concrete step as she fell. She has a concussion."

Perry swore and blasted the horn as two jaywalkers ran across the street in front of the van. "She's lucky— the gunman must have seen her collapse and thought he had killed her."

The traffic was at a standstill near the hospital.

"It must be the Saturday visitors," Perry said. He straightened his arms against the steering wheel and stretched his back. "You know that bullet was meant for you, not Kirsten."

Sonya nodded. "Yes. Keith thinks so too. But who would want to shoot me? And for what reason?"

"It's got to be connected to the diamond story. I wouldn't put anything past those Brazilians."

"There's nothing I know that they could be scared of. I've racked my brains, but I can't think of a thing. Maybe Kirsten will give me a clue when I see her."

"How much time do you think you'll have with her? Was Blair heading straight back after your interview?"

"I don't think so. She looked exhausted, even though she got a few hours' sleep at Donna's. And Bella was on the way up when I came down. I suspect Bella and Irina will keep Blair busy for a while. Kirsten and I should have plenty of time to chat," Sonya said through gritted teeth.

The van was cut off by an ambulance that swerved

in front of it. Perry swore as he jammed on the brakes. Sonya could feel his growing irritation and didn't want to cope with it.

"I'll get out here; it'll be quicker for me to walk the rest of the way. You can turn and go up York Avenue; the traffic should be lighter there."

She grabbed her bag, opened the door, and climbed out.

"Watch yourself," Perry shouted out the window at her. Sonya turned and waved, giving him as big a smile as she could manage. The street was full of people; she felt in no danger.

She stopped at the fruit vendor outside the hospital and bought a basket of seedless grapes. They would be easy for Kirsten to pick at and would meet her stringent food requirements.

The hospital's lobby and hallways were crowded; it took a good ten minutes to get up to Kirsten's room. Sonya paused in the doorway to look at the young woman in the high hospital bed. Kirsten seemed to be asleep; her body looked small and frail under the stiff-looking sheet and blanket. Her left shoulder was heavily bandaged and each arm was tethered to an IV drip. Sonya realized that Kirsten was being given blood as well as a clear fluid of some kind.

Perhaps Sonya had made a noise; Kirsten turned her head and looked toward the door. She smiled when she saw Sonya. As Sonya stepped into the room, she saw that Kirsten was holding back tears.

"Oh, Sonya, I am so pleased to see you," Kirsten said. "I can't talk to anyone about what happened—no one understands!"

This was a new Kirsten, an emotionally fragile young woman in dire need of comfort. Sonya put the grapes on the night table and pulled a chair close to the bed.

Kirsten took Sonya's hand as she went on. "I keep replaying the memories. I have to tell you. As I came out of the elevator, I heard a voice call 'Over here' from the back of the garage. It wasn't Perry's voice, it was deeper and kind of muffled, but I ran that way anyway. I wanted to get that videotape for you.

"The next thing I remember is waking up in the emergency ward with the medics bending over me."

"Kirsten," Sonya said firmly, "you have to stop thinking about it and give yourself time to recover. You've had surgery, gotten drugs—you have to let your body and mind rest."

The intern began to cry. "I'm so glad you're here," she said in a tight voice. "I've been worrying about you. I was frightened the gunman would go after you again."

Sonya leaned forward and ran her hand over the red curls that looked so much like her own. "Shush, calm down, Kirsten. I'm perfectly all right. Now, for once in your life, do what you are told. Rest."

As she spoke, she saw Kirsten reach for a tissue and determinedly wipe her eyes. "I feel okay, Sonya, really I do. My shoulder doesn't hurt much, and the nurse said that I'm young and I'll recover fast." She gave a little giggle. "So there. You won't get rid of me that easily."

Sonya smiled back.

"If I hadn't taken your coat it never would have happened. But now your wonderful plaid coat has a big hole in it and my blood all over it. It was a beautiful coat. So sixties."

Kirsten had been admiring that coat for weeks, but it was probably better that she never know that Sonya had been on the point of giving it to her. Sonya said, "Well, it's bad luck about the coat, sixties or not. Don't worry about it. If I decide to keep it, I know a great dry cleaner who can remove the blood and repair the hole. No one will ever know what happened."

"But it will never be the same to you. It will always remind you of how stupid I was."

Sonya squeezed her hand gently, trying to comfort the younger woman.

Kirsten seemed to gather herself and said, "What's happening to the story? I want to keep working on it."

"Forget it . . . the story will be fine." Kirsten's face crumpled and Sonya quickly backtracked a bit, not wanting to upset her. "There'll be other stories. You'll have plenty of work to keep you busy.

"Everyone thinks you've been very brave. People are saying you've got the courage and brains of your famous grandfather and you'll be around the network for a long time."

Kirsten shook her head violently, then winced in pain. "How can I forget the story when it involves my family? Nothing will be fine until the police find Wade's killer. They've got to find out who gave Wade the sleeping pills and who tried to shoot you." Kirsten's voice was rising. Sonya began to fear that the nurse would come to scold her about upsetting the patient and insist she leave.

"Kirsten, if you don't calm down I'll have to go." Sonya waited a moment while Kirsten calmed herself, then continued. "You texted me about a problem you didn't want your mother to know about. What is it?"

"I think my mother murdered Wade," Kirsten said in a rush. "She's always hated him. She called him a wastrel, said he'd taken advantage of everyone in the family, particularly Harold. She said we would all be better off if he were dead."

Sonya was taken aback. Was Kirsten out of her mind because of the drugs she'd been given or did she mean what she said? It was hard to believe that the woman Sonya had just interviewed was capable of murder.

"Do you really believe your mother killed Wade? I think it's highly unlikely, from what I know of her. She strikes me as an intelligent, well-balanced woman."

Kirsten looked at her closely. "Have you interviewed her?"

"Yes, this morning," Sonya said with a nod.

"I bet she turned on the charm for you. That's not what she's really like. She always says she's so concerned about me, but the truth is that she spends much more time looking after Harold. She's crazy about him and would do anything to protect him.

"Harold never had much money while Wade got a lot and spent it all, living the high life. Plus, my mother hated Wade popping in and out of the kitchen as if he owned it. She said that having him so close was the worst part of living in the apartment."

This was the first time Sonya had heard Kirsten say such negative things about her mother. She doubted Blair was the monster Kirsten made her out to be, but the younger woman's vitriol made her wonder how much of what she'd seen that morning had been an act. She didn't know Blair well enough to make a true judgment of her yet.

Keith had said that the police had found a spoon under the bed and believed that the sleeping pills had been mixed into Wade's ice cream. Blair was the member of the family in the best position to have done that. She had the know-how and plenty of opportunity. But it seemed to Sonya that Blair was too smart to use a method that would cause her to be the most obvious suspect.

"I must say your mother seemed happy with her family, her cooking, and her television appearances. I think she's more interested in opening a restaurant than in committing murder."

"Yes, we all know about the restaurant," Kirsten said bitterly. "That's the only thing she talks about—what it will look like, how special the menu will be; she's even designed the staff's uniforms.

"She's made me miserable all my life because I'm not interested in recipes. When I was a kid, she forced me to help her in the kitchen even though she knew I didn't want to. Now she tries to make me eat. She cooks fattening things and insists I put them in my mouth. She says her food is nourishing and just what I need." She began to cry again.

"It's awful! I hate to go into the kitchen or be anywhere near her. I feel like I have to sneak around to get a few morsels of what I can stand to eat.

"Harold's a beast. He hates me because he and Mom couldn't have children. And because Wade was my friend." The power of her emotions distorted Kirsten's face.

Sonya tried to soothe her, knowing that her awkward attempt would likely fail. She wanted to feel sympathy for the intern, but still felt mostly annoyance at her histrionics.

"Kirsten, come on. Your mother loves you. She wants only the best for you." Kirsten glared at her and Sonya sighed.

"I want you to really investigate Wade's murder. Find out if my mother's guilty. I'll go crazy lying here thinking that she killed Wade and then tried to kill you. Promise me you'll do it."

Sonya picked up her bag and pushed the chair away from the bed. "I promise I'll do what I can. Now I'm leaving you to rest. I mean it—try to put all of this out of your mind."

She bent and kissed Kirsten on the cheek, then left. Of course she would investigate the murder—Kirsten hadn't had to ask. The whole case was fascinating. Anyone in the family might be the killer.

Chapter 27

SATURDAY, 2:15 P.M.
Sonya's office

Sonya looked at the pile of unlogged tapes on her desk and shuddered. If only Kirsten was there; she liked logging tapes and was fast at it. Deciding to ignore the tapes for now, Sonya switched on the computer, created a new file, and typed in the names of the members of Wade Bruckheimer's family.

One of them had to be the murderer, but it was almost thirty-six hours since the murder, and she had no clues as to which one.

Sonya started thinking about the attack on Kirsten. The shot was meant to kill. But it was meant for her, not Kirsten. Why? What did the attacker think she knew? She began to type, setting down her thoughts.

It had to revolve around the diamond. Apart from Kirsten, Wade had been the only family member who'd wanted the stone sold. It was the fastest way for him to get his hands on a lot of money. But though he would have spent that money on Bella, she didn't want him to sell the stone. Not at auction in the U.S., anyway.

By Kirsten's account, Bella came from a family of thugs. Her beauty was money in the bank for them. She had set her cap for Wade, thinking he was rich, and had manipulated him until he proposed. Then, when the money began to run out, reality had set in.

If Bella could get Wade to turn the diamond over to her, her family would have no trouble selling it. They had plenty of connections in Brazil, where jewelry was an important industry. They'd probably get more for the stone through a privately arranged sale than Wade would achieve at auction. They'd also get the power that accompanied being in control of such a magnificent gem.

According to Kirsten, Bella's brother Rico managed Bella's life. She regularly turned to him for advice and did what he told her to. Kirsten had told Sonya that Rico had promised to come to New York after Wade's death, but that Bella now insisted that he had not turned up.

Sonya wondered if he had secretly arrived and was watching from the sidelines. Or if he'd sent a hit man instead. Maybe he had orchestrated both Wade's murder and Bella's reactions.

During their interview, Bella had mentioned Rico several times, as if trying to make it clear that he had had nothing to do with her since Wade's murder. That was strange to Sonya, given that she had been told that Bella rarely made a move without Rico's consent. And if he hadn't phoned her, why hadn't she called him? If Bella was as desperately lonely and afraid as she claimed, it would be natural to turn to her own family.

According to Bella, Rico had told her to get a lawyer. In Sonya's opinion, that was a natural move for a woman in Bella's position. A lawyer would certainly be necessary if the Bruckheimers got tough, which they were likely to do. Yet—again, according to Bella— Rico had not followed up on this advice. Bella had no legal representation. Sonya decided that Bella's story about her brother rang false.

When she had interviewed Bella, Sonya had thought she'd played the role of grieving widow to the hilt, except for the moment when she rushed into Kirsten's arms. The embrace appeared unnatural, but Sonya had put the blame on Kirsten. Now she wondered if she had been mistaken, if Bella was the one who was forcing the emotion, perhaps at Rico's instruction.

If Bella had murdered Wade, it seemed likely that her family was behind it.

Then there was the attempted murder to consider. If she was the intended victim, not Kirsten, why would Rico have targeted her? Even if he was upset about Bella's interview, that was no reason to murder the show's producer.

Uncle Jorge was next on Sonya's list. He could have killed Wade to stop the auction, but would he have hired someone to kill Sonya? She wondered if he even knew who she was.

Her cell phone rang. It was Keith, asking where she was. She heard the anger in his voice when she admitted she was at the office. "Is anybody else there?" he asked.

"It's Saturday lunchtime, you can't expect the place to be crowded."

"Are you alone?" She hesitated and he jumped into the silence. "Yes, you are, I can tell by the way you are avoiding giving me a direct answer." She heard him bang his fist on his desk in frustration. "That hit man got into the building once. He can get in again and find you. We still don't know who he is, but we're pretty sure that he's probably planning to take a second shot at you. You promised to be careful. I told you to stay with people all the time."

Sonya tried to calm him. "I am being careful. I'm not a fool. The receptionist is here, and a couple of editors are around." She heard him grunt in disapproval and added, sweetly, "I'm hungry. Do you have time for a quick bite? You can protect me while I eat."

She expected him to be angry when they met at his favorite deli at Sixty-Third and Madison, but his mood had changed. He put his arm around her waist and pulled her to him.

"I don't know what I'd do if I lost you." He nuzzled her hair as they walked to an empty booth. "You mean a lot more to me than you realize."

She didn't speak until the waiter came and took their orders: cheese, lettuce, and tomato on a roll for her and pastrami on rye for him. Keith insisted that deli food was the best of New York. He knew everyone in the city. In fact the first meal they had shared had been takeout deli sandwiches on a bench in Central Park.

"What's new?" she asked, anxious not to get into the security problem again.

"Not much. It's too early to come to conclusions. We have to wait for more tests to come in. You know that."

He always gave her noncommittal, nonspecific answers. Keith was a good cop who divulged as little as possible, even to her. It was irritating, but she told herself she did the same when her research dug up information she knew he would love to have. He'd been drilled not to trust the media, and she was a journalist. And for her part, she couldn't be seen as someone who leaked information to the police—it would cost her many interviews.

"Well, Kirsten's made a quick recovery," she said. "I saw her earlier today."

"Did she tell you much?"

Sonya shook her head. "Assuming that Kirsten had already been questioned by the police, she answered truthfully. The barest details. She saw nothing; just heard a voice and ran toward it. She's annoyed with herself because she says she is a journalist, and ought to remember more." Sonya gave a quick laugh.

Keith nodded. "Yeah, that's what she told us. But I thought she was close to recalling something else. Maybe when her concussion improves it'll come back to her."

The server slapped down their sandwiches. Sonya watched Keith bite into his pastrami on rye and waited until he swallowed.

"Did you get much from the attorney?" she asked. "For instance, did he say how the brothers, Wade and Harold, got on?"

"Apparently very well, when you think of the differences in their personalities and ages. Wade was social; a spendthrift whose main goal was to enjoy life. Harold is a solid engineer, highly respected. As far as we can tell from talking to their friends, Wade was proud of Harold. When they were both younger, they bonded during the holidays they spent together with the Dias family in Brazil. It looks like Harold's mom, Irina, put a stop to the joint vacations when she thought the boys were getting too close. The gossip is that Irina's a control freak who didn't want her only child straying too far."

"Interesting," Sonya commented. "What did the attorney say about the diamond? What happens to it now?"

Keith continued to eat. He's hiding something and trying to figure out how much he can share, Sonya thought. She did her best to be patient and quiet while he finished half of his sandwich.

"The attorney didn't give us much, and you know I can't tell you everything he said. But the bottom line is that Douglas Bruckheimer left nearly everything to Irina—except the diamond. There's a provision in the will that says it has to stay in Esperanza's bloodline, so it went directly to Wade.

"Wade never objected to Irina wearing the stone or to her giving everyone the impression that the diamond belonged to her. At least not until he married Bella and ran so short of money that he decided to sell the gem. Now the Braganza's future depends on what's in Wade's will." Keith smiled in a way that told Sonya that she wouldn't be hearing about Wade's will from him.

"So Wade did have every right to sell the diamond," Sonya said pensively. "But the provision that the stone has to stay with Esperanza's bloodline might have an impact. That might allow the Dias family to claim it, or Bella, if she's pregnant with Wade's child. . . ."

Keith grinned again. "Is that enough to keep you thinking?"

Sonya grinned back. "Definitely. If Douglas left everything to Irina, then Harold shouldn't be too short of money—assuming his mother shares her wealth with him." She ate a few bites, then added, "But I think she spends most of her money on herself. She's crazy about jewelry and antiques. Kirsten said that she's far from generous."

"I wonder if she gets any money from her father. He's a rich developer from Cincinnati who is suspected of having connections with the local mob. Nothing ever proven, of course." Keith looked intently at Sonya. "Did you know that Irina's mother was murdered and that the Cincinnati police have always suspected her father was the killer?"

"Yes," Sonya said, nodding. "I researched it. Irina stood up for him in court." She shook her head, wondering how that early trauma had impacted Irina. "What about Bella? Anything new about her?"

There was a pause while Keith once again decided how much to tell her. "Did I mention that we checked the calls she made the night of the murder? She definitely called her brother Rico in São Paulo. Bella hung up at two fifteen A.M. and Harold called nine-one-one at two thirty. The problem is, we don't know when Bella went upstairs to get help. There was a lot of confusion, understandably, and no one remembers exactly what time they did what, so there is some time not accounted for."

He sighed and Sonya saw that he was exhausted. She looked into his green eyes and smiled, warmed by the knowledge that even though he was working, he had time for her. They finished their meal and left the diner.

"It's time for you to go home and get some rest—I wish I could, and you didn't get as much sleep as I did. You'll be safe there, and if you want me, you can call me on my cell."

He looped his arm around her waist and kept it there as he hailed a cab. Once she was seated, he leaned over and gave the driver the address of her apartment.

"Straight home now," he said. "I want to know you're safe."

"Okay," Sonya said. As the cab pulled away, her mind raced. She was now sure that Bella let Rico tell her what to do. Which meant that she had lied about the details of the night of Wade's death. Why would she lie, when it was reasonable that she call her brother when she found her husband's body?

Sonya leaned forward. "Driver, I've changed my mind." She told him to drop her at the network offices. She had a lot of thinking and more interviews to do.

Who should she call first?

Harold.

She was eager to hear what he had to say about Wade's will.

Glancing up, she realized she had nearly reached the office and fired off a text to Perry, letting him know it was time to go back to work.

Chapter **28**

Perry was making good time negotiating East Side traffic, once again on the way to the Bruckheimer apartment building. How many times today had he loaded and unloaded the van?

"It's been a wild Saturday and I'm sorry I've had to keep you on call all day," Sonya apologized. "I know you like your weekends off. You could have asked another cameraman to cover."

"No way, no way," he insisted. "This is my story too, you know, and no other guy is going to get his video in it."

Sonya laughed. "Perry, seriously, I just don't know what I'd do without you."

Obviously pleased, he grinned.

He pulled up in front of the imposing apartment building where the Bruckheimers lived. "Well, here we are again. Which apartment this time?"

"Irina's," she answered. "Well, Irina, Harold, and Blair's. Same place we were before, only this time, I'll be interviewing Harold, and I doubt we'll use the kitchen." She climbed out of the van.

"See you upstairs," Perry said.

As before, the doorman announced her. Sonya found Harold waiting for her when she stepped off the elevator.

"I'm happy to meet you," Harold said with what impressed Sonya as forced enthusiasm. "Come in, come in. My wife told me about your interview earlier today. She said it went well and that she gave you information about the diamond.

"I'm not sure what I can tell you that she didn't," he said hesitantly, "though I'm happy to help if I can."

"No worries. Everyone has a slightly different take on the same events."

"Just remember, I'm no television personality like my wife."

That's for sure, thought Sonya. His voice was flat and his manner somewhat withdrawn, but Harold was a good-looking man, with a face and build that would work on camera. He had an old-fashioned, conservative look and was neatly dressed in a brown tweed jacket, forest-green corduroy trousers, and brown sweater vest over a dark green shirt. He seemed the opposite of his flamboyant half-brother, Wade.

"Will we do the interview in the kitchen? You did Blair's there."

"Kirsten told me that you have a home office. How about that?"

"Well," he hesitated, "I guess so. But it's a mess."

"Like mine," said Sonya with a laugh. "Sounds perfect. Can I see it?"

He led her down a dark hallway, past a series of closed doors. As she walked, Sonya noticed that one door was ajar. Curious, she looked in and glimpsed a room filled with antiques and dominated by an elaborate bed. Probably Irina's, she thought. She paused for a moment to try to get a better look, but with a firmness she had not detected before, Harold took her by the arm and encouraged her to move along.

"That's my mother's bedroom," he said softly. "She may be resting and you wouldn't want to disturb her. My office is just down the hall." He gestured at a nearby door.

With the two rooms so close, Sonya thought, Harold and Irina probably see each other frequently. She wondered if Irina bothered to knock.

As if he had read her thoughts, Harold offered, "Though we share an apartment, we all lead our own lives. My mother, Blair, and I are all so busy."

He opened the door to his office and ushered Sonya in. Contrary to his earlier statement, the room was in complete order. The largest piece of furniture was a dark wood partner's desk with a matched pair of wooden in- and out-boxes. Sonya moved closer, studying the desktop. A leather-trimmed blotter was centered in the main workspace and surrounded by an assortment of decorative items: a colorful glass paperweight; a fountain pen in a holder that was mounted on a small marble base—a small brass plate on the base was engraved DOUGLAS BRUCKHEIMER; two ornate silver frames— the larger and more ornate held a photo of Irina, the other displayed a picture of Blair. Harold's high-backed executive chair was upholstered in the same brown leather as the pair of side chairs set opposite the desk. Bookshelves, uniformly filled with leather-bound volumes, lined the walls. It was the perfect setting for Harold.

He seated himself behind the desk and drew Sonya's attention to the pen and holder. "As you can see, this belonged to my father. So did this office. I inherited it."

"It's beautiful," Sonya said. She wondered if Harold really used this office or if he just wanted to impress her. "We'll set up in here for the interview. I should check on my cameraman; he was taking the back elevator."

Sonya's hopes of getting a chance to check out Irina's bedroom were dashed when Harold said, "I'll go with you," and accompanied her into the hall. As they walked back toward the entry area, Sonya noticed that the door to Irina's room was now closed.

Perry was waiting at the front door; they collected him and returned to the office. Harold hovered over them as Perry set up his equipment. When the cameraman said he needed to bring in an additional light that he'd left in the front hall, Sonya was amused to see Harold standing in the center of the room, clearly faced with a dilemma. Should he stay, to prevent Sonya's snooping, or go with Perry, who might wander into some forbidden spot? He chose to stay with Sonya.

She decided to make sure Harold understood her concern for Kirsten. She told him that she'd visited earlier in the day and ended with, "I just can't get over my having put her in danger."

Harold nodded. "It must be disturbing to know that

someone is still out to harm you. Have you any idea who it might be?"

"No," she said. "I know the police are doing a full investigation, including forensic analysis of the bullet and casing." Sonya thought she heard him draw a breath and widen his eyes and decided to make sure to ask about the murder attempt during the interview.

Perry had come back and finished the lighting. He now asked Harold to sit. "We're ready, Sonya. Any time."

She took a seat in one of the side chairs, opened her notebook, and began. "I understand that Wade's widow was the first to find his body. She went to you for help. Tell me about it."

He bit his lower lip nervously. After a pause, he took out a crisp white handkerchief and wiped his forehead. Sonya knew that he was buying time to organize his thoughts, but she couldn't force him to speak, so she waited until Harold finally spoke.

"Bella came running up the stairs, shouting that Wade was dead. As I told the police, I went down to Wade's apartment to see for myself, and found that his bird was also dead. I called nine-one-one. When the medics arrived, they tried to revive him. The police came and told me to stay away from the body. They took a statement from me."

He sat back and smiled, apparently satisfied with his answer. Despite his initial hesitation, it was obvious that Harold had told this story before and it was now well-practiced.

Sonya chose her next question carefully.

"Why did you refuse to let the family into the bedroom to see Wade's body?"

"Who told you that?" he snapped. "It's not true. Naturally, I tried to protect the murder scene. I knew the police would insist on that and they thanked me for doing the right thing." He frowned. "I thought this interview was about the diamond. If you have questions about Wade's death, ask the police."

"Harold, it seems that there is some confusion over who actually owns the Braganza. Your mother wears it, but Wade was going to sell it. I've heard that the Brazilian part of the family would like to have it. Your wife told me that you would get at least part of the income from the sale. Can you clarify the situation for me?"

"I'm afraid I can't say much about that. The Braganza did belong to my brother, Wade, but now that he's dead, the ownership and sale of the stone is a matter to be handled by his estate. While I will be taking care of that, I'm not at liberty to share any information yet."

"Will the diamond be sold? I understand that important objects like the Braganza are often sent on tour, to Hong Kong, Geneva, London, and other major cities to increase interest in an auction. Will that happen to the Braganza?"

He appeared to be about to answer and then to think better of it. Sonya realized that it would be practically impossible for her to get a spontaneous, unguarded answer from him.

Harold smiled slightly and said, "I have to repeat that I can't answer that question. I have to talk to the attorney and the auction house before I can make any comment on a potential tour or sale."

Sonya decided to ask once more, to see if she could

rattle him. She took a more direct approach. "Are you authorized to deal with the sale?"

"Why not?" Harold replied defensively. "Wade was my brother—and I'm sure to be the executor of his estate."

"I see. But what about your mother—how does she feel about selling the diamond?"

"If you want to know how she feels, you should ask her. I told you, I am not going to talk about that. Do you have any other questions?"

Clearly, his temper was rising. How would Donna handle him, Sonya asked herself. Change the subject and go easy, then return to hard questions later.

"I'd like to talk about your brother, Wade."

Harold's voice softened and his face relaxed. "He was my brother and I loved him. I can't tell you how much I miss him. I keep expecting to go into his apartment and find him there. And he loved me too."

"He was your half-brother, wasn't he? His mother was Esperanza Dias and yours is Irina Bruckheimer."

"Yes, but that wasn't a problem between us. Wade was ten years older than me and he always took care of me. He was a great older brother. I knew nothing about his mother except that she was a kind of legend. Everyone said how wonderful she was, how beautiful. I'm sorry I never knew her." He gave a short laugh as he continued. "But if she had lived, my father would never have married my mother, and I wouldn't be here, would I?"

"No, I guess not," Sonya agreed. "Your mother and father met in New York, didn't they?"

"Yes. My grandfather lived in Cincinnati, but my mother moved here. He was against my mother and father's marriage at first, but it turned out well. Granddad still lives in Ohio. He's getting older." Harold paused and then said, "He's not feeling so well right now."

"Did you and Wade ever discuss his Brazilian family or his mother, Esperanza?"

"You couldn't avoid it, with her picture hanging in his apartment. My father also often spoke of her. I think Wade was Father's favorite son because he was Esperanza's child." There was a flicker of some emotion in Harold's eyes, though his voice stayed smooth and calm. He shrugged lightly as he said, "But that wasn't a problem between Wade and me. We were brothers. We had a special relationship."

Sonya was not convinced by his expression of family solidarity. Instinct told her that Harold resented Wade. With the possible exception of Kirsten, she had not found anyone in the family who genuinely liked Wade.

"Did you share Wade's interest in birds?"

"You mean his parrot? I thought Cacao was great. Maybe a little noisy, and it could be nasty. But I liked it."

"Did you think it strange that the parrot was killed at the same time as your brother?"

"Not if Wade committed suicide. He was devoted to Cacao and I don't think that he would have trusted Cacao to anyone else. Better dead than not loved, I think." Harold said this with little visible emotion; so much, Sonya thought, for Wade being his adored older brother.

"You think it was suicide?" she pressed.

"Yes," Harold said flatly. She could see that she'd get no shot of a tearful, grieving man today.

"Did Wade get along with your mother?"

"They had their differences."

"How did your mother feel about Cacao? Did she and the bird get along?"

Harold stiffened; she could see fresh wariness in his eyes. "What are you suggesting?" he demanded. "That my mother had something to do with Wade's death?"

"Not at all . . . just trying to get more background." She smiled. "Did Irina like the parrot?"

"I don't know," Harold admitted. "I don't think any of us liked the mess Cacao could make, but Wade mostly kept him downstairs. So Bella would be the one to talk to about that."

"Do you have any thoughts about who might want to harm your brother?"

"Of course not," he replied angrily. Then he seemed to have a second thought. "You might look into Bella's family in Brazil."

"What do you mean?"

"They're a rough bunch. Wade told me he had made a deal with them to bring birds into the country, to be sold as pets, and there was some kind of trouble. Wade got out of it, as he always did, with his uncle Jorge's help. But he made enemies.

"Wade also told me his uncle wanted the Braganza back in Brazil." Harold's tight smile told Sonya that he was pleased to have deflected suspicion onto others.

"Do you think Bella's family might have hired whoever shot your stepdaughter, Kirsten?" That hit home, Sonya thought, when she saw Harold's eyes widen fractionally. It was hard to tell under Perry's lights, but it looked like he'd gone pale as well.

"I'm not saying anything more," he replied, his voice shaking. "I don't know who could have wanted to shoot Kirsten."

"Please," Sonya said quickly, "just a few more questions—about Kirsten. How does she get along with her mother and with you?"

"Sonya, she's our dearest treasure. We both love her. I've tried to be a good father to her—certainly better than her birth father. I know she has her faults, but underneath she's a fine woman."

"So you have a good relationship with her?"

"When Blair and I married, Kirsten was very young and I was delighted to have a little girl in my life, especially once Blair and I found out that we couldn't have children. She looked to me as her father and we spent a lot of time together.

"She liked going to the zoo and so did I," Harold said, beaming. "Kirsten has a natural talent for drawing and she'd usually bring a pad with her and draw the animals or the trees in Central Park. I thought she should study art, but television is what she has her eye on."

"Do the two of you still spend time together?"

"Sadly, no. And it's disappointing. As she got older, there were the expected differences—you know how teenagers can be. She began to say that I wasn't her real father, things like that. When I asked her to come to the park with me, to maybe do a little drawing, she wasn't interested. We grew apart, but I still love her."

"Have you been to the hospital to see her?"

"Not yet. I wanted to go right away, of course, but

Blair insisted only one of us go at a time. She doesn't want Kirsten to get too excited."

"Do you know of any reason why anyone would try to kill Kirsten?"

"No. Of course not. I thought they were after you?" Harold asked, looking closely at Sonya.

"Yes, that's what the police think," Sonya said, as calmly as possible. She signaled to Perry to stop rolling. "Harold, I have what we need. Thank you for doing this interview."

She began to gather her things. Harold had successfully stonewalled her most of the time, but some of what he'd said, and how he'd said it, had sparked some connections and questions in her mind. She wanted to write them down as quickly as possible, but not in front of him.

As soon as the TV lights were off, Harold got out of his chair and came to stand near Sonya. "What parts of my interview will you use?" he asked.

"I don't know yet," she answered truthfully. "I'll have to look at your interview, and Blair's, and any other footage we have, before we make any decisions." She turned to Perry. "Take your time getting the equipment together. I'll see you downstairs."

"I hope what I told you was useful," Harold persisted.

"It was," Sonya said. "I definitely learned some new things from what you said."

Harold's face tensed. "What did you learn?"

Sonya tried to cover her slip. "Just some small details that help to fill out the story—like you and Kirsten going to the zoo together. Thanks again. Now I have to go." She left quickly, passing Irina's still-closed bedroom door on the way.

In the elevator, Sonya told herself that she had learned one thing for certain. Harold Bruckheimer was a liar.

Chapter 29

SATURDAY, 6:00 P.M.
The Bruckheimers' Fifth Avenue apartment

"Will she ever finish that interview and come down?"
Jorge asked Elenora. "There's a draft on this lobby sofa,
and I'm getting tired of waiting."

Her reply began with a series of light, encouraging
pats on his hand. "Be patient. We don't want to miss her."

Blair had told Elenora that Harold would be interviewed that afternoon at around four o'clock. That gave
the Diases the opportunity to meet Sonya Iverson, but
they didn't want her to think that they were lying in
wait for her. They decided it would seem more natural
if they ran into each other by chance. Even if it wasn't
by chance at all.

Jorge had given the doorman some cash and asked
him to ring their apartment when the newspeople arrived. When word had come, Jorge had found himself
suddenly curious about how the people on Fifth Avenue
were reacting to the presence of the network van. What
if the neighbors connected the van with Wade's murder? He didn't want anyone gossiping about his nephew.

He and Elenora went downstairs, dressed as if they were going for a walk. Outside the building, they found a small group of passersby gathered near the van, watching the cameraman finish unloading.

Someone asked the man what program he was shooting. Jorge was pleased at the cameraman's polite and discreet reply, "This is for *The Donna Fuller Show*." No mention of the Bruckheimer or Dias families.

To avoid attracting attention, Jorge took Elenora's arm and they crossed Fifth Avenue to sit on one of the benches outside the stone wall that framed Central Park. From there, they watched the front door of their apartment building. Once the cameraman was inside, the little crowd quickly dispersed.

The Diases sat in a comfortable silence for some time. Jorge's attention was drawn to the many dog walkers passing by and pausing to pick up their animals' waste.

"Can you imagine how it would be if someone from Brazil saw me bending down to clean what a dog put in the street?" Jorge asked. "I certainly would never have a dog in this city—and if I did, one of the servants would walk it."

"Nonsense," Elenora responded, "you love dogs, and you would do anything necessary to care for your dog. Besides, here, everyone does it. And it's the law." She gave his arm an affectionate squeeze.

"No, my dear Elenora, you are mistaken. If I found myself with a troublesome, demanding cur, I would dispose of it."

"Jorge, please don't talk that way."

Why did she so rarely take his side on anything,

even in such simple matters? How was it that after so many years of marriage, she still failed to understand what was important to him? If she knew what he had done to preserve the family's wealth and power, what would she say?

Elenora suddenly said, "Jorge, what are we doing? If we stay here, we might not get across the street in time to catch her. We should wait in the lobby."

Jorge had to admit that she was right. He stood and drew his wife to her feet. "Let's go."

They crossed Fifth Avenue midblock, weaving quickly through the tangle of cars that had stopped for a red light.

The doorman smoothly opened the door for them and the Diases passed into the lobby. Now they had to find a place to sit where they could still "run into" Donna Fuller's producer. Elenora guided Jorge to the sofa at the side of the lobby.

As they waited, he closed his eyes and tried to rest, but continued to seethe. It was true that Elenora's warnings had often kept him from having unwise confrontations, but he resented her advice. As he grew older, her constant interference made him feel less and less in charge of his life. How would she have handled the discussion with Wade? Would it still have gotten so tragically out of hand?

His thoughts were interrupted by a sharp squeeze on his arm. "There she is," Elenora hissed, "just out of the elevator."

They rose quickly. "May we speak to you for a moment?" Jorge asked as they approached the small, red-haired woman.

"Certainly. I'm Sonya Iverson," she said, offering her hand.

"We are pleased to have run into you," Jorge said, introducing himself and Elenora.

"I recognize you, Mr. Dias," Sonya said. "In my research, I found several pictures of you and the Dias family. This must be a hard time for you. My condolences on the death of your nephew."

"Yes, it is difficult, but we are strong."

"I'm so glad to have run into you; I was considering calling you for an interview. Do you have time to sit and talk now? I won't be leaving until my cameraman comes down with his equipment, and that will take a few minutes. If we move to the back of the lobby, we should have some privacy."

Jorge looked at Elenora for her reaction. She smiled and said, "It would be good to chat now."

They moved away from the elevator and took seats. Jorge began, "How lucky that we ran into you by chance."

"Yes, by chance. Very lucky," she responded as she pulled out her notebook. Jorge saw a flicker of her eyelids and realized that she was more perceptive than he had expected. Clearly she was aware that they had been waiting for her. He began to try to explain, but Elenora spoke first.

"Ms. Iverson, the truth is we have been hoping to talk to you and that is why we were waiting here in the lobby. My husband spoke as he did because he thought you might resent our intruding."

Jorge felt a hot wave of anger. He took Elenora's hand and squeezed it tightly. Her slight gasp confirmed that he had hurt her. Perhaps now she understood that she was to remain silent.

"My wife is right. We wanted to talk with you," he said.

"I understand. Did you have a specific reason?"

Jorge tried to swallow before he continued, but his mouth was dry. His voice felt tight and it cracked slightly as he spoke. "We want you to cancel the story on the Braganza."

He studied her face, looking for her reaction, but saw no indication of how she had taken his blunt request. He felt compelled to continue.

"Let me explain. This diamond is part of our country's history. Though Esperanza brought it to the United States, she always meant to return it to Brazil. Unfortunately, her untimely death prevented that. Her husband, Douglas, claimed the diamond as part of his wife's estate and escaped with it to New York."

"Escaped? That's not quite how I heard it from your nephew, Wade, before his death."

"He was a liar," Jorge snarled, angry that Sonya had challenged him. Unsettled, he allowed his true feelings about Wade to show.

Sonya looked astounded by his vehemence.

Elenora intervened, speaking almost inaudibly. "Sonya, forgive us. My husband didn't mean that. Jorge loved Wade and supported him. You can see he is passionate about this stone and its importance to Brazil. He and Wade occasionally argued over it, which was painful for him. And he has not been well."

"I understand. But tell me why you don't want me to do the story."

Jorge explained, "*The Donna Fuller Show* is very powerful. If you do this story, I am convinced the publicity will cause the auction price to go up. We want to buy the Braganza for our museum, but unfortunately, my family and our friends have limited resources, and if it is too costly, we would lose it."

"But the story is no longer just about the diamond. There is Wade's death to take into account. I am almost certain we'll be airing the story."

Jorge felt Elenora's elbow press against his arm, her way of warning him not to lose his temper again. He felt trapped between the two women—one trying to tame his natural instincts and the other not interested in what was so important to him. In Brazil, the media would be more responsive.

"Perhaps you could slant the story to support our position that the Braganza should go back to Brazil? That's the correct thing to do, the fairest thing."

Sonya began to stand, gathering her notepad and bag. "Mr. Dias, you are being offensive. As a journalist, I must pursue the story wherever it takes me."

Elenora spoke quickly, holding out her hand to delay the newswoman's departure. "I am sorry. Of course, you must do the story as you wish. But perhaps you could arrange for Señor Dias to state his position about the diamond's importance to Brazil and about the Dias family being the stone's rightful owners?"

Sonya relaxed into her chair. "Yes, fair enough. I can't promise to include what he says, but I want to do a balanced piece, so I'll interview him and see where we go from there."

"Good. Thank you," said Elenora.

Jorge's anger had grown more intense as his wife took charge and the women came to their agreement, but he continued to restrain himself. When this conversation was over, he would have it out with Elenora and send her back to Brazil on the next plane.

"Yes, I agree," he said, as enthusiastically as he could manage. He couldn't resist adding, "And I advise you to be fair."

Ignoring his threat, Sonya replied, "Can you answer some questions for me now? They will help me prepare for our interview."

"What questions?" Jorge asked.

"When did you last see Wade?"

"As I told the police, I saw him when I first arrived, on the night he died."

"So you must have been the last person to see him alive," Sonya said.

"That could be true, but it is possible that someone else saw him later. We have connecting, but separate apartments."

"And why didn't he sell the diamond to you?"

Jorge exploded. "Young woman, that is between me and my nephew. What kinds of questions are these? You are not the police. I don't have to answer such questions about him."

This time Sonya did not react to his outburst. Jorge wondered if she thought he was all bluster and no action. She merely said, "That's true, but I need some background on your relationship with Wade if we're going to do an interview."

She is clever, he thought, and I must be careful. "All

right, but you must understand that I will not answer all your questions."

Sonya continued, "How did you feel when he said he would sell the diamond at auction instead of letting your family buy it?"

"Naturally, I was upset. It was a matter of family honor. My nephew did not understand that.

"We have an obligation to bring the stone back to our country. Wade only thought of himself and what he wanted. He was a greedy boy and he grew into a greedy man. He gave no thought to the commandments."

Jorge's voice rose out of control until he was practically shouting. "'Thou shalt not covet,' the Bible says. Now God has punished him. Now he is dead."

"Jorge, be calm," Elenora urged, but he ignored her, pushing her hand off his arm and pointing at Sonya.

"That horrible woman he married only made things worse. More greed, just like Irina. They want our heirlooms, things Esperanza brought to her marriage with Douglas." Jorge gasped and went on, "The painting of Esperanza . . . taken down. . . . They have no respect for our family, no appreciation for honor. But I swear to you I will have the diamond."

"And what about the Bruckheimers' claim to the stone?" Sonya asked.

Jorge tried to respond, but began to cough. Elenora held up her hand to stop Sonya. "He is not well," she said. "We should go upstairs."

"No, Elenora . . ." he said, even as she put her arm around him and helped him to his feet. He felt dizzy and short of breath.

Sonya walked with them to the elevator. "May I help you?"

"No, thank you," Elenora said. "He just needs to rest."

"I'll call in the morning about a time for the interview."

Jorge's coughing had eased and he was about to agree, but Elenora spoke first. "Yes, please call. If Jorge is feeling up to it, we'll schedule something."

Chapter 30

"I'm home," Sonya called as she let herself into her apartment.

There was no answer.

"Keith?" she tried again. Still no answer.

Her day had been so hectic, she forgot he was working overtime. She put down her bag and stood listening for a moment, suddenly feeling apprehensive.

She removed her coat, then turned the double lock on the door, and walked slowly through the apartment, stopping in each room to listen for movement.

Satisfied that she was alone, she felt foolish for having been afraid. It was exhaustion, she told herself, and worries about Kirsten. A nice long, luxurious bath would be just the thing to relax her.

While the tub filled, she left a brief report of the day on Donna's voice mail. Sonya lit her favorite lavender candle and slipped into the soothing warmth of the water as an intense aroma filled the room. She inhaled gently, then leaned back against the bath pillow and closed her eyes. She tried not to think but she couldn't clear her mind of the day's events.

Jorge Dias was an angry man. His was an unbending, aggressive belief in family honor. He was not used to being challenged and Sonya had clearly seen that only his wife's restraint kept his dangerous temper in check.

Wade had disgraced the family by selling the beach house and planning to sell the diamond. Differences between uncle and nephew might have ended in an explosive argument and murder.

But out of everything she had heard today, nothing was more astounding than Kirsten's accusation against her mother. Blair as a murderer? It seemed completely out of character for the TV chef. At the same time, Sonya could not completely dismiss the charge; she knew Blair could be tough. Incredibly, she had brought Donna near to collapse and forced her to withdraw from the story. No one had done that before.

Sonya couldn't help but wonder what Blair knew, how she had made Donna step back.

Of course, there were others, outside the family, who might have wanted Wade dead. Where a thirty- or forty-million-dollar payoff was involved, the list of suspects was large.

Sonya glanced at the clock on her bathroom wall and realized that she had been lying in the tub for nearly an hour. She got out, dried off, and put on a pair of jeans, a blouse and vest, and some comfortable walking shoes.

Keith said that he could tell her mood by the way she dressed. "My favorite is when you wear nothing," he sometimes teased.

Thinking of Keith reminded Sonya that she hoped to use him as a sounding board when he got home. Which meant that her own thoughts had to be organized. Sonya got her bag and seated herself in the comfortable, red leather armchair that was her favorite for reading and dozing. As she settled in and flipped on the bright lamp beside her, she realized that she hadn't used the chair in a long time.

She'd gotten out of the habit of sitting there because this chair was the only one in the apartment that was really big enough for Keith. She wanted him to feel comfortable in her home, so she had almost entirely given up her favorite seat.

She opened her bag and took out her reporter's notebook. Somewhere, buried in what she had heard, was the name of the murderer and the answer to why she, Sonya, had also been targeted. She began by listing each person she had interviewed: Wade, Bella, Blair, Harold.

Then she added Jorge and Elenora Dias and Irina Bruckheimer. And there she froze, astonished at her failure to book an interview with Irina. Kirsten was her contact with the family and had made the first overtures, but Sonya had not followed through as she should have. Had Kirsten deliberately omitted Irina, or had it been a simple oversight?

After a moment's thought, Sonya concluded that Kirsten also belonged on the list. Giorgio came next. He had been close to Wade for years, had been married to Blair, and might know something that the others wanted to hide.

Suddenly she heard a soft clicking noise from the

front of the apartment. Her body went rigid with fear. The sound repeated and she realized it was the front door lock. There was a lump in her throat; the relaxation from the bath had vanished. She half-rose from her chair, feeling her pulse racing.

Then Keith's voice called, "Hi, Red, it's me."

Sonya was flooded with relief. She ran to hug him. He dropped the bags he was carrying and held her as she half-sobbed, half-gasped in his embrace. "I'm here and you're safe." As Sonya's heart rate returned to normal, she pushed away from Keith and smiled though she still felt close to tears.

"I didn't realize how upset I was," she said, as a kind of apology.

"I'm sorry I had to work so late, but I've brought something to make up for it. I got the Japanese place we like to make up a couple of takeout bento boxes for us, with the promise that I bring the boxes back tomorrow."

She opened the bags on the dining table, revealing the beautifully prepared boxes and a large container of miso soup. "I've never seen so much food in a bento box." She laughed. "You must be hungry."

While she laid out chopsticks and napkins, he opened a bottle of red wine and took two glasses to the table. "I figured you'd want a quiet dinner," he said, handing her a glass of wine. They touched glasses as Keith said, "Cheers, Red. I hope you don't mind staying in."

"Keith, it's perfect. I have so much to tell you, and I need to sort some things out."

"Sure. I've got a couple of things to tell you too. Want to start now?"

"Before you eat, you mean? No way. You're no good when you're hungry."

The food was delicious, but Sonya's mind was elsewhere. She took a few sips of soup and picked at the sashimi. She was anxious to hear what Keith had to tell her, but she held back, knowing he would be more forthcoming after he ate.

"Not hungry?" Keith asked.

"Not so much," she said with real regret, because the soup was delicious but her appetite seemed to have vanished. "I guess it's the tension."

"Would you mind if I finished your California roll?"

"Of course not," she said, refilling her wineglass. Once Keith was finished, they cleared the table. Sonya cleaned the bento boxes as best she could while Keith put the leftover soup in the refrigerator.

They sat together on the sofa. Keith smiled and said, "Want me to start?"

"You know I can hardly wait. Go!"

"Detectives from the drug unit have a plant in the crowd Bella runs with. According to our informant, Bella's friends are mostly young and rich and are big users. The night Wade was murdered, Bella was out with them and was spending more of her time with a particular guy. He's around thirty, good-looking, a former Brazilian football player. He's loaded, and the CI says he and Bella are lovers."

"I'm not surprised," Sonya said, shaking her head. "But the fact that she has a lover keeps her on the suspect list, even if she didn't have much opportunity that night."

"You are right," Keith said, nodding. "We know now that Wade died from an overdose of powerful sleeping pills that aren't available in the U.S., so our bet is that the uncle brought them from Brazil. They were ground up and blended into Wade's special ice cream."

"What about the bird?"

"Same cause of death—the examiner found traces of the pills in its stomach. Of course, Wade didn't know that his ice cream was poisoned, so he might have fed it to the bird himself."

"How long was the ice cream in the freezer?"

"Good question! The manager of the ice cream company said that Wade insisted they deliver once a month, on the first, and bring one carton for each day. Wade believed that ensured freshness. Apparently he even had the cartons lined up by date in the freezer.

"We ran tests on the remaining cartons. Only one other was contaminated with powdered sleeping pills."

"That means the murderer would not only need access to Wade's freezer," Sonya said, "but would have to know Wade's habits well enough to be able to poison cartons that Wade would probably eat before the diamond went to the auction house.

"In fact, the pills could have been put into the ice cream days ago and could have been brought into the country at any time. Jorge Dias wouldn't necessarily have had to bring them with him on this trip." Though if he'd had that many pills sitting around somewhere in his apartment, Sonya thought, then Wade's murder might have been premeditated for a long time—since before the sale of the Braganza became public knowledge.

"You got it, Red," Keith agreed. "This also proves

that Wade didn't commit suicide." He leaned over and gave her a kiss on the cheek. "The other thing about Bella is that she and her lover left the party about eleven o'clock—but the nine-one-one call about Wade didn't come in until around two A.M. But the informant says that Bella and the Brazilian often went to his place for sex, so there's nothing particularly suspicious about the gap in time."

"Anything else?" Sonya asked in her most professional tone.

Keith laughed. "Nothing more for the moment, Ms. Iverson."

Sonya sat back and looked at him. "Guess I was a little reportorial, huh?" She began to laugh. He was the only one who could make her laugh at herself and enjoy it. "Now, my turn," she said. "First, I have to tell you about Kirsten and get your take on whether I did the right thing."

She explained how she had promised Kirsten to find the murderer. "I've had misgivings about it. The rule is that a journalist should report on a story, not become part of it. Do you think I was wrong?"

"It's a professional question, and as I don't know all the rules of reporting I'll leave it up to you. Frankly, I'd prefer to see you off this story. It's not safe."

When she objected, he added, "But I know that's not an option. So I'm going to ask you again to be extra careful as you go about your investigation. Goodness knows you've uncovered a killer or two in the last few years. If you do that again just by pursuing your normal leads, then you'll have lived up to your promise. If not, then you'll still have tried your best."

She didn't want to disagree so she said nothing. His suggestion might satisfy her promise but not her sense of the ethics involved.

"Now let me see if I can sort out some facts from my interviews.

"The three apartments are connected, so anyone can get into anyone else's place. I don't know if there are locks on any of the connecting doors, but even if there are, I doubt they are ever used. Whenever I was there, whether I was in Wade's apartment or Harold and Blair's, I always had the feeling that someone was listening out of sight.

"Like when I was interviewing Wade, and Kirsten and her father, Giorgio, suddenly appeared out of nowhere. They were like two silent cats—lurking and then suddenly there.

"Wade said that they were all just one happy family, but it's clear to me that he was trying to cover up a lot of dirt. When I asked him about his uncle Jorge, at first he denied having heard from him, then told me that his uncle was expected." Sonya paused to look at her notes.

"I met Jorge and his wife today. Let me tell you, Jorge Dias has strong convictions about family honor. Even though Wade is dead, Jorge can't stop expressing his anger about his nephew, can't stop dwelling on Wade's failure to uphold the family's image."

Beside her, Keith said, "Hmm."

"There's something else that's been bothering me. Considering that Wade just died, no one in the family truly seemed to be upset or grieving, except for Kirsten. In most families, when someone dies, everyone gathers for support and cries together. The Bruckheimers went on with their lives with hardly a glitch. Even after they learned that Wade was murdered."

Keith agreed, adding, "They have the reputation for being uptight. I expect you'll see a lot more anger than grief from them as the investigation goes on."

Sonya continued, "Another thing about the uncle. The Dias family is still a powerhouse in Brazil, and through the years, they repeatedly got Wade out of trouble. You mentioned the bird exporters and their gang. They wouldn't have much love for Wade, and might be working with Bella's shady family.

"Bella could get a lot from the sale of that diamond. I doubt she has the right to sell it but if her family gets their hands on it, that won't matter." Sonya picked up her glass and took a long sip of wine.

"Now that I think about it, Wade was perfectly relaxed with me until he moved Cacao to another room. When he came back, his mood had changed—and when Kirsten and her dad interrupted my interview, they came in from that direction. Maybe they ran into Wade earlier and said something to him? Or maybe just seeing them there upset him."

"What did you find out from Bella?" Keith asked. "After all, she was Wade's wife. She should have known him best."

"I'm not sure anyone in that family really knows anyone," Sonya said with a little laugh. "But as far as Bella is concerned, Keith, you've supplied part of her motive—the Brazilian lover. I think that money is her strongest motivation, though I also want to know more about her brother Rico.

"Bella said she phoned him after she found Wade and that he was supposed to come to New York, to help her. That was days ago but there's been no sign of him in the city and now Bella says she doesn't know where he is. I researched her family and I'd say they're pretty rough and that they don't have a lot of respect for people like the Diases."

"Phone records show that Bella definitely called Rico the night Wade was murdered. I wonder if they've spoken since," Keith said musingly. "But I don't have anything to justify a new warrant."

Sonya shook her head. "When I saw Bella today, she was practically falling-down drunk. She was even confused about who got shot, me or Kirsten."

Keith grunted, then asked, "What about Harold?"

"That was interesting. I talked to Blair first, and she was evasive when I asked her who owned the diamond, who controlled it, and so forth. I don't think anyone in that family ever just tells the truth. Everyone is always hiding something. Eventually Blair said that her husband would be making all the decisions.

"Now, when I interviewed Harold, he confirmed that he was the executor of Wade's will, but he was very hesitant when I asked him about the particulars of the auction. About all he said was that he had to talk to the auction house and Wade's lawyer."

"It seems to me that there's plenty of motive to go around. Everyone in the family could use the money from the sale of the diamond."

"True. Even Blair. Even though she has some income from her show and her cookbooks, it hasn't been enough for her to realize her dream of running a restaurant. Selling the Braganza would make that possible."

"Do you think," Keith asked, "that she would commit murder to get it?"

"Who knows? I don't trust her or Harold—or any of them, to be honest.

"I still want to interview Irina. That might tell me a lot." She looked at Keith. "One thing has stuck with me all day—Bella's confusion over who was shot. It seemed so strange that she didn't know who had been attacked, especially since I was standing right there, talking to her."

"You said she was very drunk."

"True. But it makes me wonder. Is it possible that someone was really after Kirsten?" Sonya frowned. "That would put a new spin on things, wouldn't it?"

Keith said, "It's too late to start speculating on that now. Let's go to bed."

Chapter **31**

The phone sounded, an annoying buzz. Harold didn't answer. He strongly suspected it was his mother, since he hadn't spoken to her since the previous evening. Usually he called her soon after he got up each morning. Today Blair had let him sleep a little later than usual, explaining when she'd awakened him that she thought he could use the rest after dealing with Wade's estate and that Sonya Iverson person the previous day.

Harold had decided she was right and he should be easy on himself. So he shaved and showered, then put on his robe and took his time with coffee and one of Blair's superior muffins. The phone had rung a few times and he'd ignored it. Now, listening to the buzz, Harold realized that if it was Irina, she would simply continue to call back until she reached him. With a sigh, he picked up the receiver.

"Yes, Mother. What is it?" he asked, trying to hide his annoyance.

"Been trying all morning . . . reach you. Why no . . . answer?" she gasped.

"Are you all right, Mother? You sound out of breath."

"Need to see you. My bedroom. Have to talk. Hardly slept."

Hearing the panic in her voice, Harold was overwhelmed with guilt for not having called her earlier. "Mother," he said soothingly, "I'll be there as soon as I dress. Just lie down. I'm coming."

"Good. Come," she said.

Harold hung up and rushed to his closet, quickly dressing in trousers and a plain button-down shirt. Worries chased one another through his thoughts. Had she had a stroke? Was she having an asthma attack? A panic attack?

From an early age Harold had known that his mother had faced enormous challenges when she was a young girl. Her mother's brutal murder had left permanent scars on her psyche, but for the most part, Irina had balanced her fears with a steely determination to survive.

She could be difficult and erratic, but he had never heard her so upset and unable to control herself.

He knew that since Wade's death, Irina had been closeted in her bedroom. Except for the police and Harold, she had seen no one in the past two days. She had told Harold that she'd called his grandfather, Max, and that always upset her.

Years ago, Irina had told Harold, "Someday, I want you to know what Max did to my mother, your grandmother. I've written out the whole story and put it in my safety deposit box. Once I'm gone, you can read it, and then you will know what to do if Max gives you any trouble.

"You must always remember that he is a terrible man."

Harold asked for more details, but his mother had refused to tell him anything more. "It's unbearable to go through the past," she said.

He knew little of his mother's relationship with her father—just that when she asked him for anything, which she did rarely, he would be extremely cold and disinterested at first. Max would tell Irina that she should be grateful for everything he had already done for her and that she should not ask for more. Eventually he would give in to her request, but only after he had made her grovel.

What had Irina wanted from Max this time, and how much was he torturing her?

Harold walked quickly down the hall. Before he could knock on the door to his mother's bedroom, she opened it—probably she had been listening for his footsteps.

Her appearance was shocking. He was accustomed to seeing Irina made up and neatly groomed, every hair in place, dressed elegantly, but today she wore a loosely belted robe and looked disheveled and drawn. Around her neck was the gold chain on which she usually hung the Braganza; the fingers of one hand played with the links.

Irina grabbed Harold and hugged him tightly. After a long moment, Harold gently loosened her grasp and guided her slowly to her chaise. He eased her down carefully, feeling even more ashamed for not having taken her calls sooner.

"Here, Mother. Lie down. Be calm. I'm with you and I love you." He felt compelled to excuse himself. "I'm sorry I didn't hear the earlier calls. Blair forgot to wake me."

"I'm so much better now that you are here, Harold. I had nightmares—frightening things coming at me. I dreamed about your father, my father, my mother. And when I woke up, all I could think about was Kirsten."

He felt her relax against the back of the chaise. "There, that's better, Mother," he said, releasing her. He drew up a chair beside the chaise and sat down, then took Irina's hand. "How can I help?"

"Kirsten is lying in the hospital, in pain, and I know it's because of the diamond. And I keep thinking about that woman from television."

"You mean Sonya Iverson?"

"Yes. I phoned her a little while ago. She wasn't in, so I left a message asking her to call me."

"For god's sake, why?" Harold demanded.

She covered her face with her handkerchief and turned away. Harold relented immediately, taking a deep breath and trying to calm his pounding heart.

"Mother, I'm sorry I spoke that way. It's just that I was surprised to hear that you called Sonya. Why did you do that?"

"I'm afraid that the attack on Kirsten will be part of the story. She's young, with her whole life ahead of her. She must be protected. I know what reporters can do to you. I know. I know," Irina said, her voice rising.

"You can't understand." She shook her head back and forth as if that would banish any unhappy thoughts. "I remember how the newspapers treated me. I don't want that to happen to Kirsten."

"But, Mother," Harold said. She put her finger to his mouth to quiet him.

"Everywhere I went, people stared and pointed at me. It's worse today, with those horrible paparazzi. We mustn't let that happen to Kirsten." Irina sat up, faced Harold, and spoke with deadly calm. "If Sonya Iverson hurts Kirsten, I will hurt her. You know I can arrange that."

As close as they had been, Harold had never seen his mother this way. She had survived her husband's affairs and rejection, Max's cruelty, and the jealous gossip of New York society. Through it all, Irina had been determined and fierce . . . and until now, he had no idea of the emotional price she had paid.

Harold tried to reassure her. "I promise you, Mother, I'll talk to Sonya Iverson. After all, Kirsten is my stepdaughter, my responsibility. I had no idea you cared so much for her."

Irina responded, "I see myself in her." She stood up and went to the full-length mirror that stood in the corner. "When I have the Braganza for my own, perhaps I'll let her wear it sometime."

She smoothed back her hair and toyed with the gold chain, turning a loop from side to side as if the diamond was hanging from it and catching the light. Harold was astounded at the change in his mother's attitude toward Kirsten. Just the previous day, when he'd told Irina that Kirsten was in the hospital, his mother had responded with a shrug.

During Kirsten's childhood, Irina had often complained about her, about how she dressed, how she spoke, her manners, her anorexia, everything. To Harold, this had been a distressing echo of his own younger days, when he had done everything he could to please his mother. He had always felt that he'd disappointed her and he hated seeing the pattern continue with his stepdaughter.

The strain between Irina and Blair, between Irina and Kirsten, had negatively affected Harold's relationship with his family. He and Blair often fought about Irina; his defense of his mother had put a barrier between him and Kirsten.

"Yes," Irina continued. "When she is a bit better, I'll visit Kirsten in the hospital and let her know that when she is older, she can wear the stone. She'll like that. She appreciates fine things, just as I do." She sat next to Harold and cajoled, "You can arrange things, can't you? You're the executor and can do it for me."

"Of course I can, but there are still details to be settled. I have to talk to the attorney again."

"You must ensure that I can wear the Braganza to the next Black and White Ball. I can't bear the humiliation of making my entrance without it."

"Yes, Mother. When I'm executor, it will all work out."

The phone rang.

"Get that," she commanded. "I don't want to talk to anyone but Sonya Iverson. If it's anyone else, you deal with it."

Harold lifted the receiver and said hello.

An already-familiar voice replied, "Good morning,

Harold, this is Sonya Iverson. I'm returning a call from your mother."

"Yes, Sonya, my mother has asked me to speak for her for now."

"I see," Sonya said, sounding disappointed. "I was really hoping to speak to Irina directly, but as long as I have you, I'd like to get an update on what's to become of the diamond."

"I'm not sure what I can tell you, Sonya," Harold said. "I'm going to put you on speaker, so my mother can hear too." He clicked the button on the phone and confirmed that the speaker was working.

Irina made the first move. "I prefer you talk with my son. I will listen, and if I have anything to add, I will speak up. I do want to apologize for disturbing your Sunday morning."

"Not at all," Sonya replied, "I often work on Sundays in order to have a story ready for the Tuesday broadcast. In fact, I'm going to see Kirsten later today."

Irina pointed at Harold in alarm, and waved her finger back and forth with a gesture that clearly meant no.

"In fact, that's the very reason my mother called you."

"Oh? What do you mean?"

"My mother and I are worried about the effect of so much publicity on Kirsten's life. I'm sure you've noticed, since you work with her, that she has a number of health problems."

He waited for Sonya to respond, but the phone was silent.

"Miss Iverson," Irina interjected. "Let me speak frankly. I—that is, we—do not want you to include

Kirsten in the story. We do not want you to even mention her. She has had enough."

"I'm afraid, Mrs. Bruckheimer, that that is not possible. I can't promise to keep her out of the story." There was a pause, then Sonya continued. "While I have you on the phone, I have to tell you how sorry I am that you refuse to do an interview with me. I think you could shed light on the murky view many people have of your family."

Irina moved closer to the phone. Her voice rose as she said, "I have no idea what you are talking about and I strongly advise you not to express any such opinions of my family."

"I'm only sharing my observations. That's why I want to give you the chance to express your feelings on camera. For example, I was surprised to hear your concerns about Kirsten, since it was my understanding that the two of you are not close."

"How dare you . . ." Irina shouted.

Harold spoke quietly but firmly. "That's unfair, Sonya . . ."

"Well, you see what I mean," said Sonya calmly. "If you were on camera, you could clear up any misunderstandings. Kirsten seems to have a different perspective on some matters regarding your family, and if you won't talk to me, then I have to rely on her impressions."

"Very clever, Miss Iverson," Irina responded, "but I have been dealing with the press all my life and your cheap trick doesn't faze me. I want you to know I have powerful, determined friends, who would not—and I repeat—*not* be happy to hear that you have refused my

reasonable request to respect Kirsten's privacy and protect her future. I want you to think that over carefully
before you include her in your tabloid program."

"I do hear you, and I will keep your threat in mind."

"No threat, Miss Iverson," Irina countered, "just
something, as you say, to keep in mind. Anyway, we'll
be seeing Kirsten this afternoon and advise her not to
cooperate with you. Now, good-bye." She signaled
Harold to push the button ending the call.

After a moment of silence, Irina took a deep breath
and said, "Sonya Iverson seems more strong willed than
I expected. I don't like it. Let's see Kirsten as early as
possible this afternoon. I want to put a stop to this Iverson woman once and for all."

She kissed him on the cheek. "Now go, dear, and let
me fix myself up." She swept into the bathroom.

Harold felt relieved. There was the Irina he knew,
back again.

Chapter 32

Sonya had never seen Sabrina look so worried. She hesitated in the doorway, obviously unsure whether to come in. "What is it?" Sonya asked firmly. "Don't stand there like a homeless pigeon. Come in and tell me what's on your mind."

Sabrina smiled, walked in, and sat opposite Sonya. "It's not what's on my mind—it's what's on the mind of your faithful cameraman. And for once, you'd better pay attention to what I've got to say about him."

Sonya broke in. "Don't start that again. I've told you to quit the matchmaking. Perry's a good friend and I respect his work, but if you want to get him married, then marry him yourself."

Sabrina gave her a hard look. "Cool it, will you? You almost got a bullet through your heart on Friday night. We're both just trying to protect you."

Sonya looked at the makeup artist's full, round face. As she often did, Sabrina had given herself a highly stylized appearance, painting her face dead white and placing a perfect circle of bright red rouge on each cheek. She looked freaky but Sonya knew that underneath Sabrina had plenty of common sense.

"I'm sorry, Sabrina," she said. "Go on."

"Well." She hesitated for moment, then said, "Perry feels that in a way he's responsible for the shooting."

Sonya couldn't resist a laugh. "That's ridiculous. Perry wouldn't hurt a fly."

"He thinks he met the hit man and told him a lot about you."

"What?" Sonya sat bolt upright in her chair in shock.

"You know that pub around the corner where the techs hang out? A few days ago, Perry met some guy there who said he was writing a screenplay about a TV producer. They had a few drinks together—well, maybe more than a few drinks. Perry said the guy asked him a lot of questions, supposedly to get background information for his movie."

"Why isn't Perry telling me this, Sabrina?"

"He's in a complete panic and says he's too ashamed. I think he feels he betrayed you and put your life in jeopardy."

Sonya thought back to the previous day, when she and Perry had worked together on the interview with Harold Bruckheimer. Now that she focused on it, she realized that they hadn't really talked much, that Perry hadn't kidded with her as usual.

"When did this happen?"

"Friday night, after work." Sabrina shook her head. "He'll tell you the rest himself now that I've broken the ice. He said if I spoke to you first, that would make it easier on him."

Sonya put her head between her hands and pressed her palms to her temples. Her mind was racing.

"I can't believe this. Perry meets a total stranger and gives him enough information about how we operate to let him figure out how to try to shoot me?"

Thinking of what Perry had done made her feel sick to her stomach. She trusted Perry completely.

"Sabrina, I don't know what to say. How could Perry betray me like that? We have tons of security in place at the office and he didn't stop to think before opening his mouth!" She took a deep breath to calm herself. "I'm sick about this. I feel as if I never want to see him again."

She reached across the desk and took Sabrina's hand. "Thank you for being such a friend to me and letting me know what he did."

"Oh, honey, stop it," Sabrina said, patting her hand. "You're overreacting. Perry would never harm you intentionally. He had too many drinks. Just give him a chance. He's waiting in the cafeteria to talk to you. Let me call and tell him to come up."

Sonya shook her head. "No."

"Oh, Sonya grow up," Sabrina said sharply. She picked up the phone and dialed.

Sonya had managed to compose herself by the time Perry appeared, looking utterly shamefaced. She stood up to greet him, determined not to let him see how hurt she was, and put her hand casually on his shoulder. "Come, sit down, and tell me everything."

"Oh, god, Sonya, I feel awful. I had no idea what the guy was up to," Perry said mournfully. "But maybe I'm wrong. Maybe he had nothing to do with the shooting." He took the chair next to Sabrina.

"Let's have every detail," Sonya said.

"It's like this; I went to the regular bar to have a few beers, like I often do after work. This guy was a stranger, but I saw him talking to a couple of the cameramen, so I thought he was one of the regulars. After a while he drifted over to me. He said his name was Arthur Singer and that he was writing a movie script about a TV producer, and could I answer some questions."

Perry spoke slowly and carefully. It irritated Sonya, and she interrupted to insist he get on with his story. "Did you ask him why he wanted to talk to you?"

"No. I assumed the other guys told him I could give him some of the information he wanted."

"So you have no idea whether he came to the bar just to talk to you?"

Perry shook his head. "No." He leaned forward and spoke earnestly. "Listen, Sonya, he did nothing to suggest he was up to anything. He was just an average guy, about five eleven, brown hair, short cut, wire-rimmed glasses, slim Levi's, black leather jacket. He bought me a couple of drinks and we talked. Like any two guys in a bar. "

"What did he ask you and what did you tell him?"

Perry's face turned red and he shifted in his chair.

Sabrina held up her hand. "Slow down, Sonya. Give Perry a chance to think. This isn't the Inquisition."

Sonya wasn't moved. "I don't mean to upset you, Perry, but if a hit man can figure out how to try to kill me after talking to you in a bar for a few minutes, we have a big problem."

Perry reached into his jacket pocket and took out a sheet of paper covered with his neat handwriting. "I've written down some of the things he asked about. For starters, your routine at the office. When you came in the morning, when you left at night. Was there any pattern?"

Sabrina broke in, "Those questions would make me suspicious."

Looking even more embarrassed, Perry shook his head. "I know, Sabrina, they should have set me off. The guy could have been a crazed fan. But those weren't his first questions, and he seemed so normal—I didn't feel like he was pumping me for information. It was just a conversation.

"And how could I have known he was a hit man? It's not like he gave me a business card that said PAID AS-SASSIN." It was a terrible joke and no one laughed.

Sonya took the paper from Perry. The questions dealt with every aspect of her working life. Arthur Singer was not interested in her as a person, but how she operated as a producer.

"Interesting list. If he was working on a screenplay, this would be a lot of help."

"He was really interested in Kirsten's job too," Perry said. "He wanted to know how she was treated by the regular staff. What she did exactly. How much time you spent with her. I got the impression that he was thinking that some young sexy actress could get a starring role if his movie was ever made.

"I said that you both worked long hours," Perry continued. "Then Arthur asked me to tell him about that day, about everything we'd done. He said it would give him a good idea about an average workday. So I told him. And I told him that you and Kirsten were still upstairs, still working."

"The call from the garage," Sonya said. "That wasn't you. But the hit man learned how to do it from you."

Perry lowered his eyes, avoiding Sonya's gaze as he continued. "Yes. I told him about the systems we have for handling tapes and how things sometimes go wrong." He looked up at Sonya then, red-faced. "I probably said that, if I had something I'd forgotten to give you, I'd call your office and you'd either come or, more likely, send an intern to get it."

"Are you sure you said that?"

"I'm sure I said something, but I'm not sure what."

"Anything else?" Sonya asked, her anger rising.

"We'd swapped phone numbers in the bar. Later, when my head had cleared, I realized that I had told him some stuff I probably shouldn't have. So I gave him a call, to let him know that the information I'd given him was strictly confidential. But the number he gave me was no good—the person who answered had never heard of Arthur Singer."

"You see," Sabrina said, "Arthur Singer left no traces behind him."

Sonya sat quietly for a moment, thinking through all she had heard.

"And it wasn't me he was after," she said slowly.

Chapter 33

SUNDAY, 12:30 P.M.
A local restaurant

Sonya picked up her handbag, slipped it over her shoulder, and headed out the office door. She and Keith had already planned to meet for lunch. She was glad, because she wanted to tell him about Perry's encounter right away. The police would have to interview Perry as part of their investigation.

They were meeting at a local deli—another deli, she thought with a sigh. And she knew that he'd want to talk to her about a trip he was planning to take with his teenage daughters. She loved Keith, but she hadn't yet met his children and wasn't sure their first encounter should be a vacation together. From what she'd heard of the girls, Sonya suspected they were somewhat spoiled—Keith and his ex-wife seemed to give them everything they set their sights on.

Sonya had no desire to be a doting stepmother and felt that Keith's girls were too old and too set in their ways to accept her as a parent. She had not been looking forward to trying to get out of joining Keith for this vacation. Now she had something else to talk to him about, and horrible as it would be to tell him Perry's story, it would also be a relief.

She wasn't sure Keith would accept her belief that the hit man had been after Kirsten, not her. But she was convinced that she was right.

Keith's face lit up when he saw Sonya enter the coffee shop. He put his arm around her and kissed her on the top of the head as he pulled her toward him. "I've ordered the usual for you," he said. "The waitress reserved a table in the back for us, so we can talk."

Though it was Sunday, the deli was busy because of its generous brunch specials. Sonya followed Keith as he threaded his way through the crowded tables. He had a well-proportioned body and moved with a lanky grace. Sonya loved to watch him.

"The news is all good," he said as he pulled out a chair for her. "I've arranged for time off in two weeks. The Maine coast is great at this time of year. We'll drive up to Stonington, a little lobstermen's village on Deer Isle.

"Since the girls have been living in Southern California for a while, they haven't seen the leaves change color in years. I think they'll like driving up, and then we can go fishing like we used to. Maybe we'll even go whale watching."

Sonya could tell that he was about to ask if she was coming. She didn't want to give him an answer, so she changed the subject.

"I need to talk to you about the shooting and the Bruckheimer story."

Keith looked annoyed, then put his hand on hers and replied, "Okay. I want to tie up this murder and get you out of danger."

She related Perry's story about the man in the bar and told Keith how hurt she was. She could tell that he was thinking like a cop when he said, "Don't be too hard on him, Red. Perry's in love with you.

"I'm willing to bet that this Arthur Singer was buying the beers. You've told me that usually Perry doesn't drink much. I guess he ended up not knowing what he was saying."

The waitress arrived with their sandwiches. Keith bit into his and grunted with pleasure before he spoke.

"We can't assume anything until we've got more information, and I'll send someone to talk to Perry, but it's a pretty thin lead. Sure, it's possible that Singer is the hit man, but he could just be a nosy writer."

"Then what about the phone number? Why did he give Perry a wrong number?"

Keith shrugged. "It could've been a simple mistake. A slip of the tongue. If they were both drinking for at least a couple of hours, it's easy to imagine what state they were in."

Sonya wasn't convinced. "I still think Singer's connected to the shooting."

"It does all seem to add up neatly. But what's the motive for killing you? We keep coming back to that. What did you do, or what do you know that would make some Bruckheimer want you dead?"

Time to tell Keith the rest of her theory. Sonya began slowly. "Perry told Singer that I would probably send an intern for a stray tape. And the more I thought about it, the more I understood that no one would ever mistake Kirsten for me. We may have the same color hair and I know she was wearing my coat, but she's much taller than I am and much skinnier.

"Plus, Keith, I'm thirty-nine years old and even in a parking garage, I don't think I look anything like an intern. So if the hit man was after me, he wouldn't have fired at Kirsten. No. I have no doubt that he was after her. I don't know why, but I'm sure there's a motive. I just have to figure out what it is."

His face lit up. "You're right," said Keith. "Red, you are one smart cookie and I love you." He leaned over the table and brushed his fingers against her cheek. "Well, I've got my work cut out for the day. I've decided to talk to Perry myself and get him to go through some mug books and sit down with a sketch artist. Let's see if we can find this Arthur Singer, or at least figure out what he looks like. And I'll follow up on that phone number."

He signaled for the check. "Sonya, tell me when can I expect a decision about our holiday. I need to confirm the reservations as soon as I can. If I leave it until the last minute the best rooms will be taken, and I want everything to be perfect. They're great girls. I don't expect you to love them yet, but I hope that if you spend some time together, you'll enjoy being with them."

Sonya felt trapped. "Keith, don't you think I should at least meet your daughters before we spend two weeks together? It's not fair to them or to me—we're strangers to one another. Let's have dinner when they arrive. Then you spend a week with them, without me. The girls haven't seen you for months and shouldn't have to compete with your girlfriend for your time and attention."

Frowning, Keith picked up his mug and drained the dregs of his coffee. She saw the disappointment on his face. "Think about it, please, Keith. Surely you want us to get off on the right foot together. I'm not trying to avoid them. I'm being realistic. I've been through this before, remember? Let's discuss it tonight when we're both more relaxed."

Keith huffed a sigh and said, "Any idea where I can find Perry?"

"He's working today so he can't be far away. Let me give you the number."

Keith called, listened for a moment, and then said, "Voice mail."

Sonya said, "When I get back to the office, I'll find him and tell him to call you."

"Do you have to go back to work? Even if the hit man was after Kirsten, I'm still not convinced you're safe. I'd worry less about you if I knew you were at home, behind a double-locked door."

"What happened with Kirsten was a violation of our security procedures, but Keith, I really think I'm safer at work—where there are plenty of other people around, even on a Sunday—than I would be alone at the apartment," Sonya said. "Stop worrying. I'll be fine."

Keith escorted her to the network building. They parted at the reception desk, where Keith asked how many people were in the building that day. The receptionist said, "Don't worry, Detective. Since the shooting, we've doubled the number of guards patrolling the place. Sonya will be fine."

In the elevator, Sonya began to think more seriously about the idea that the hit man had been after Kirsten. Why would anyone want to kill her? Maybe someone thought Kirsten knew who'd murdered Wade. Sonya began to compile a new list of suspects in her mind. As soon as she got to her desk, she'd lay them out and start making notes.

When she pushed open her office door, she jumped in surprise. Perry was lounging in her chair with his feet on the desk.

"Why didn't you answer your phone?" she snapped. "Keith wants to question you."

"Is that who that was? I didn't want to answer, in case it was Arthur Singer again, using some new number." He got up and moved away from Sonya's chair, then perched on the corner of her desk. "I wanted to know if we were okay now," he said softly.

Sonya was tired of reassuring him, especially because she still wasn't sure if they were "okay" yet. "Perry, let's move on," she said. "Let me ask you: do you believe Singer was after me or Kirsten?"

"I don't know, but after we talked this morning, I began to think it was Kirsten."

"Why?"

"All the questions he asked about Kirsten and what she did. He was interested in every detail, and when I thought about it, that seemed strange, because Kirsten is just an intern."

"I've come to the same conclusion. After all, who would benefit from my death? No one. Donna would assign somebody else to finish the story.

"On the other hand, Kirsten was close to Wade

Bruckheimer. What did she know, and who would benefit from seeing her dead?"

Perry shook his head and shrugged. "I don't know."

Sonya's mind was racing. "Blair? Or maybe Harold, who can't seem to get his hands on the estate even though he's Wade's executor.

"What about Irina—she had plenty of opportunity to get to Wade. She threatened me earlier today. And for Irina, the fate of the diamond was more than enough motive."

"But where did the hit man come from?" Perry interrupted.

Sonya said, "I think there are several possibilities, but most likely there's a Brazilian connection through either Jorge or Bella."

"I'd put my money on Jorge Dias. We know he brought Wade sleeping pills."

"He may have had the pills, but I doubt that he had the opportunity to put them in the ice cream—or that he would stoop to handling the poison himself. And Wade was a direct blood relative, a Dias. Bella's another story. She had every chance to do it, and she also had access to Wade's pills."

"But why would she want someone to shoot Kirsten?"

"I don't know." Sonya sat bolt upright as fear stabbed through her. "I don't think Kirsten is safe at the hospital. Let's get over there right now."

She grabbed her bag, her coat, and her phone. Perry opened the door and they ran down the hall. Sonya worked the speed-dial on her phone. She was terrified.

Chapter 34

SUNDAY, 2:00 P.M.
Kirsten's hospital room

"Why doesn't Kirsten answer?" Sonya said when her call went to voice mail. She disconnected and immediately redialed. "Answer the damned phone!"

They were in Perry's van, trying desperately to get across town from the network offices. A parade on Fifth Avenue made negotiating through what should have been light Sunday traffic extremely slow.

"There's one of these parades every weekend. Something should be done about them. They make the city impossible," Perry complained.

"I know. I'm just worried that Kirsten is alone."

"Didn't you say there's a security guard stationed outside her room?"

"Yes, but I think I know who arranged to shoot Kirsten. And if I'm right they'll try to kill her again. And the security guard might not know to stop them." She tried to reach Keith but was once again sent to voice mail. Sonya nearly snarled as she redialed.

"First I thought that Wade's murder and the attack

on Kirsten had been done by the same person, but then I realized that in a family like the Bruckheimers, there are lots of reasons why someone might want another relative out of the way. Who was desperate enough to want Kirsten dead, and why? Who could find a hit man at a moment's notice? Those were the two questions I had to answer."

Perry maneuvered through the crowd, then leaned out the window to shout his thanks to the traffic cop who waved him across the avenue.

"It has something to do with the Braganza, doesn't it? Somehow, Kirsten could affect where the diamond wound up."

"Exactly," Sonya agreed. "And what's the only way Kirsten could do that?" Laying it out like this for Perry only increased her conviction that she was right about everything.

"You've got me," he said as he steered the van through a group of jaywalkers. Sonya knew he was focused on driving, though to her the answer seemed obvious.

"She could inherit it." Perry took his eyes off the road for an instant to shoot Sonya a look.

"You mean Wade left the diamond to Kirsten, not Bella?"

"That's what I believe," Sonya said.

"That got me thinking about who in the family could easily hire a hit man," Sonya continued. "Jorge, Bella, and Irina seem the most likely candidates. And even though Jorge knew that Wade wanted to sell the stone, I'm sure he thought that Wade's will would return the diamond to the Diases, as Esperanza supposedly wanted." Sonya shook her head. "I know that doesn't make complete sense, but Jorge Dias seems to operate using a very personal kind of logic."

Perry grunted at her to continue.

"The more I've learned about Irina, the less likely I think she is as a suspect. Irina is genuinely worried about Kirsten. She didn't want her to be exposed in the press. She wants to protect her, not hurt her.

"Besides, Wade was already dead and Irina was certain that Harold, as executor of Wade's estate, would hold onto the diamond for her. So that lets Irina out, I think.

"As for Bella, she wanted everything she could get from Wade, but she's too much of a partygoer to seriously want to kill someone. Rico, her brother, sounds like a different story, and no one knows where he is right now, so that's still a possibility. And he might have been able to set up the hit, even if he didn't pull the trigger himself."

"Rico's from Brazil, right?" Perry asked.

"Yes," Sonya confirmed.

"So whoever Arthur Singer was, he wasn't Rico."

"Good point," Sonya said. She tried Kirsten's number again. It was busy. She kept hitting redial until Kirsten answered. Sonya practically sobbed with relief when she heard the intern's voice. "Are you okay? Has any stranger come into your room? Have you gotten any unusual calls?"

Kirsten sounded puzzled as she replied, "No strangers, no strange calls. The doctor was just here. He told me I'm a model patient." She giggled.

"I've been trying to reach you for ages. Why didn't you answer?" Sonya demanded.

"I turned my cell off when the doctor came in. The only other call I've gotten today was from Harold. He and Irina are on their way. Irina's bringing a pile of fashion magazines for me, he said."

Sonya kept her tone casual to hide her anxiety. "Right, I knew that. Perry and I are fighting traffic, but we'll be there soon."

"Sonya, do you have any news about Uncle Wade's murderer? I haven't heard a word."

"Let's not talk about it on the phone."

"Okay. I understand." She hesitated for a moment, then blurted, "Sonya, I was crazy when I told you that my mother murdered Wade."

"We'll talk about that when I see you, Kirsten."

"I know you won't be able say much in front of the others, so if they get here early, will you hang around after they leave? I have to know what you've found out." Sony heard renewed anxiety in Kirsten's voice.

The van stopped and Perry announced, "We're here."

Sonya told Kirsten, "I'm right downstairs. I'll see you in a couple of minutes." She hung up, then turned to Perry and said, "Thank you."

"Parking around here isn't going to be easy," Perry said, "but I'll be up as soon as I can."

Sonya jumped out of the van and raced through the lobby to the elevators. When she got out on the seventh floor, she paused to look into the waiting room. Was there a hit man among the visitors?

She shook her head. She was acting crazy. How could she possibly tell?

Kirsten's room was opposite the nurses' station. A hospital security guard stood outside the door. Sonya wished he was a cop.

Entering the room, she found Kirsten alone, sitting up in bed with her arm in a sling. She was pale and drawn but looked better than she had the last time Sonya had visited. She welcomed Sonya with a smile.

"Oh, I'm so glad you're here. I feel so guilty about accusing Mom of murdering Wade. It must have been the concussion or maybe the painkillers."

"Or a combination of both," Sonya said as she sat down and took Kirsten's free hand. "Rest assured, your mother did not kill Wade."

Relief flooded Kirsten's face. "I knew it. I was just being spiteful. I get angry about the way she and Harold treat me."

Sonya nodded. "Well, you were right about her feelings toward Wade. Blair really disliked him, but that doesn't mean she would kill him. She hoped to get her hands on some part of money from the sale of the diamond, but that's true of almost everyone in the family.

"And why would she try to kill you? She's your mother and she loves you."

"Yes, I know," Kirsten said.

"We'll just keep your accusation to ourselves. When I interview you, I won't bring it up."

"You want to interview me? Really?" Kirsten's eyes had gone wide in surprise.

"Yes," Sonya said.

"What should I wear?"

The two women looked at each other and burst out laughing.

The door swung open behind Sonya and she turned to see Harold standing in the doorway, holding an enormous bunch of long-stemmed red roses. Irina stood beside him, holding a plastic bag emblazoned with the logo of the hospital gift shop. Sonya expected that contained the promised fashion magazines.

"Where shall we put these?" Harold asked, stepping into the room.

"Here, there, and everywhere, and don't bother with vases," Irina gushed. She set the plastic bag on Kirsten's bedside table, then turned to Harold and took the roses from him. She scattered the blooms everywhere—on Kirsten's bed, the nightstand, the tray table, even the second, empty bed in the room. Finished, she threw up her arms, and with a sweeping gesture cried, "Voilà!"

Sonya and Kirsten were speechless. After a long moment, Kirsten stuttered her thanks. Sonya felt like coughing—the roses' scent was almost overpowering.

Irina leaned over and kissed Kirsten on the forehead. "I wanted you to know how much we love you."

"This is awesome," Kirsten said.

Sonya caught sight of Perry at the door and waved him in. "This is quite an impressive sight."

Perry grinned at Kirsten. "I've got to say you look great in a hospital gown."

Speaking had made Irina suddenly aware of them. "You are intruding on our privacy," the woman said imperiously. "You should go. We have family matters to discuss."

"No," Kirsten objected. "They're staying. I was shot, but the guy was after Sonya. She has a right to know everything."

Sonya shook her head. "You're wrong, Kirsten," she said calmly. "The hit man wanted to kill you, not me."

"Me? That's crazy." The young woman looked shocked. "Who would want to kill me?"

"I'm not sure," Sonya said. "But Perry had an interesting encounter with a guy who asked him a lot of questions about me—but also about you."

"He wanted to know all about your workday, your schedule, things like that," Perry put in.

"This is all nonsense," Harold said flatly. "The killer mistook her for you, Miss Iverson. It's obvious—you look exactly alike."

Sonya snorted. "Look again and you'll find that we don't. Kirsten is five inches taller than me and she was wearing high wedges. Sure, she had borrowed my checkered coat—but most of the photos of me on the Internet show me in a black-and-white-checked coat, not the brightly colorful one Kirsten had borrowed that night. There was nothing about the coat that identified the wearer as Sonya Iverson.

"A hired assassin has to have an excellent eye. He has to hit the right target, even in a dark parking garage. He would know the difference between me and Kirsten."

"But Sonya, why would anyone try to kill me?" Kirsten asked again.

"That's what I keep asking myself. Who would benefit from your death? What did shooting you have to do with the sale of the Braganza?"

Irina broke in. "Don't be stupid," she almost hissed.

"What happened to Kirsten had nothing to do with the Braganza."

Sonya had stepped away from Kirsten's bedside when Irina and Harold had arrived; now she moved closer to Kirsten. "No, Mrs. Bruckheimer, it had everything to do with the diamond." A glance at Harold's twisted face told her she was right.

"Harold, you are Wade's executor," Irina said, turning to her son. "What does Kirsten have to do with the diamond?"

Harold was silent.

"Well?" Irina demanded.

Harold looked down and said in a choking voice, "Mother, Wade left the Braganza to Kirsten."

"What? What are you saying? The Braganza belongs to this child?" Irina grabbed Harold's arm. "You are the executor, Harold. You control the diamond."

"No, Mother," he said, pulling away from her. "I am not the executor of Wade's will."

"But you told me . . ."

"No, I didn't. I said, 'when I was executor.' I was trying to work it out."

Irina grabbed his arm again and swung him around to face her. "Who is the executor?" she demanded. "Who?"

"It's the person Wade trusted most," Sonya said slowly as the realization came to her. "It's Giorgio . . . Kirsten's father."

Harold nodded, staring at the floor. "She's right. The attorney told me that six months ago, Wade found out that Bella had a lover. He changed his will at that time. He made Giorgio Sacco the executor and left Kirsten the Braganza."

Irina screamed, "The Braganza is mine, mine, not Kirsten's!" She lunged at the woman in the hospital bed, grabbing at her injured arm. "You can't have it," she shrieked as she picked up half a dozen roses and whipped them across Kirsten's face. Kirsten jerked away from her and slid out of the bed, landing hard on the floor.

Harold pulled his mother back. She spun in his grasp and punched him in the face. He howled in pain and threw her onto the spare bed, then leaned over her and slapped her across the face. Irina writhed under him.

Perry and Sonya rushed to Kirsten and lifted her onto her bed; Sonya supported the younger woman's injured arm and shoulder. A nurse ran in, followed by the security guard.

"Mother," Harold shouted as he held her down on the second bed, "stop!"

Her face knotted with fury, Irina cried, "We murdered Wade for the Braganza but it was all for nothing, nothing!"

Harold smacked her again. "Shut up! Stop screaming." He yelled, "I've had enough of you and your demands about the Braganza. I decided to kill Kirsten because with her dead I would have inherited the diamond. Then I would have sold it, and finally I would have enough money to be free of you."

The nurse had taken charge of Kirsten. The security guard was moving toward Harold. Sonya saw the nurse hit the panic button and asked, quickly, "How did you find the hit man?"

"My grandfather got him for me." He gave a harsh laugh. Irina looked stunned. "That's right, Mother, I asked your father for help. And he gave it to me, no questions asked."

More medical personnel and another security guard raced into the room. The security officer said, "I called the police. They're on the way."

One of the nurses said, "Everyone out, immediately. We have to take care of the patient." She hit another button on the bed's control panel and asked that a doctor be paged. A moment later, the announcement echoed in the hall.

Sonya saw blood seeping through the bandages on Kirsten's shoulder. Kirsten was terrified, panting, her eyes wild. Perry was trailing after the security team, who were hustling Harold and Irina out of the room, but Sonya reached for her intern's hand and squeezed it hard.

"Calm down," she said. "It's going to be all right."

Kirsten looked at Sonya. "The Braganza is evil. It has caused so much death and destruction. If it is really mine, I'm sending it back to Brazil where it belongs. I'll sell it to Uncle Jorge and give some of the money to Mom to open her restaurant."

"That's great, just what you should do," Sonya said, reassuringly.

The doctor entered the room.

"Time to go," the nurse said, more kindly than before.

"All right," Sonya said, releasing Kirsten's hand. "Kirsten, I'll call your mother and tell her to come right away."

"Thank you," Kirsten said. As Sonya opened the door, Kirsten said, "Don't forget to come back tomorrow to do my interview."

Sonya shook her head in disbelief. Kirsten's step-father had tried to kill her, had killed Wade, and Kirsten was thinking about going on television. Sonya could not understand her.

Chapter 35

She had gone from the hospital directly to her office. Her first call was to Keith. He'd already heard about the incident at the hospital and wasn't surprised to learn that she would be working late, writing the story.

Then she'd called Donna to fill her in, ending with, "I have a good angle on the story now. I'm approaching it from the point of view of how each member of the family had been motivated by greed. Kirsten is a major part of the story."

"Blair will like that," Donna had said, relief evident in her voice.

"I've gotten permission to interview Kirsten at the hospital tomorrow and Perry and I got some good shots of Irina and Harold being taken out of the hospital by the police."

"Wonderful," Donna answered. "I'll take a look in the morning to see if I have suggestions. I think there's enough here for a whole show." Then she'd ordered

Sonya to go home. Sonya had agreed, but had worked for another half an hour before heading out.

She'd walked into her apartment and headed straight for the bathroom. She was in the middle of a long, hot shower when Keith arrived. They shouted greetings at each other, then Keith said, "I'll just wait patiently for you in my favorite red chair." Then he added, teasing, "But hurry up."

He was sitting there when Sonya came out of the bedroom in her favorite robe. He handed her a glass of wine as she took a seat on the arm of the chair.

"How did you figure it all out?" he asked. "For a long time, I thought Jorge Dias was the most obvious suspect. But you didn't."

"That's right," Sonya said. "Jorge was only briefly a suspect for me. He arrived the evening Wade was killed. He wouldn't have had the time to crush the pills, soften the ice cream, mix in the poison, and have the ice cream refreeze before Wade got home.

"And he would have had to do all that without being discovered, while Wade was in the apartment. It just wasn't reasonable."

"Okay, Red," said Keith. "What about Bella?"

"The grieving widow? She had more to lose than gain by Wade's death. Besides, Kirsten was her only friend in the family and they seemed to genuinely like each other. As a matter of fact, that relationship made me briefly wonder if Kirsten was a suspect." Sonya laughed at herself.

"But Bella couldn't be sure what she'd inherit if Wade died. She didn't know if he knew about her lover, didn't know what the will said. What she did know was that if Wade sold the diamond, she'd be able to get her hands on a lot of cash." She paused to kiss Keith, then said, "Your turn. What's your theory on Blair Bruckheimer?"

"A no-brainer. She'd never harm Kirsten. Wade, maybe. Kirsten, no."

"I figured the same. But something about Blair really shook up Donna. I don't know what it was, and I'm probably better off not knowing." She sighed.

"What made you decide Harold was the murderer?"

"At first, it was just my gut feeling that somehow he would benefit from Kirsten's death. And he made a slipup during his interview.

"He said that he'd heard from his grandfather that he wasn't feeling well. But Kirsten had told me that Max Lundell had nothing to do with his grandson, so how could Harold know that Max was ill? Only if they had been in touch recently.

"Max had told Irina that he wouldn't buy the diamond for her. Harold knew that—Irina had told him. He had already helped his mother kill Wade. He wanted his mother's love, had always been desperate, and he knew he couldn't get it without the Braganza." She shuddered. "You should have seen them today at the hospital."

"Do you really think they murdered Wade together?" Keith asked.

"Maybe. Harold would do almost anything his mother asked of him, and I'm not sure she's the type to mess around with ice cream, even if she was going to use it to kill someone. But she might have done it and then told Harold about her victory over Wade.

"Harold knew that Kirsten stood between them and the stone. He didn't tell his mother—he just tried to solve the problem, with Max's help. Getting rid of Kirsten would have been a cheap way to get Irina off his back."

"But then Max would have had his claws into Harold forever," Keith said. "I don't think Harold Bruckheimer knows who Max Lundell really is."

"I know this sounds crazy, Keith, but I feel sorry for Irina, in a way. That diamond gave her what she needed most—it made her feel important—gave her self-esteem."

Sonya got up and took both wineglasses to the kitchen sink. "It's time for bed," she said.

Keith got up and followed her into the bedroom. There would be time the next day to write her story, to figure out what she was going to say to Keith about his daughters, to do the interview with Kirsten. But now, she had a sexy man in her bedroom and she intended to take full advantage of that.